£1. 21-98
Smith's Discount

The Just – William Collection

This collection has been specially selected for W H Smith.

The complete list of *William* books published by Macmillan Children's Books is as follows:

Also available:

Just—William
a facsimile of the first (1922) edition

The William Companion
by Mary Cadogan

Just William's World – a pictorial map
by Gillian Clements and Kenneth Waller

What's Wrong with Civilizashun
by William Brown (and Richmal Crompton)

All are available from your local branch of W H Smith.

"NOW YOU MUTH PLAY WITH ME," LISPED VIOLET
ELIZABETH, SWEETLY.
"I DON'T PLAY LITTLE GIRL'S GAMES," ANSWERED THE
DISGUSTED WILLIAM.

(*See page 293*)

The Just – William Collection

RICHMAL CROMPTON

Illustrated by Thomas Henry

WH SMITH

EXCLUSIVE
· BOOKS ·

3 5 7 9 10 8 6 4

This collection, first published 1991,
specially produced for W H Smith by
MACMILLAN CHILDREN'S BOOKS
A division of Macmillan Publishers Limited
London and Basingstoke
Associated companies throughout the world

ISBN 0-333-56698-X

Printed and bound in Great Britain by
Cox & Wyman Ltd, Reading, Berkshire

Contents

The Show

The Outlaws sat around the old barn, plunged in deep thought. Henry, the oldest member (aged 12¼) had said in a moment of inspiration:

"Let's think of—sumthin' else to do—sumthin' quite fresh from what we've ever done before."

And the Outlaws were thinking.

They had engaged in mortal combat with one another, they had cooked strange ingredients over a smoking and reluctant flame with a fine disregard of culinary conventions, they had tracked each other over the country-side with gait and complexions intended to represent those of the aborigines of South America, they had even turned their attention to kidnapping (without any striking success), and these occupations had palled.

In all its activities the Society of Outlaws (comprising four members) aimed at a simple, unostentatious mode of procedure. In their shrinking from the glare of publicity they showed an example of unaffected modesty that many other public societies might profitably emulate. The parents of the members were unaware of the very existence of the society. The ill-timed and tactless interference of parents had nipped in the bud many a cherished plan, and by bitter experience the

Outlaws had learnt that secrecy was their only protec-
tion. Owing to the rules and restrictions of an unsympathetic world that orders school hours from 9 to 4 their
meetings were confined to half-holidays and occasionally Sunday afternoons.

William, the ever ingenious, made the first suggestion.

"Let's shoot things with bows an' arrows same as real
outlaws used to," he said.

"What things?" and

"What bows an' arrows?" said Henry and Ginger
simultaneously.

"Oh, anything—birds an' cats an' hens an' things—
an' buy bows an' arrows. You can buy them in shops."

"We can make them," said Douglas, hopefully.

"Not like you can get them in shops. They'd shoot
crooked or sumthin' if we made them. They've got to be
jus' so to shoot straight. I saw some in Brook's window,
too, jus' right—jus' same as real outlaws had."

"How much?" said the outlaws breathlessly.

"Five shillings—targets for learnin' on before we
begin shootin' real things an' all."

"Five shillings!" breathed Douglas. He might as well
have said five pounds. "We've not got five shillings.
Henry's not having any money since he broke their
drawing-room window an' Ginger only has 3*d*. a week
an' has to give collection an' we've not paid for the
guinea pig yet, the one that got into Ginger's sister's hat
an' she was so mad at, an'——"

"Oh, never mind all that," said William, scornfully.
"We'll jus' get five shillings."

"How?"

"Well," uncertainly, "grown-ups can always get
money when they want it."

"How?" again.

William disliked being tied down to details.

"Oh—bazaars an' things," impatiently.

"Bazaars!" exploded Henry. "Who'd come to a bazaar if we had one? Who would? Jus' tell me that if you're so clever! Who'd come to it? Besides, you've got to sell things at a bazaar, haven't you? What'd we sell? We've got nothin' to sell, have we? What's the good of havin' a bazaar with nothin' to sell and no one to buy it? Jus' tell me that!

Henry always enjoyed scoring off William.

"Well—shows an' things," said William desperately.

There was a moment's silence, then Ginger repeated thoughtfully. "Shows!" and Douglas, whose eldest brother was home from college for his vacation, murmured self-consciously, "By Jove!"

"We *could* do a show," said Ginger. "Get animals an' things an' charge money for lookin' at them."

"Who'd pay it?" said Henry, the doubter.

"Anyone would. You'd pay to see animals, wouldn't you?—real animals. People do at the Zoo, don't they? Well, we'll get some animals. That's easy enough, isn't it?"

A neighbouring church clock struck four and the meeting was adjourned.

"Well, we'll have a show an' get money and buy bows an' arrows an' shoot things," summed up William, "an' we'll arrange the show next week."

William returned home slowly and thoughtfully. He sat on his bed, his hands in his pockets, his brow drawn into a frown, his thoughts wandering in a dreamland of wonderful "shows" and rare exotic beasts.

Suddenly from the next room came a thin sound that gathered volume till it seemed to fill the house like the roaring of a lion, then died gradually away and was followed by silence. But only for a second. It began again—a small whisper that grew louder and louder, became a raucous bellow, then faded slowly away to rise again after a moment's silence. In the next room William's mother's Aunt Emily was taking her after-noon nap. Aunt Emily had come down a month ago for a week's visit and had not yet referred to the date of her departure. William's father was growing anxious. She was a stout, healthy lady, who spent all her time recovering from a slight illness she had had two years ago. Her life held two occupations, and only two. These were eating and sleeping. For William she possessed a subtle but irresistible fascination. Her stature, her appetite, her gloom, added to the fact that she utterly ignored him, attracted him strongly.

The tea bell rang and the sound of the snoring ceased abruptly. This entertainment over, William descended to the dining-room, where his father was addressing his mother with some heat.

"Is she going to stay here for ever, or only for a few years? I'd like to know, because——"

Perceiving William, he stopped abruptly, and William's mother murmured:

"It's so nice to have her, dear."

Then Aunt Emily entered.

"Have you slept well, Aunt?"

"Slept!" repeated Aunt Emily majestically. "I hardly expect to sleep in my state of health. A little rest is all I can expect."

"Sorry you're no better," said William's father sardonically.

"*Better?*" she repeated again indignantly. "It will be a long time before I'm better."

She lowered her large, healthy frame into a chair, carefully selected a substantial piece of bread and butter and attacked it with vigour.

"I'm going to the post after tea," said William's mother. "Would you care to come with me?"

Aunt Emily took a large helping of jam.

"You hardly expect me to go out in the evening in my state of health, surely? It's years since I went out after tea. And I was at the post office this morning. There were a lot of people there, but they served me first. I suppose they saw I looked ill."

William's father choked suddenly and apologised, but not humbly.

"Though I must say," went on Aunt Emily, "this place does suit me. I think after a few months here I should be a little stronger. Pass the jam, William."

The glance that William's father fixed upon her would have made a stronger woman quail, but Aunt Emily was scraping out the last remnants of jam and did not notice.

"I'm a bit over-tired to-day, I think," she went on. "I'm so apt to forget how weak I am and then I overdo it. I'm ready for the cake, William. I just sat out in the sun yesterday afternoon and sat a bit too long and over-tired myself. I ought to write letters after tea, but I don't think I have the strength. Another piece of cake, William. I'll go upstairs to rest instead, I think. I hope you'll keep the house quiet. It's so rarely that I can get a bit of sleep."

William's father left the room abruptly. William sat on and watched, with fascinated eyes, the cake disappear, and finally followed the large, portly figure upstairs and sat down in his room to plan the "show" and incidentally listen, with a certain thrilled awe, for the sounds from next door.

The place and time of the "show" presented no little

difficulty. To hold it in the old barn would give away to the world the cherished secret of their meeting place. It was William who suggested his bedroom, to be entered, not by way of the front door and staircase, but by the less public way of the garden wall and scullery roof. Ever an optimist, he affirmed that no one would see or hear. The choice of a time was limited to Wednesday afternoon, Saturday afternoon, and Sunday. Sunday at first was ruled out as impossible. But there were difficulties about Wednesday afternoon and Saturday afternoon. On Wednesday afternoon Ginger and Douglas were unwilling and ungraceful pupils at a dancing class. On Saturday afternoon William's father gardened and would command a view of the garden wall and scullery roof. On these afternoons also Cook and Emma, both of a suspicious turn of mind, would be at large. On Sunday Cook and Emma went out, William's mother paid a regular weekly visit to an old friend and William's father spent the afternoon on the sofa, dead to the world.

Moreover, as he pointed out to the Outlaws, the members of the Sunday School could be waylaid and induced to attend the show and they would probably be provided with money for collection. The more William thought over it, the more attractive became the idea of a Sunday afternoon in spite of superficial difficulties; therefore Sunday afternoon was finally chosen.

The day was fortunately a fine one, and William and the other Outlaws were at work early. William had asked his mother, with an expression of meekness and virtue that ought to have warned her of danger, if he might have "jus' a few friends" in his room for the afternoon. His mother, glad that her husband should be spared his son's restless company, gave willing permission.

By half-past two the exhibits were ready. In a cage by the window sat a white rat painted in faint alternate stripes of blue and pink. This was Douglas' contribution, handpainted by himself in water colours. It wore a bewildered expression and occasionally licked its stripes and then obviously wished it hadn't. Its cage bore a notice printed on cardboard:

> RAT FROM CHINA
> RATS ARE ALL LIKE
> THIS IN CHINA

Next came a cat belonging to William's sister, Smuts by name, now imprisoned beneath a basket-chair. At the best of times Smuts was short-tempered, and all its life had cherished a bitter hatred of William. Now, enclosed by its enemy in a prison two feet square, its fury knew no bounds. It tore at the basket work, it flew wildly round and round, scratching, spitting, swearing. Its chair bore the simple and appropriate notice:

> WILD CAT

William watched it with honest pride and prayed fervently that its indignation would not abate during the afternoon.

Next came a giant composed of Douglas upon Ginger's back, draped in two sheets tied tightly round Douglas's neck. This was labelled:

> GENWIN GIANT

Ginger was already growing restive. His muffled voice was heard from the folds of the sheets informing the other Outlaws that it was a bit thick and he hadn't known it would be like this or he wouldn't have done it, and anyway he was going to change with Douglas half time or he'd chuck up the whole thing.

The next exhibit was a black fox fur of William's mother's, to which was fortunately attached a head and several feet, and which he had surreptitiously removed from her wardrobe. This had been tied up, stuffed with waste paper and wired by William till it was, in his eyes, remarkably lifelike. As the legs, even with the assistance of wire, refused to support the body and the head would only droop sadly to the ground, it was perforce exhibited in a recumbent attitude. It bore marks of sticky fingers and of several side slips of the scissors when William was cutting the wire, but on the whole he was justly proud of it. It bore the striking but untruthful legend:—

> ### BEAR SHOT
> ### BY OUTLAWS
> ### IN RUSHER

Next came:

> ### BLUE DOG

This was Henry's fox terrier, generally known as Chips. For Chips the world was very black. Henry's master mind had scorned his paint box and his water colours. Henry had "borrowed" a blue bag and dabbed it liberally over Chips. Chips had, after the first wild frenzied struggle, offered no resistance. He now sat, a picture of black despair, turning every now and then a melancholy eye upon the still enraged Smuts. But for him cats and joy and life and fighting were no more. He was abject, shamed—a blue dog.

William himself, as showman, was an imposing figure. He was robed in a red dressing-gown of his father's that trailed on the ground behind him and over whose cords in front he stumbled ungracefully as he walked. He had cut a few strands from the fringe of a rug and glued them to his lips to represent moustaches. They fell in two straight lines over his mouth. On his head was a tinsel crown, once worn by his sister as Fairy Queen.

The show had been widely advertised and all the neighbouring children had been individually canvassed, but under strict orders of secrecy. The threats of what the Outlaws would do if their secret were disclosed had kept many a child awake at night.

William surveyed the room proudly.

"Not a bad show for a penny, I *should* say. I guess there aren't many like it, anyway. Do shut up talkin', Ginger. It'll spoil it all, if folks hear the giant talking out of his stomach. It's Douglas that's got to do the giant's *talking*. Anyone could see that. I say, they're comin'! Look! They're comin'! Along the wall!'

There was a thin line of children climbing along the wall in single file on all fours. They ascended the scullery roof and approached the window. These were the first arrivals who had called on their way to Sunday School.

Henry took their pennies and William cleared his throat and began:—

"White rat from China, ladies an' gentlemen, pink an' blue striped. All rats is pink an' blue striped in China. This is the only genwin China rat in England—brought

FINEST SHOW ON ERTH 1D

WILLIAM WAS AN IMPOSING FIGURE.

over from China special las' week jus' for the show. It lives on China bread an' butter brought over special, too.''

"Wash it!" jeered an unbeliever. "Jus' wash it an' let's see it then."

"Wash it?" repeated the showman indignantly. "Its gotter be washed. It's washed every morning an' night same as you or me. China rats have gotter be washed or they'd die right off. Washin' 'em don't make no difference to their stripes. Anyone knows that that knows anything about China rats, I guess."

He laughed scornfully and turned to Smuts. Smuts had grown used to the basket chair and was settling down for a nap. William crouched down on all fours, ran his fingers along the basket-work, and, putting his face close to it, gave vent to a malicious howl. Smuts sprang at him, scratching and spitting.

"Wild cat," said William triumphantly. "Look at it! Kill anyone if it got out! Spring at their throats, it would, an' scratch their eyes out with its paws an' bite their necks till its teeth met. If I jus' moved away that chair it would spring out at you." They moved hastily away from the chair, "and I bet some of you would be dead pretty quick. It could have anyone's head right off with bitin' and scratchin'. Right off—separate from their bodies!"

There was an awe-stricken silence.

Then:

"Garn! It's Smuts. It's your sister's cat!"

William laughed as though vastly amused by this idea.

"Smuts!" he said, giving a surreptitious kick to the chair that infuriated its occupant still more. "I guess there wouldn't be many of us left in this house if Smuts was like this."

They passed on to the giant.

"A giant," said William, re-arranging the tinsel crown, which was slightly too big for him. "Real giant. Look at it. As big as two of you put together. How d'you think he gets in at doors and things? Has to have everything made special. Look at him walk. Walk, Ginger."

Ginger took two steps forward. Douglas clutched his shoulders and murmured anxiously, "By Jove!"

"Go on," urged William scornfully, "That's not walkin'."

The goaded Ginger's voice came from the giant's middle regions!

"If you go on talkin' at me, I'll drop him. I'm just about sick of it."

THE GOADED GINGER'S VOICE CAME FROM THE GIANT'S MIDDLE REGIONS.

"All right," said William hastily.

"Anyway it's a giant," he went on to his audience. "A jolly fine giant."

"It's got Douglas's face," said one of his audience.

William was for a moment at a loss.

"Well," he said at last, "giant's got to have some sort of a face, hasn't it? Can't not have a face, can it?"

The Russian Bear, which had often been seen adorning the shoulders of William's mother and was promptly recognised, was greeted with ribald jeers, but there was no doubt as to the success of the Blue Dog. Chips advanced deprecatingly, blue head drooping, and blue tail between blue legs, making abject apologies for his horrible condition. But Henry had done his work well. They stood around in rapt admiration.

"Blue dog," said the showman, walking forward proudly and stumbling violently over the cords of the dressing gown. "Blue dog," he repeated, recovering his balance and removing the tinsel crown from his nose to his brow. "You never saw a blue dog before, did you? No, and you aren't likely to see one again, neither. It was made blue special for this show. It's the only blue dog in the world. Folks 'll be comin' from all over the world to see this blue dog—an' thrown in in a penny show! If it was in the Zoo you'd have to pay a shilling to see it, I bet. It's—it's jus' luck for you it's here. I guess the folks at the Zoo wish they'd got it. Tain't many shows have blue dogs. Brown an' black an' white—but not blue. Why, folks pay money jus' to see shows of ornery dogs—so you're jus' lucky to see a blue dog *an'* a dead bear from Russia *an'* a giant, *an'* a wild cat, *an'* a China rat for jus' one penny."

After each speech William had to remove from his mouth the rug fringe which persisted in obeying the force of gravity rather than William's idea of what a moustache should be.

"It's jus' paint. Henry's gate's being painted blue," said one critic feebly, but on the whole the Outlaws had scored a distinct success in the blue dog.

Then, while they stood in silent admiration round the unhappy animal, came a sound from the next door, a gentle sound like the sighing of the wind through the trees. It rose and fell. It rose again and fell again. It increased in volume with each repetition, till at its height it sounded like a wild animal in pain.

"What's that?" asked the audience breathlessly.

William was slightly uneasy. He was not sure whether this fresh development would add lustre or dishonour to his show.

"Yes," he said darkly to gain time, "what is it? I guess you'd like to know what it is!"

"Garn! It's jus' snorin'."

"Snorin'!" repeated William. "It's not ornery snorin', that isn't. Jus' listen, that's all! You couldn't snore like that, I bet. Huh!"

They listened spellbound to the gentle sound, growing louder and louder till at its loudest it brought rapt smiles to their faces, then ceasing abruptly, then silence. Then again the gentle sound that grew and grew.

William asked Henry in a stage whisper if they oughtn't to charge extra for listening to it. The audience hastily explained that they weren't listening, they "jus' couldn't help hearin'."

A second batch of sightseers had arrived and were paying their entrance pennies, but the first batch refused to move. William, emboldened by success, opened the door and they crept out to the landing and listened with ears pressed to the magic door.

Henry now did the honours of showman. William stood, majestic in his glorious apparel, deep in thought. Then to his face came the faint smile that inspiration brings to her votaries. He ordered the audience back into the showroom and shut the door. Then he took off his shoes and softly and with bated breath opened Aunt Emily's door and peeped within. It was rather a close afternoon, and she lay on her bed on the top of her eiderdown. She had slipped off her dress skirt so as not to crush it, and she lay in her immense stature in a blouse and striped petticoat, while from her open mouth issued the fascinating sounds. In sleep Aunt Emily was not beautiful.

William thoughtfully propped up a cushion in the doorway and stood considering the situation.

In a few minutes the showroom was filled with a silent, expectant crowd. In a corner near the door was a new notice:

> PLACE FOR TAKING
> OFF SHOES AND TAKING
> OTH OF SILENCE

William, after administering the oath of silence to a select party in his most impressive manner, led them shoeless and on tiptoe to the next room.

From Aunt Emily's bed hung another notice:

> FAT WILD WOMAN
> TORKIN NATIF
> LANGWIDGE

They stood in a hushed, delighted group around her bed. The sounds never ceased, never abated. William only allowed them two minutes in the room. They came out reluctantly, paid more money, joined the end of the queue and re-entered. More and more children came to see the show, but the show now consisted solely in Aunt Emily.

The China rat had licked off all its stripes; Smuts was fast asleep; Ginger was sitting down on the seat of a chair and Douglas on the back of it, and Ginger had insisted at last on air and sight and had put his head out where the two sheets joined; the Russian Bear had fallen on to the floor and no one had picked it up; Chips lay in a disconsolate heap, a victim of acute melancholia—and no one cared for any of these things. New-comers passed by them hurriedly and stood shoeless in the queue outside Aunt Emily's room eagerly awaiting their turn. Those who came out simply went to the end again to wait another turn. Many returned home for more money, for Aunt Emily was 1d. extra and each visit after the first, ½d. The Sunday School bell pealed forth its summons, but no one left the show. The vicar was depressed that evening. The attendance at Sunday School had been the worst on record. And still Aunt Emily slept and snored with a rapt, silent crowd around her. But William could never rest content. He possessed ambition that would have put many of his elders to shame. He cleared the room and re-opened it after a few minutes, during which his clients waited in breathless suspense.

When they re-entered there was a fresh exhibit. William's keen eye had been searching out each detail of the room. On the table by her bed now stood a glass containing teeth, that William had discovered on the washstand, and a switch of hair and a toothless comb,

that William had discovered on the dressing-table.
These all bore notices:

FAT WILD WOMAN'S TEETH	FAT WILD WOMAN'S HARE	FAT WILD WOMAN'S KOME

Were it not that the slightest noise meant instant
expulsion from the show (some of their number had
already suffered that bitter fate) there would have been
no restraining the audience. As it was, they crept in,
silent, expectant, thrilled, to watch and listen for the
blissful two minutes. And Aunt Emily never failed
them. Still she slept and snored. They borrowed money
recklessly from each other. The poor sold their dearest
treasures to the rich, and still they came again and again.
And still Aunt Emily slept and snored. It would be
interesting to know how long this would have gone on,
had she not, on the top note of a peal that was a pure
delight to her audience, awakened with a start and
glanced around her. At first she thought that the cluster
of small boys around her was a dream, especially as they
turned and fled precipitately at once. Then she sat up
and her eye fell upon the table by her bed, the notices,
and finally upon the petrified horror-stricken showman.
She sprang up and, seizing him by the shoulders, shook
him till his teeth chattered, the tinsel crown fell down,
encircling ears and nose, and one of his moustaches fell
limply at his feet.

"You wicked boy!" she said as she shook him, "you
wicked, *wicked*, *wicked* boy!"

He escaped from her grasp and fled to the showroom,

where, in sheer self-defence, he moved a table and three chairs across the door. The room was empty except for Henry, the blue dog, and the still sleeping Smuts. All that was left of the giant was the crumpled sheets. Douglas had, with an awe-stricken "By Jove!" snatched up his rat as he fled. The last of their clients was seen scrambling along the top of the garden wall on all fours with all possible speed.

Mechanically William straightened his crown.

"She's woke," he said. "She's mad wild."

He listened apprehensively for angry footsteps descending the stairs and his father's dread summons, but none came. Aunt Emily could be heard moving about in her room, but that was all. A wild hope came to him that, given a little time, she might forget the incident.

"Let's count the money—" said Henry at last.

They counted.

"Four an' six!" screamed William. "Four an' six! Jolly good, I *should* say! An' it would only have been about two shillings without Aunt Emily, an' I thought of her, didn't I? I guess you can all be jolly grateful to me."

"All right," said Henry unkindly. "I' not envying you, am I? You're welcome to it when she tells your father."

And William's proud spirits dropped.

Then came the opening of the fateful door and heavy steps descending the stairs.

William's mother had returned from her weekly visit to her friend. She was placing her umbrella in the stand as Aunt Emily, hatted and coated and carrying a bag, descended. William's father had just awakened from his peaceful Sunday afternoon slumber, and, hearing his wife, had come into the hall.

Aunt Emily fixed her eye upon him.

"Will you be good enough to procure a conveyance?"

she said. "After the indignities to which I have been subjected in this house I refuse to remain in it a moment longer."

Quivering with indignation she gave details of the indignities to which she had been subjected. William's mother pleaded, apologised, coaxed. William's father went quietly out to procure a conveyance. When he returned she was still talking in the hall.

"A crowd of vulgar little boys," she was saying, "and horrible indecent placards all over the room."

He carried her bag down to the cab.

"And me in my state of health," she said as she followed him. From the cab she gave her parting shot.

"And if this horrible thing hadn't happened, I might have stayed with you all the winter and perhaps part of the spring."

William's father wiped his brow with his handkerchief as the cab drove off.

"How dreadful!" said his wife, but she avoided meeting his eye. "It's—it's *disgraceful* of William," she went on with sudden spirit. "You must speak to him."

"I will," said his father determinedly. "William!" he shouted sternly from the hall.

William's heart sank.

"She's told," he murmured, his last hope gone.

"You'd better go and get it over," advised Henry.

"William!" repeated the voice still more fiercely.

Henry moved nearer the window, prepared for instant flight if the voice's owner should follow it up the stairs.

"Go on," he urged. "He'll only come up for you."

William slowly removed the barricade and descended the stairs. He had remembered to take off the crown and dressing gown, but his one-sided moustache still hung limply over his mouth.

His father was standing in the hall.

"What's that horrible thing on your face?" he began.

"Whiskers," answered William laconically.

His father accepted the explanation.

"Is it true," he went on, "that you actually took your friends into your aunt's room without permission and hung vulgar placards around it?"

William glanced up into his father's face and suddenly took hope. Mr. Brown was no actor.

"Yes," he admitted.

"It's disgraceful," said Mr. Brown, "*disgraceful!* That's all."

But it was not quite all. Something hard and round slipped into William's hand. He ran lightly upstairs.

"Hello!" said Henry, surprised. "That's not taken long. What——"

William opened his hand and showed something that shone upon his extended palm.

"Look!" he said. "Crumbs! Look!" It was a bright half-crown.

from *Just—William*

William and White Satin

"I'd simply love to have a page," murmured Miss Grant wistfully. "A wedding seems so—second-rate without a page."

Mrs. Brown, her aunt and hostess, looked across the tea-table at her younger son, who was devouring iced cake with that disregard for consequences which is the mark of youth.

"There's William," she said doubtfully. Then, "You've had quite enough cake, William."

Miss Grant studied William's countenance, which at that moment expressed intense virtue persecuted beyond all bearing.

"*Enough!*" he repeated. "I've had hardly any yet. I was only jus' beginning to have some when you looked at me. It's a plain cake. It won't do me any harm. It's a plain cake. It won't do me any harm. I wu'nt eat it if it'd to me any harm. Sugar's *good* for you. Animals eat it to keep healthy. *Horses* eat it an' it don't do 'em any *harm*, an' poll parrots an' things eat it an' it don't do 'em any——"

"Oh, don't argue, William," said his mother wearily.

William's gift of eloquence was known and feared in his family circle.

Then Miss Grant brought out the result of her study of his countenance.

"He's got such a—*modern* face!" she said. "There's something essentially mediæval and romantic about the idea of a page."

Mrs. Brown (from whose house the wedding was to take place) looked worried.

"There's nothing mediæval or romantic about William," she said.

"Well,"—Miss Grant's intellectual face lit up—"what about his cousin Dorita. They're about the same age, aren't they? Both eleven. Well, the *two* of them in white satin with bunches of holly. Don't you think? Would you mind having her to stay for the ceremony?" (Miss Grant always referred to her wedding as "the ceremony.") "If you don't have his hair cut for a bit, he mightn't look so bad?"

William had retired to the barden with his three bosom friends—Ginger, Henry, and Douglas—where he was playing his latest game of mountaineering. A plank had been placed against the garden wall, and up this scrambled the three, roped together and wearing feathers in their caps. William was wearing an old golf cap of his mother's, and mentally pictured himself as an impressive and heroic figure. Before they reached the top they invariably lost their foothold, rolled down the plank and fell in a confused and bruised heap at the bottom. The bruises in no way detracted from the charm of the game. To William the fascination of any game consisted mainly in the danger to life and limb involved. The game had been suggested by an old alpenstock which had been thoughtlessly presented to William by a friend of Mr. Brown's. The paint of the staircase and upstairs corridor had been completely ruined before the family knew of the gift, and the alpenstock had been confiscated for a week, then restored on the condition that it was not to be brought into the house. The result was the game of mountaineering up the plank. They carried the alpenstock in turns, but William had two turns running to mark the fact that he was its proud possessor.

Mrs. Brown approached William on the subject of his prospective rôle of page with a certain apprehension. The normal attitude of William's family towards William was one of apprehension.

"Would you like to go to Cousin Sybil's wedding?" she said.

"No, I wu'nt," said William without hesitation.

"Wouldn't you like to go dressed up?" she said.

"Red Injun?" said William with a gleam of hope.

"Er—no, not exactly."

"Pirate?"

"Not quite."

"I'd go as a Red Injun, or I'd go as a Pirate," he said firmly, "but I wu'nt go as anything else."

"A page," said Miss Grant's clear, melodious voice, "is a mediæval and romantic idea, William. There's the glamour of chivalry about it that should appeal strongly to a boy of your age."

William turned his inscrutable countenance upon her and gave her a cold glare.

They discussed his costume in private.

"I've got a pair of lovely white silk stockings," said his mother. "They'd do for tights, and Ethel has got a satin petticoat that's just beginning to go in one place. I should think we could make some sort of costume from that, don't you? We'll buy some more white satin and get some patterns."

"WOULD YOU LIKE TO GO TO COUSIN SYBIL'S WEDDING?" SHE
ASKED. "NO, I WU'NT," SAID WILLIAM WITHOUT HESITATION.

"No, I won't wear Ethels' ole clothes," said William smouldering. "You all jus' want to make me look ridiclus. You don't care how ridiclus I look. I shall be ridiclus all the rest of my life goin' about in Ethel's ole clothes. I jus' won't do it. I jus' won't go to any ole weddin'. No, I *don't* want to see Cousin Sybil married, an' I jus' *won't* be made look ridiclus in Ethel's ole clothes."

They reasoned and coaxed and threatened, but in vain. Finally William yielded to parental authority and went about his world with an air of a martyr doomed to the stake. Even the game of mountaineering had lost its charm and the alpenstock lay neglected against the garden wall. The attitude of his select circle of friends was not encouraging.

"Yah! *Page!* Who's goin' to be a *page?* Oh, crumbs. A page all dressed up in white. *Dear* little Willie. Won't he look swe-e-e-et?"

Life became very full. It was passed chiefly in the avenging of insults. William cherished a secret hope that the result of this would be to leave him disfigured for life and so unable to attend the wedding. However, except for a large lump on his forehead, he was none the worse. He eyed the lump thoughtfully in his looking-glass and decided that with a little encouragement it might render his public appearance in an affair of romance an impossibility. But the pain which resulted from one heroic effort at banging it against the wall caused him to abandon the plan.

Dorita arrived the next week, and with her her small brother, Michael, aged three. Dorita was slim and graceful, with a pale little oval face and dark curling hair.

Miss Grant received her on the doorstep.

"Well, my little maid of honour?" she said in her flute-like tones. "Welcome! We're going to be such friends—you and me and William—the bride" (she blushed and bridled becomingly) "and her little page and her little maid of honour. William's a boy, and he's just a *leetle* bit thoughtless and doesn't realise the romance of it all. I'm sure you will. I see it in your dear little face. We'll have some lovely talks together." Her eyes fell upon Michael and narrowed suddenly. "He'd look sweet, too, in white satin, wouldn't he?" turning to Mrs. Brown. "He could walk between them. . . . We could buy some more white satin. . . ."

When they had gone the maid of honour turned dark, long-lashed, demure eyes upon William.

"Soft mug, that," she said in clear refined tones, nodding in the direction of the door through which the tall figure of Miss Grant had just disappeared.

William was vaguely cheered by her attitude.

"Are you keen on this piffling wedding affair? she went on carelessly, "'cause I jolly well tell you I'm not."

William felt that he had found a kindred spirit. He unbent so far as to take her to the stable and show her a field-mouse he had caught and was keeping in a cardboard box.

"I'm teachin' it to dance," he confided, "an' it oughter fetch a jolly lot of money when it can dance proper. Dancin' mice do, you know. They show 'em on the stage, and people on the stage get pounds an' pounds every night, so I bet mice do, too—at least the folks the mice belong to what dance on the stage. I'm teachin' it to dance by holdin' a biscuit over its head and movin' it about. It bit me twice yesterday." He proudly displayed his mutilated finger. "I only caught it yesterday. It oughter learn all right to-day," he added hopefully.

Her intense disappointment, when the only trace of the field-mouse that could be found was the cardboard box with a hole gnawed at one corner, drew William's heart to her still more.

He avoided Henry, Douglas and Ginger. Henry, Douglas and Ginger had sworn to be at the church door to watch William descend from the carriage in the glory of his white satin apparel, and William felt that friendship could not stand the strain.

He sat with Dorita on the cold and perilous perch of the garden wall and discussed Cousin Sybil and the wedding. Dorita's language delighted and fascinated William.

"She's a soppy old luny," she would remark sweetly, shaking her dark curls. "The soppiest old luny you'd see in any old place on *this* old earth, you betcher life! She's made of sop. I wouldn't be found dead in a ditch with her—wouldn't touch her with the butt-end of a barge-pole. She's an assified cow, she is. Humph!"

"Those children are a *leetle* disappointing as regards character—to a child lover like myself," confided Miss Grant to her intellectual *fiancé*. "I've tried to sound their depths, but there are no depths to sound. There is none of the mystery, the glamour, the 'clouds of glory' about them. They are so—so material."

The day of the ordeal drew nearer and nearer, and William's spirits sank lower and lower. His life seemed to stretch before him—youth, manhood, and old age—dreary and desolate, filled only with humiliation and shame. His prestige and reputation would be blasted for ever. He would no longer be William—the Red Indian, the pirate, the dare-devil. He would simply be the Boy Who Went to a Wedding Dressed in White Satin. Evidently there would be a surging crowd of small boys at the church door. Every boy for miles round who knew William even by sight had volunteered the information that he would be there. William was to ride with Dorita and Michael in the bride's carriage. In imagination he already descended from the carriage and heard the chorus of jeers. His cheeks grew hot at the thought. His life for years afterwards would consist solely in the avenging of insults. He followed the figure of the blushing bride-to-be with a baleful glare. In his worst moments he contemplated murder. The violence of his outburst when his mother mildly suggested a wedding present to the bride from her page and maid of honour horrified her.

"I'm bein' made look ridiclus all the rest of my life," he ended. "I'm not givin' her no present. I know what I'd *like* to give her," he added darkly.

"Yes, and I *do*, too."

Mrs. Brown forebore to question further.

The day of the wedding dawned coldly bright and sunny. William's expressions of agony and complaints of various startling symptoms of serious illnesses were ignored by his experienced family circle.

Michael was dressed first of the three in his minute white satin suit and sent down into the morning-room to play quietly. Then an unwilling William was captured from the darkest recess of the stable and dragged pale and protesting to the slaughter.

"Yes, an' I'll *die* pretty soon, prob'ly," he said pathetically, "and then p'r'aps you'll be a bit sorry, an' I shan't care."

In Michael there survived two of the instincts of primitive man, the instinct of foraging for food and that of concealing it from his enemies when found. Earlier in the day he had paid a visit to the kitchen and found it

"SHE'S A SOPPY OLD LUNY!" DORITA REMARKED SWEETLY.

empty. Upon the table lay a pound of butter and a large bag of oranges. These he had promptly confiscated and, with a fear of interruption born of experience, he had retired with them under the table in the morning-room. Before he could begin his feast he had been called upstairs to be dressed for the ceremony. On his return (immaculate in white satin) he found to his joy that his treasure trove had not been discovered. He began on the butter first. What he could not eat he smeared over his face and curly hair. Then he felt a sudden compunction and tried to remove all traces of the crime by rubbing his face and hair violently with a woolly mat. Then he sat down on the Chesterfield and began the oranges. They were very yellow and juicy and rather overripe. He crammed them into his mouth with both little fat hands at once. He was well aware, even at his tender years, that life's sweetest joys come soonest to an end. Orange juice mingled with wool fluff and butter on his small round face. It trickled down his cheeks and fell on to his white lace collar. His mouth and the region round it were completely yellow. He had emptied the oranges out of the bag all around him on the seat. He was sitting in a pool of juice. His suit was covered with it, mingled with pips and skin, and still he ate on.

His first interruption was William and Dorita, who came slowly downstairs holding hands in silent sympathy, two gleaming figures in white satin. They walked to the end of the room. They also had been sent to the morning-room with orders to "play quietly" until summoned.

"*Play?*" William had echoed coldly. "I don't feel much like *playing.*"

They stared at Michael, openmouthed and speechless. Lumps of butter and bits of wool stuck in his curls and adhered to the upper portion of his face. They had been washed away from the lower portion of it by orange juice. His suit was almost covered with it. Behind he was saturated with it.

"*Crumbs!*" said William at last.

"*You'll* catch it," remarked his sister.

Michael retreated hastily from the scene of his misdeeds.

"Mickyth good now," he lisped deprecatingly.

They looked at the seat he had left—a pool of crushed orange fragments and juice. Then they looked at each other.

"*He'll* not be able to go," said Dorita slowly.

Again they looked at the empty orange-covered Chesterfield and again they looked at each other.

"Heth kite good now," said Michael hopefully.

Then the maid of honour, aware that cold deliberation often kills the most glorious impulses, seized William's hand.

"Sit down. *Quick!*" she whispered sharply.

Without a word they sat down. They sat till they felt the cold moisture penetrate to their skins. Then William heaved a deep sigh.

"*We* can't go now," he said.

Through the open door they saw a little group coming—Miss Grant in shining white, followed by William's mother, arrayed in her brightest and best, and William's father, whose expression revealed a certain weariness mingled with a relief that the whole thing would soon be over.

"Here's the old sardine all togged up," whispered Dorita.

"William! Dorita! Michael!" they called.

Slowly William, Dorita and Michael obeyed the summons.

When Miss Grant's eyes fell upon the strange object that was Michael, she gave a loud scream.

"*Michael!* Oh, the *dreadful* child!"

She clasped the centre of the door and looked as though about to swoon.

Michael began to sob.

"*Poor* Micky," he said through his tears. "He feelth tho thick."

They removed him hastily.

"Never mind, dear," said Mrs. Brown soothingly, "the other two look sweet."

But Mr. Brown had wandered further into the room and thus obtained a sudden and startling view of the page and maid of honour from behind.

"What? Where?" he began explosively.

William and Dorita turned to him instinctively, thus providing Mrs. Brown and the bride with the spectacle that had so disturbed him.

The bride gave a second scream—shriller and wilder than the first.

"Oh, what have they done? Oh, the *wretched* children! And just when I wanted to feel *calm*. Just when all depends on my feeling *calm*. Just when——"

"We was walkin' round the room an' we sat down on the Chesterfield and there was this stuff on it an' it came on our clothes," explained William stonily and monotonously and all in one breath.

"*Why* did you sit down," said his mother.

"We was walkin' round an' we jus' felt tired and we sat down on the Chesterfield and there was this stuff on it an' it came on——"

"Oh, *stop!* Didn't you *see* it there?"

William considered.

"Well, we was jus' walking round the room," he said, 'an' we jus' felt tired and we sat——"

"*Stop* saying that."

"Couldn't we make *cloaks?*" wailed the bride, "to hang down and cover them all up behind. It wouldn't take long——"

Mr. Brown took out his watch.

"The carriage has been waiting a quarter of an hour already," he said firmly. "We've no time to spare. Come along, my dear. We'll continue the investigation after the service. You can't go, of course, you must stay at home now," he ended, turning a stern eye upon William. There was an unconscious note of envy in his voice.

"And I did so *want* to have a page," said Miss Grant plaintively as she turned away.

Joy and hope returned to William with a bound. As the sound of wheels was heard down the drive he turned head over heels several times on the lawn, then caught

"THERE WAS THIS STUFF ON THE CHESTERFIELD, AND IT CAME ON OUR CLOTHES," WILLIAM EXPLAINED STONILY ALL IN ONE BREATH.

sight of his long-neglected alpenstock leaning against a wall.

"Come on," he shouted joyfully. "I'll teach you a game I made up. It's mountaineerin'."

She watched him place a plank against the wall and begin his perilous ascent.

"You're a mug," she said in her clear, sweet voice. "I know a mountaineering game worth ten of that old thing."

And it says much for the character and moral force of the maid-of-honour that William meekly put himself in the position of pupil.

It must be explained at this point that the domestics of the Brown household were busy arranging refreshments in a marquee in the garden. The front hall was quite empty.

In about a quarter of an hour the game of mountaineering was in full swing. On the lowest steps of the staircase reposed the mattress from William's father's and mother's bed, above it the mattress from Miss Grant's bed, above that the mattress from William's bed, and on the top, the mattress from Dorita's bed. In all the bedrooms the bedclothes lay in disarray on the floor. A few nails driven through the ends of the mattresses into the stairs secured the stability of the "mountain." Still wearing their robes of ceremony, they scrambled up in stockinged feet, every now and then losing foothold and rolling down to the pile of pillows and bolsters (taken indiscriminately from all the beds) which was arranged at the foot of the staircase. Their mirth was riotous and uproarious. They used the alpenstock in turns. It was a great help. They could get a firm hold on the mattresses with the point of the alpenstock. William stood at the top of the mountain,

THEY USED THE ALPENSTOCK IN TURNS—IT WAS A GREAT HELP.

hot and panting, his alpenstock in his hand, and paused for breath. He was well aware that retribution was not far off—was in the neighbouring church, to be quite exact, and would return in a carriage within the next few minutes. He was aware that an explanation of the yellow stain was yet to be demanded. He was aware that this was not a use to which the family mattresses could legitimately be put. But be cared for none of these

things. In his mind's eye he only saw a crowd of small
boys assembled outside a church door with eager eyes
fixed on a carriage from which descended—Miss Grant,
Mrs. Brown, and Mr. Brown. His life stretched before
him bright and rose-coloured. A smile of triumph
curved his lips.

"Yah! Who waited at a church for someone what
never came? Yah!"

"I hope you didn't get a bad cold waitin' for me on
Wednesday at the church door."

"Some folks is easy had. I bet you all believed I was
coming on Wednesday."

Such sentences floated idly through his mind.

"I say, my turn for that stick with the spike."

William handed it to her in silence.

"I say," she repeated, "what do you think of this
marriage business?"

"Dunno," said William laconically.

"If I'd got to marry," went on the maid of honour,
"I'd as soon marry *you* as anyone."

"I wu'nt mind," said the page gallantly. "But," he
added hastily, "in ornery clothes."

"Oh, yes," she lost her foothold and rolled down to
the pile of pillows. From them came her voice muffled,
but clear as ever. "You betcher life. In ornery clothes."

from *Just—William*

William's New Year's Day

William went whistling down the street, his hands in his pockets. William's whistle was more penetrating than melodious. Sensitive people fled shuddering at the sound. The proprietor of the sweet-shop, however, was not sensitive. He nodded affably as William passed. William was a regular customer of his—as regular, that is, as a wholly inadequate allowance would permit. Encouraged William paused at the doorway and ceased to whistle.

"'Ullo, Mr. Moss!" he said.

"'Ullo, William!" said Mr. Moss.

"Anythin' cheap to-day?" went on William hopefully.

Mr. Moss shook his head.

"Twopence an ounce cheapest," he said.

William sighed.

"That's awful *dear*," he said.

"What isn't dear? Tell me that. What isn't dear?" said Mr. Moss lugubriously.

"Well, gimme two ounces. I'll pay you tomorrow," said William casually.

Mr. Moss shook his head.

"Go on!" said William. "I get my money to-morrow. You know I get my money to-morrow."

"Cash, young sir," said Mr. Moss heavily. "My terms is cash. 'Owever," he relented, "I'll give you a few over when the scales is down to-morrow for a New Year's gift."

"Honest Injun?"

"Honest Injun."

"Well, gimme them now then," said William.

Mr. Moss hesitated.

"They wouldn't be no New Year's gift then, would they?" he said.

William considered.

"I'll eat 'em to-day but I'll *think* about 'em tomorrow," he promised. "That'll make 'em a New Years's gift."

Mr. Moss took out a handful of assorted fruit drops and passed them to William. William received them gratefully.

"An' what good resolution are you going to take to-morrow?" went on Mr. Moss.

William crunched in silence for a minute, then,

"Good resolution?" he questioned. "I ain't got none."

"You've got to have a good resolution for New Year's Day," said Mr. Moss firmly.

"Same as giving up sugar in tea in Lent and wearing blue on Oxford and Cambridge Boat Race Day?" said William with interest.

"Yes, same as that. Well, you've got to think of some fault you'd like to cure and start to-morrow."

William pondered.

"Can't think of anything," he said at last. "You think of something for me."

"You might take one to do your school work properly," he suggested.

William shook his head.

"No," he said, "that wun't be much fun, would it? Crumbs! It *wun't!*"

"Or—to keep your clothes tidy?" went on his friend.

William shuddered at the thought.

"Or to—give up shouting and whistling."

William crammed two more sweets into his mouth and shook his head very firmly.

"Crumbs, No!" he ejaculated indistinctly.

"Or to be perlite."

"Perlite?"

"Yes. 'Please' and 'thank you,' and 'if you don't mind me sayin' so,' and 'if you excuse me contradictin' of you,' and 'can I do anything for you?' and such like."

William was struck with this.

"Yes, I might be that," he said. He straightened his collar and stood up. "Yes, I might try bein' that. How long has it to go on, though?"

"Not long," said Mr. Moss. "Only the first day gen'rally. Folks gen'rally give 'em up after that."

"What's yours?" said William, putting four sweets into his mouth as he spoke.

Mr. Moss looked round his little shop with the air of a conspirator, then leant forward confidentially.

"I'm goin' to arsk 'er again," he said.

"Who?" said William mystified.

"Someone I've arsked regl'ar every New Year's Day for ten year."

"Asked what?" said William, gazing sadly at his last sweet.

"Arsked to take me. o' course," said Mr. Moss with an air of contempt for William's want of intelligence.

"Take you where?" said William. "Where d'you want to go? Why can't you go yourself?"

"Ter *marry* me, I means," said Mr. Moss, blushing slightly as he spoke.

"Well," said William with a judicial air, "I wun't have asked the same one for ten years. I'd have tried someone else. I'd have gone on asking other people, if I wanted to get married. You'd be sure to find someone that wouldn't mind you—with a sweet-shop, too. She must be a softie. Does she *know* you've got a sweet-shop?"

Mr. Moss merely sighed and popped a bull's eye into his mouth with an air of abstracted melancholy.

*   *   *

The next morning William leapt out of bed with an expression of stern resolve. "I'm goin' to be p'lite," he remarked to his bedroom furniture. "I'm going' to be p'lite all day."

He met his father on the stairs as he went down to breakfast.

"Good mornin', Father," he said, with what he fondly imagined to be a courtly manner. "Can I do anything for you to-day?"

His father looked down at him suspiciously.

"What do you want now?" he demanded.

William was hurt.

"I'm only bein' p'lite. It's—you know—one of those things you take on New Year's Day. Well, I've took one to be p'lite."

His father apologised. "I'm sorry," he said. "You see, I'm not used to it. It startled me."

At breakfast William's politeness shone forth in all its glory.

"Can I pass you anything, Robert?" he said sweetly.

"GOOD MORNIN', FATHER," SAID WILLIAM WITH WHAT HE FONDLY
IMAGINED TO BE A COURTLY MANNER.

His elder brother coldly ignored him. "Going to rain again," he said to the world in general.

"If you'll 'scuse me contradicting of you Robert," said William, "I heard the milkman sayin' it was goin' to be fine. If you'll 'scuse me contradictin' you."

"Look here!" said Robert angrily, "Less of your cheek!"

"Seems to me no one in this house understands wot bein' p'lite is," said William bitterly. "Seems to me one might go on bein' p'lite in this house for years an' no one know wot one was doin'.."

His mother looked at him anxiously.

"You're feeling quite well, dear, aren't you?" she said. "You haven't got a headache or anything, have you?"

"No. I'm bein' *p'lite*," he said irritably, then pulled himself up suddenly. "I'm quite well, thank you, Mother dear," he said in a tone of cloying sweetness.

"Does it hurt you much?" inquired his brother tenderly.

"No thank you, Robert," said William politely.

After breakfast he received his pocket-money with courteous gratitude.

"Thank you very much, Father."

"Not at all. Pray don't mention it, William. It's quite all right," said Mr. Brown, not to be outdone. Then, "It's rather trying. How long does it last?"

"What?"

"The resolution."

"Oh, bein' p'lite! He said they didn't often do it after the first day."

"He's quite right, whoever he is," said Mr. Brown. "They don't."

"He's goin' to ask her again," volunteered William.

"Who ask who what?" said Mr. Brown, but William had departed. He was already on his way to Mr. Moss's shop.

Mr. Moss was at the door, hatted and coated, and gazing anxiously down the street.

"Goo' mornin' Mr. Moss," said William politely.

Mr. Moss took out a large antique watch.

"He's late!" he said. "I shall miss the train. Oh, dear! It will be the first New Year's Day I've missed in ten years."

William was inspecting the sweets with the air of an expert.

"Them pink ones are new," he said at last. "How much are they?"

"Eightpence a quarter. Oh, dear, I shall miss the train."

"They're very small ones," said William disparagingly. "You'd think they'd be less than that—small ones like that."

"Will you—will you do something for me and I'll *give* you a quarter of those sweets."

William gasped. The offer was almost too munificent to be true.

"I'll do *anythin'* for that," he said simply.

"Well, just stay in the shop till my nephew Bill comes. 'E'll be 'ere in two shakes an' I'll miss my train if I don't go now. 'E's goin' to keep the shop for me till I'm back an' 'e'll be 'ere any minute now. Jus' tell 'im I 'ad to run for to catch my train an' if anyone comes into the shop before 'e comes jus' tell 'em to wait or to come back later. You can weigh yourself a quarter o' those sweets."

Mr. Moss was certainly in a holiday mood. William pinched himself just to make sure that he was still alive and had not been translated suddenly to the realms of the blest.

Mr. Moss, with a last anxious glance at his watch, hurried off in the direction of the station.

William was left alone. He spent a few moments indulging in roseate day dreams. The ideal of his childhood—perhaps of everyone's childhood—was realised. He had a sweet-shop. He walked round the shop with a conscious swagger, pausing to pop into his mouth a Butter Ball—composed, as the label stated, of pure farm cream and best butter. It was all his—all those rows and rows of gleaming bottles of sweets of every size and colour, those boxes and boxes of attractively arranged chocolates. Deliberately he imagined himself as their owner. By the time he had walked round the shop three times he believed that he was the owner.

At this point a small boy appeared in the doorway. William scowled at him.

"Well," he said ungraciously, "what d'you want?" Then, suddenly remembering his resolution, "*Please* what d'you want?"

"Where's Uncle?" said the small boy with equal ungraciousness. "'Cause our Bill's ill an' can't come."

William waved him off.

"That's all right," he said. "You tell 'em that's all right. That's quite all right. See? Now, you go off!"

The small boy stood, as though rooted to the spot. William pressed into one of his hands a stick of liquorice and into the other a packet of chocolate.

"Now, you go *away*! I don't *want* you here. See? You *go away* you little—assified cow"!

William's invective was often wholly original.

The small boy made off, still staring and clutching his spoils. William started to the door and yelled to the retreating figure, "if you don't mind me sayin' so."

He had already come to look upon the Resolution as a kind of god who must at all costs be propitiated. Already the Resolution seemed to have bestowed upon him the dream of his life—a fully-equipped sweet-shop.

He wandered round again and discovered a wholly new sweetmeat called Cokernut Kisses. Its only drawback was its instability. It melted away in the mouth at once. So much so that almost before William was aware of it he was confronted by the empty box. He returned to the more solid charms of the Pineapple Crisp.

He was interrupted by the entrance of a thin lady of uncertain age.

"Good morning," she said icily. "Where's Mr. Moss?"

William answered as well as the presence of five sweets in his mouth would allow him.

"I can't hear a word you say," she said—more frigidly than ever.

William removed two of his five sweets and placed them temporarily on the scale.

"Gone," he said laconically, then murmured vaguely, "thank you," as the thought of the Resolution loomed up in his mind.

"Who's in charge?"

"Me," said William ungrammatically.

She looked at him with distinct disapproval.

"Well, I'll have one of those bars of chocolates."

William looking round the shop, realised suddenly that his own depredations had been on no small scale. But there was a chance of making good any loss that Mr. Moss might otherwise have sustained.

He looked down at the twopenny bars.

"Shillin' each," he said firmly.

She gasped.

"They were only twopence yesterday."

"They're gone up since," said William brazenly, adding a vague, "if you'll kin'ly 'scuse me sayin' so."

"Gone up——?" she repeated indignantly. "Have you heard from the makers they're gone up?"

"Yes'm," said William politely.

"When did you hear?

"This mornin'—if you don't mind me saying so."

William's manner of fulsome politeness seemed to madden her.

"Did you hear by post?"

"Yes'm. By post this mornin'."

She glared at him with vindictive triumph.

"I happen to live opposite, you wicked, lying boy, and I know that the postman did not call here this morning."

William met her eye calmly.

"No, they came round to see me in the night—the makers did. You cou'n't of heard them," he added hastily. "It was when you was asleep. If you'll 'scuse me contradictin' of you."

It is a great gift to be able to lie so as to convince other people. It is a still greater gift to be able to lie so as to convince oneself. William was possessed of the latter gift.

"I shall certainly not pay more than twopence," said his customer severely, taking a bar of chocolate and laying down twopence on the counter. "And I shall report this shop to the Profiteering Committee. It's scandalous. And a pack of wicked lies!"

William scowled at her.

"They're a *shillin'*," he said. "I don't want your nasty ole tuppences. I said they was a *shillin'*."

He followed her to the door. She was crossing the street to her house. "You—you ole *thief!*" he yelled after her, though, true to his Resolution, he added softly with dogged determination, "if you don't mind me sayin' so."

"I'll set the police on you," his late customer shouted angrily back across the street. "You wicked, blasphemous boy!"

William put out his tongue at her, then returned to the shop and closed the door.

Here he discovered that the door, when opened, rang a bell, and, after filling his mouth with Liquorice All Sorts, he spent the next five minutes vigorously opening and shutting the door till something went wrong with the mechanism of the bell. At this he fortified himself with a course of Nutty Footballs and, standing on a chair, began ruthlessly to dismember the bell. He was disturbed by the entry of another customer. Swallowing a Nutty Football whole, he hastened to his post behind the counter.

The newcomer was a little girl of about nine—a very dainty little girl, dressed in a white fur coat and cap and long white gaiters. Her hair fell in golden curls over her white fur shoulders. Her eyes were blue. Her cheeks were velvety and rosy. Her mouth was like a baby's. William had seen this vision on various occasions in the town, but had never yet addressed it. Whenever he had seen it, his heart in the midst of his body had been even as melting wax. He smiled—a self-conscious, sheepish smile. His freckled face blushed to the roots of his short stubby hair. She seemed to find nothing odd in the fact of a small boy being in charge of a sweet-shop. She came up to the counter.

"Please, I want two twopenny bars of chocolate."

Her voice was very clear and silvery.

Ecstasy rendered William speechless. His smile grew wider and more foolish. Seeing his two half-sucked Pineapple Crisps exposed upon the scales, he hastily put them into his mouth.

She laid four pennies on the counter.

William found his voice.

"You can have lots for that," he said huskily. "They've gone cheap. They've gone ever so cheap. You can take all the boxful for that," he went on recklessly. He pressed the box into her reluctant hands. "An'— what else would you like? You jus' tell me that. Tell me what else you'd like?"

"Please, I haven't any more money," gasped a small, bewildered voice.

"*Money* don't matter," said William. "Things is cheap to-day. Things is awful cheap to-day. *Awful* cheap! You can have—anythin' you like for that fourpence. Anythin' you like."

"'Cause it's New Year's Day?" said the vision, with a gleam of understanding.

"Yes," said William, "'cause it's that."

"Is it your shop?"

"Yes," said William with an air of importance. "It's all my shop."

She gazed at him in admiration and envy.

"I'd love to have a sweet-shop." she said wistfully.

"Well, you take anythin' you like," said William generously.

She collected as much as she could carry and started towards the door. "*Sank* you! Sank you ever so!" she said gratefully.

William stood leaning against the door in the easy attitude of the good-natured, all-providing male.

"*MONEY* DON'T MATTER," SAID WILLIAM. "THINGS IS CHEAP
TO-DAY. AWFUL CHEAP!"

"It's all right," he said with an indulgent smile. "Quite
all right. Quite all right." Then, with an inspiration born
of memories of his father earlier in the day. "Not at all.
Don't menshun it. Not at all. Quite all right."
He stopped, simply for lack of further expressions,

and bowed with would-be gracefulness as she went through the doorway.

As she passed the window she was rewarded by a spreading effusive smile in a flushed face.

She stopped and kissed her hand.

William blinked with pure emotion.

He continued his smile long after its recipient had disappeared. Then absent-mindedly he crammed his mouth with a handful of Mixed Dew Drops and sat down behind the counter.

As he crunched Mixed Dew Drops he indulged in a day dream in which he rescued the little girl in the white fur coat from robbers and pirates and a burning house. He was just leaping nimbly from the roof of the burning house, holding the little girl in the white fur coat in his arms, when he caught sight of two of his friends flattening their noses at the window. He rose from his seat and went to the door.

"'Ullo, Ginger! 'Ullo, Henry!" he said with an unsuccessful effort to appear void of self-consciousness.

They gazed at him in wonder.

"I've gotta shop," he went on casually. "Come on in an' look at it."

They peeped round the door-way cautiously and, reassured by the sight of William obviously in sole possession, they entered, openmouthed. They gazed at the boxes and bottles of sweets. Aladdin's Cave was nothing to this.

"Howd' you get it, William?" gasped Ginger.

"Someone gave it me," said William. "I took one of them things to be p'lite an' someone gave it me. Go on," he said kindly. "Jus' help yourselves. Not at all. Jus' help yourselves an' don't menshun it."

They needed no second bidding. With the unerring

instinct of childhood (not unsupported by experience) that at any minute their Eden might be invaded by the avenging angel in the shape of a grown-up, they made full use of their time. They went from box to box, putting handfuls of sweets and chocolates into their mouths. They said nothing, simply because speech was, under the circumstances, a physical impossibility. Showing a foresight for the future, worthy of the noble ant itself, so often held up as a model to childhood, they filled pockets in the intervals of cramming their mouths.

A close observer might have noticed that William now ate little. William himself had been conscious for some time of a curious and inexplicable feeling of coldness towards the tempting dainties around him. He was, however, loth to give in to the weakness, and every now and then he nonchalantly put into his mouth a Toasted Square or a Fruity Bit.

It happened that a loutish boy of about fourteen was passing the shop. At the sight of three small boys rapidly consuming the contents, he became interested.

"What yer doin' of?" he said indignantly, standing in the doorway.

"You get out of my shop," said William valiantly.

"*Yer* shop?" said the boy. "Yer bloomin' well pinchin' things out o' someone else's shop, *I* can see. 'Ere, gimme some of them."

"You get *out!*" said William.

"Get out *yerself!*" said the other.

"If I'd not took one to be p'lite," said William threateningly, "I'd knock you down."

"Yer would, would yer?" said the other, beginning to roll up his sleeves.

"Yes, an' I would, too. You get out." Seizing the nearest bottle, which happened to contain Acid Drops, he began to fire them at his opponent's head. One hit him in the eye. He retired into the street. William, now a-fire for battle, followed him, still hurling Acid Drops with all his might. A crowd of boys collected together. Some gathered Acid Drops from the gutter, others joined the scrimmage. William, Henry, and Ginger carried on a noble fight against heavy odds.

It was only the sight of the proprietor of the shop coming briskly down the side-walk that put an end to the battle. The street boys made off (with what spoils they could gather) in one direction and Ginger and Henry in another. William, clasping an empty Acid Drop bottle to his bosom, was left to face Mr. Moss.

Mr. Moss entered and looked round with an air of bewilderment.

"Where's Bill?" he said.

"He's ill," said William. "He couldn't come. I've been keepin' shop for you. I've done the best I could." He looked round the rifled shop and hastened to propitiate the owner as far as possible. "I've got some money for you," he added soothingly, pointing to the four pennies that represented his morning's takings. "It's not much," he went on with some truth, looking again at the rows of emptied boxes and half-emptied bottles and the *débris* that is always and everywhere the inevitable result of a battle. But Mr. Moss hardly seemed to notice it.

"Thanks, William," he said almost humbly. "William, she's took me. She's goin' ter marry me. Isn't it grand? After all these years!"

"I'm afraid there's a bit of a mess," said William, returning to the more important matter.

Mr. Moss waved aside his apologies.

"It doesn't matter, William," he said. "Nothing

matters to-day. She's took me at last. I'm goin' to shut shop this afternoon and go over to her again. Thanks for staying, William."

"Not at all. Don't menshun it," said William nobly. Then, "I think I've had enough of that bein' p'lite. Will one mornin' do for this year, d'you think?"

"Er—yes. Well, I'll shut up. Don't you stay, William. You'll want to be getting home for lunch."

Lunch? Quite definitely William decided that he did not want any lunch. The very thought of lunch brought with it a feeling of active physical discomfort which was much more than mere absence of hunger. He decided to go home as quickly as possible, though not to lunch.

"Goo'-bye," he said.

"Good-bye," said Mr. Moss.

"I'm afraid you'll find some things gone," said William faintly; "some boys was in."

"That's all right, William," said Mr. Moss, roused again from his rosy dreams. "That's quite all right."

But it was not "quite all right" with William. Reader, if you had been left, at the age of eleven, in sole charge of a sweet shop for a whole morning, would it have been "all right" with you? I trow not. But we will not follow William through the humiliating hours of the afternoon. We will leave him as, pale and unsteady, but as yet master of the situation, he wends his homeward way.

from *Just—William*

William Leads a Better Life

If you go far enough back it was Mr. Strong, William's form master, who was responsible for the whole thing. Mr. Strong set, for homework, more French than it was convenient for William to learn. It happened that someone had presented William with an electric motor, and the things one can do with an electric motor are endless.

Who would waste the precious hours of a summer evening over French verbs with an electric motor simply crying out to be experimented on? Certainly not William.

It wasn't as if there was any *sense* in French verbs. They had been deliberately invented by someone with a grudge against the race of boys—someone probably who'd slipped on a concealed slide or got in the way of a snowball or foolishly come within the danger zone of a catapult. Anyway, whoever it was had devised a mean form of revenge by inventing French verbs and, somehow or other, persuading schoolmasters to adopt them as one of their choicest tortures.

"Well, I never *will* wanter use 'em," said William to his mother when she brought forward the time-honoured argument. "I don't wanter talk to *any* French folks, an' if they wanter talk to me they can learn English. English's 's easy 's easy to talk. It's *silly* havin' other langwidges. I don' see why all the other countries shun't learn English 'stead of us learnin' other langwidges with no *sense* in 'em. English's *sense*."

This speech convinced him yet more firmly of the foolishness of wasting his precious hours of leisure on such futile study, so he devoted all his time and energy to the electric motor. There was some *sense* in the electric motor. William spent a very happy evening.

In the morning, however, things somehow seemed different. He lay in bed and considered the matter. There was no doubt that Mr. Strong could make himself extremely disagreeable over French verbs.

William remembered that he had threatened to make himself more disagreeable than usual if William did not know them "next time". This was "next time" and William did not know them. William had not even attempted to learn them. The threats of Mr. Strong had seemed feeble, purposeless, contemptible things last night when the electric motor threw its glamour over the whole world. This morning they didn't. They seemed suddenly much more real than the electric motor.

But surely it was possible to circumvent them. William was not the boy to give in weakly to any fate. He heard his mother's door opening, and, assuming an expression of intense suffering, called weakly, "Mother." Mrs. Brown entered the room fully dressed.

"Aren't you up yet, William?" she said: "Be quick or you'll be late for school."

William intensified yet further his expression of suffering.

"I don' think I feel quite well enough to go to school

this morning, mother, dear," he said faintly.

Mrs. Brown looked distressed. He had employed the ruse countless times before, but it never failed of its effect upon Mrs. Brown. The only drawback was that Mr. Brown, who was still about the house, was of a less trustful and compassionate nature.

Mrs. Brown smoothed his pillow. "Poor little boy," she said tenderly, "where is the pain?"

"All over," said William, playing for safety.

"Dear! dear!" said Mrs. Brown, much perturbed, as she left the room. "I'll just go and fetch the thermometer."

William disliked the thermometer. It was a soulless, unsympathetic thing. Sometimes, of course, a hot-water bottle, judiciously placed, would enlist its help, but that was not always easy to arrange.

To William's dismay his father entered the room with the thermometer.

"Well, William," he said cheerfully, "I hear you're too ill to go to school. That's a great pity, isn't it. I'm sure it's a great grief to you?"

William turned up his eyes. "Yes, father," he said dutifully and suspiciously.

"Now where exactly is the pain and what sort of pain is it?"

William knew from experience that descriptions of non-existent pains are full of pitfalls. By a master-stroke he avoided them.

"It hurts me to talk," he said.

"What sort of pain does it hurt you with?" said his father brutally.

William made some inarticulate noises, then closed his eyes with a moan of agony.

"I'll just step round and fetch the doctor," said Mr.

Brown, still quite cheerful.

The doctor lived next door. William considered this a great mistake. He disliked the close proximity of doctors. They were equally annoying in real and imaginary diseases.

William made little brave reassuring noises to inform his father that he'd rather the doctor wasn't troubled and it was all right, and please no one was to bother about him, and he'd just stay in bed and probably be all right by the afternoon. But his father had already gone.

William lay in bed and considered his position.

Well, he was going to stick to it, anyway. He'd just make noises to the doctor, and they couldn't say he hadn't got a pain where he said he had if they didn't know where he said he had one. His mother came in and took his temperature. Fate was against him. There was no hot-water bottle handy. But he squeezed it as hard as he could in a vague hope that that would have some effect on it.

"It's normal, dear," said his mother, relieved. "I'm so glad."

He made a sinister noise to imply that the malady was too deep-seated to be shown by an ordinary thermometer.

He could hear the doctor and his father coming up the stairs. They were laughing and talking. William, forgetting the imaginary nature of his complaint, felt a wave of indignation and self-pity.

The doctor came in breezily. "Well, young man," he said, "what's the trouble?"

William made his noise. By much practice he was becoming an expert at the noise. It implied an intense desire to explain his symptoms, thwarted by physical incapability, and it thrilled with suffering bravely endured.

"Can't speak—is that it?" said the doctor.

"Yes, that's it," said William, forgetting his *rôle* for the minute.

"Well—open your mouth, and let's have a look at your throat," said the doctor.

William opened his mouth and revealed his throat. The doctor inspected the recesses of that healthy and powerful organ.

"I see," he said at last. "Yes—very bad. But I can operate here and now, fortunately. I'm afraid I can't give an anæsthetic in this case, and I'm afraid it will be rather painful—but I'm sure he's a brave boy."

William went pale and looked around desperately, French verbs were preferable to this.

"I'll wait just three minutes," said the doctor kindly. "Occasionally in cases like this the patient recovers his voice quite suddenly." He took out his watch. William's father was watching the scene with an air of enjoyment that William found maddening. "I'll give him just three minutes," went on the doctor, "and if the patient hasn't recovered the power of speech by then, I'll operate——"

The patient decided hastily to recover the power of speech.

"I can speak now," he said with an air of surprise. "Isn't it funny? I can talk quite ordinary now. It came on quite sudden."

"No pain anywhere?" said the doctor.

"No," said the patient quickly.

The patient's father stepped forward.

"Then you'd better get up as quickly as you can," he said. "You'll be late for school, but doubtless they'll know how to deal with that."

They did know how to deal with that. They knew, too, how to deal with William's complete ignorance on the subject of French verbs. Excuses (and William had many—some of them richly ingenious) were of no avail. He went home to lunch embittered and disillusioned with life.

"You'd think knowin' how to work a motor engine'd be more *useful* than sayin' French verbs," he said. "S'pose I turned out an engineer—well, wot use'd French verbs be to me 'n I'd *have* to know how to work a motor engine. An' I was so ill this mornin' that the doctor wanted to do an operate on me, but I said I *can't* miss school an' get all behind the others, an' I came, awful ill, an' all they did was to carry on something terrible 'cause I was jus' a minute or two late an' jus' ha'n't had time to do those old French verbs that aren't no *use* to anyone——"

Ginger, Henry and Douglas sympathised with him for some time, then began to discuss the history lesson. The history master, feeling for the moment as bored with Edward the Sixth as were most of his class, had given them a graphic account of the life of St. Francis of Assisi. He had spent the Easter holidays at Assisi. William, who had been engaged in executing creditable caricatures of Mr. Strong and the doctor, had paid little attention, but Ginger remembered it all. It had been such a welcome change from William the Conqueror. William began to follow the discussion.

"Yes, but why'd he do it?" he said.

"Well, he jus' got kind of fed up with things an' he had visions an' things an' he took some things of his father's to sell to get money to start it——"

"*Crumbs!*" interpolated William. "Wasn't his father mad?"

"Yes, but that din't matter. He was a saint, was Saint Francis, so he could sell his father's things if he liked, an' he 'n his frien's took the money an' got funny long sort of clothes an' went an' lived away in a little house by themselves, an' he uster preach to animals an' to people an' call everythin' 'brother' an' 'sister', and they cooked all their own stuff to eat an'——"

"Jolly fine it sounds," said William enviously, "an' did their people let 'em?"

"They couldn't stop 'em," said Ginger. "An' Francis, he was the head one, an' the others all called themselves Franciscans, an' they built churches an' things."

They had reached the gate of William's house now and William turned in slowly.

"G'bye till this afternoon," called the others cheerfully.

Lunch increased still further William's grievances. No one inquired after his health, though he tried to look pale and ill, and refused a second helping of rice pudding with a meaning, "No, thank you, not to-day. I would if I felt all right, thank you very much." Even that elicited no anxious inquiries. No one, thought William, as he finished up the rice pudding in secret in the larder afterwards, no one else in the world, surely, had such a callous family. It would just serve them right to lose him altogether. It would just serve them right if he went off like St. Francis and never came back.

He met Henry and Ginger and Douglas again as usual on the way to school.

"Beastly ole 'rithmetic," said Henry despondently.

"Yes, an' then beastly ole jography," sighed Douglas.

"Well," said William, "let's not go. I've been

thinkin' a lot about that Saint man. I'd a lot sooner be a saint an' build things an' cook things an' preach to things than keep goin' to school an' learnin' the same ole things day after day an' day after day—all things like French verbs without any *sense* in them. I'd much sooner be a saint, wun't you?"

The other Outlaws looked doubtful, yet as though attracted by the idea.

"They wun't let us," said Henry.

"They can't stop us bein' saints," said William piously, "an' doin' good an' preachin'—not if we have visions, an' I feel's if I could have visions quite easy."

The Outlaws had slackened their pace.

"What'd we have to do first?" said Ginger.

"Sell some of our father's things to get money," said William firmly. "'S all right," he went on, anticipating possible objections, "he did, so I s'pose anyone can if they're settin' out to be saints—of course it would be different if we was jus' stealin', but bein' saints makes it diff'rent. Stands to reason saints can't steal."

"Well, what'd we do *then?*" said Douglas.

"Then we find a place an' get the right sort of clothes to wear——"

"Seems sort of a waste of money," said Henry sternly, "spendin' it on *clothes*. What sort of clothes were they?"

"He showed us a picture," said Ginger, "don' you remember? Sort of long things goin' right down to his feet."

"Dressing-gowns'd do," said Douglas excitedly.

"No, you're thinkin' of detectives," said Henry firmly; "detectives wear dressing-gowns."

"No," said William judicially. "I don' see why dressing-gowns shun't do. Then we can save the money an' spend it on things to eat."

"Where'll we live?"

"We oughter build a place, but till we've built it we can live in the old barn."

"Where'll we get the animals to preach to?"

"Well, there's a farm just across the way from the barn, you know. We can start on Jumble an' then go on to the farm ones when we've had some practice."

"An' what'll we be called? We can't be the Outlaws now we're saints, I s'pose?"

"What were they called?"

"Franciscans. . . . After Francis—he was the head one."

"Well, if there's goin' to be any head one," said William in a tone that precluded any argument on the subject, "if there's going to be any head one, I'm going to be him."

None of them denied to William the position of leader. It was his by right. He had always led, and he was a leader they were proud to follow.

"Well, they just put 'cans' on to the end of his name," said Henry. "Franciscans. So we'll be William-cans——"

"Sounds kind of funny," said Ginger dubiously.

"I think it sounds jolly fine," said William proudly. "I vote we start to-morrow, 'cause it's rather late to start to-day, an' anyway, it's Saturday to-morrow, so we can get well started for Monday, 'cause they're sure to make a fuss about our not turnin' up at school on Monday. You all come to the old barn d'rectly after breakfast to-morrow an' bring your dressing-gowns an' somethin of your father's to sell——"

The first meeting of the Williamcans was held directly after breakfast the next morning. They had all left notes dictated by William on their bedroom mantelpieces announcing that they were now saints and had left home for ever.

They deposited their dressing-gowns on the floor of the old barn and then inspected the possessions that they had looted from their unsuspecting fathers. William had appropriated a pair of slippers, not because he thought their absence would be undetected (far from it) or because he thought they would realise vast wealth (again far from it), but it happened that they were kept in the fender-box of the morning-room, and William had found himself alone there for a few minutes that morning, and slippers can be concealed quite easily beneath one's coat. He could have more easily appropriated something of his mother's, but William liked to do things properly. Saint Francis had sold something of his father's, so Saint William would do the same. Douglas took from his pocket an inkstand, purloined from his father's desk; Ginger had two ties and Henry a pair of gloves.

They looked at their spoils with proud satisfaction.

"We oughter get a good deal of money for *these*," said William. "How much did *he* get, d'you know?"

"No, he never said," said Ginger.

"We'd better not put on our saint robes yet—not till we've been down to the village to sell the things. Then we'll put 'em on an' start preachin' an' things."

"Din' we oughter wear round-hoop-sort-of-things on our heads?" said Henry. "They do in pictures. What d'you call 'em?—Halos."

"You don' get *them* till you're dead," said Ginger with an air of wisdom.

"Well, I don't see what good they are to anyone *dead*," said Henry, rather aggrieved.

"No, we've gotter do things *right*," said William sternly. "If the real saints waited till they was dead, we will, too. Anyway, let's go an' sell the things first. An' remember call everything else 'brother' or 'sister'."

"Everything?"

"Yes—*he* did—the other man did."

"You've gotter call me *Saint* William now, Ginger."

"All right, you call me Saint Ginger."

"All right, I'm goin' to—Saint Ginger——"

"Saint William."

"All right."

"Well, where you goin' to sell the slippers?"

"Brother slippers," corrected William. "Well, I'm goin' to sell brother slippers at Mr. Marsh's 'f he'll buy 'em."

"An' I'll take brother ties along, too," said Ginger. "An' Henry take brother gloves, an' Douglas brother inkstand."

"Sister inkstand," said Douglas. "William——

"Saint William," corrected William, patiently.

"Well, Saint William said we could call things brother *or* sister, an' my inkstand's goin' to be sister."

"Swank!" said St. Ginger severely, "always wanting to be diff'rent from other people!"

Mr. Marsh kept a second-hand shop at the end of the village. In his window reposed side by side a motley collection of battered and despised household goods.

He had a less optimistic opinion of the value of brothers slippers and ties and gloves and sister inkstand than the saints.

He refused to allow them more than sixpence each.

"Mean!" exploded St. William indignantly as soon as they had emerged from Mr. Marsh's dingy little sanctum to the village street and the light of day. "I call

him sim'ly *mean*. That's what *I* call him."

"I s'pose now we're saints," said St. Ginger piously, "that we've gotter forgive folks what wrong us like that."

"I'm not goin' to be *that* sort of a saint," said St. William firmly.

Back at the barn they donned their dressing-gowns, St. Henry still grumbling at not being able to wear the "little hoop" on his head.

"Now what d'we do *first?*" said St. Ginger energetically, as he fastened the belt of his dressing-gown.

"Well, anyway, why can't we cut little bits of our hair at the top like they have in pictures?" said St. Henry disconsolately, "that'd be better than *nothin'*."

This idea rather appealed to the saints. St. Douglas discovered a penknife and began to operate at once on St. Henry, but the latter saint's yells of agony soon brought the proceedings to a premature end.

"Well, *you* s'gested it," said St. Douglas, rather hurt, "an' I was doin' it as gently as I could."

"*Gently!*" groaned Henry, still nursing his saintly head. "You were tearing it out by the roots."

"Well, come *on!*" said St. Ginger impatiently, "let's begin now. What did you say we were goin' to do first?"

"Preachin' to animals is the first thing," said William in his most business-like manner. "I've got Brother Jumble here. Ginger—I mean St. Ginger, you hold Brother Jumble while I preach to him 'cause he's not used to it, an' he might try to run away, an' St. Henry an' St. Douglas go out an' preach to birds. The St. Francis man did a lot of preachin' to birds. They came an' sat on his arms. See if you can gettem to do that. Well now, let's start. Ginger—I mean St. Ginger—you catch hold of Brother Jumble."

Henry and Douglas departed. Douglas's dressing-gown, made by a thrifty mother with a view to Douglas's further growth, was slightly too big and tripped him over every few steps. Henry's was made of bath towelling and was rather conspicuous in design. They made their way

ST. WILLIAM STOOD UP TO PREACH TO THE RELUCTANT
JUMBLE. "DEARLY BELOVED JUMBLE," HE BEGAN.

slowly across a field and into a neighbouring wood.

St. Ginger encircled the reluctant Jumble with his arms, and St. William stood up to preach.

"Dearly beloved Jumble——" he began.

"Brother Jumble," corrected St. Ginger, with triumph. He liked to catch the founder of the order tripping.

Jumble, under the delusion that something was expected of him, sat up and begged.

"Dearly beloved Brother Jumble," repeated William. He stopped and cleared his throat in the manner of all speakers who are not sure what to say next.

Jumble, impatient of the other saint's encircling arms, tried another trick, that of standing on his head. Standing on his head was the title given to the performance by Jumble's owner. In reality it consisted of rubbing the top of his head on the ground. None of his legs left the ground, but William always called it "Jumble standing on his head", and was inordinately proud of it.

"Look at him," he said, "isn't that jolly clever? An' no one told him to. Jus' did it without anyone tellin' him to. I bet there's not many dogs like him. I bet he's the cleverest dog there is in England. I wun't mind sayin' he's the cleverest dog there is in the world. I wun't——"

"I thought you was preachin' to him, not talkin' about him," said St. Ginger, sternly. Ginger, who was not allowed to possess a dog, tired occasionally of hearing William sing the praises of his.

"Oh, yes," said St. William with less enthusiasm. "I'll start all over again. Dearly beloved Brother Jumble—I say, what did that St. Francis *say* to the animals?"

"Dunno," said St. Ginger vaguely, "I s'pect he jus' told 'em to—well, to do good an' that sort of thing."

"Dearly beloved Brother Jumble," said William again, "you mus'—do good an—an' stop chasin' cats. Why," he said proudly, "there's not a cat in this village that doesn't run when it sees Jumble comin'. I bet he's the best dog for chasin' cats anywhere round *this* part of England. I bet——"

Jumble, seizing his moment for escape, tore himself from St. Ginger's unwary arms, and leapt up ecstatically at William.

"Good old Jumble," said the saint affectionately. "Good old boy!"

At this point the other two saints returned.

"Well, did you find any birds?" said St. William.

"There was heaps of birds," said St. Douglas in an exasperated tone of voice, "but the minute I started preachin' they all flew off. They din' seem to know how to *act* with saints. They din' seem to know they'd got to sit on our arms an' things. Made us feel *mad*—anyway, we gotter thrush's egg and Henry—I mean St. Henry—jus' wanted one of those——"

"Well," said St. William rather sternly, "I don' think it's the right thing for saints to do—to go preachin' to birds an' then takin' their eggs—I mean their brother eggs."

"There was *lots* more," said Henry. "They *like* you jus' takin' one. It makes it less trouble for 'em hatchin' 'em out."

"Well, anyway," said William, "let's get on with this animal business. P'raps the tame ones'll be better. Let's go across to Jenks' farm an' try on them."

They crept rather cautiously into the farmyard. The feud between Farmer Jenks and the Outlaws was one of long standing. He would probably not realise that the Williamcans were a saintly organisation whose every

WILLIAM WAS ALREADY STRIKING AN ATTITUDE BEFORE HIS CONGREGATION OF COWS

action was inspired by a love of mankind. He would probably imagine that they were still the old unregenerate Outlaws.

"I'll do brother cows," said St. William, "an' St. Ginger do brother pigs, and St. Douglas do brother goats, an' St. Henry do sister hens."

They approached their various audiences. Ginger leant over the pigsty. Then he turned to William, who was already striking an attitude before his congregation of cows, and said: "I say, what've I gotter *say* to 'em?"

At that moment brother goat, being approached too nearly by St. Douglas, butted the saintly stomach, and St. Douglas sat down suddenly and heavily. Brother goat, evidently enjoying this form of entertainment, returned to the charge. St. Douglas fled to the accompaniment of an uproarious farmyard commotion.

Farmer Jenks appeared, and, seeing his old enemies, the Outlaws, actually within his precincts, he uttered a yell of fury and darted down upon them. The saints fled swiftly, St. Douglas holding up his too flowing robe as he went. Brother goat had given St. Douglas a good start and he reached the farm first.

FARMER JENKS UTTERED A YELL OF FURY AND
BORE DOWN UPON THE OUTLAWS. DOUGLAS
FLED SWIFTLY.

"Well," said St. William, panting, "I've *finished* with preachin' to animals. They must have changed a good bit since *his* time. That's all *I* can say."

"Well, what'll we do *now?*" said St. Ginger.

"I should almost think it's time for dinner," said William. "Must be after two, I should think."

No one knew the time. Henry possessed a watch which had been given to him by a great-uncle. Though it may possibly have had some value as an antique, it had not gone for over twenty years. Henry, however, always wore it, and generally remembered to move its hands to a correct position whenever he passed a clock. This took a great deal of time and trouble, but Henry was proud of his watch and liked it to be as nearly right as possible. He consulted it now. He had put it right by his family's hall clock as he came out after breakfast, so its fingers stood at half-past nine. He returned it to his pocket hastily before the others could see the position of the fingers.

"Yes," he said, with the air of an oracle, "it's about dinner-time." Though they all knew that Henry's watch had never gone, yet it had a certain prestige.

"Well, we've gotter *buy* our dinner," said William. "S'pose two of us goes down to the village, an' buys it now with the two shillings we got for sellin' our fathers' things. We've gotter buy all our meals now like what *they* did."

"Well, how d'we get the money when we've finished this? We can't go *on* sellin' our fathers' things. They'd get so mad."

"We beg from folks after that," said Ginger, who was the only one who had paid much attention to the story of the life of St. Francis.

"Well, I bet they won't give us much if *I* know 'em," said William bitterly. "I bet both folks *an'* animals must've been nicer in those times."

It was decided that Douglas and Henry should go
down to the village to purchase provisions for the meal.
It was decided also that they should go in their dressing-
gowns.

"*They* always did," said Ginger firmly, "and folks
may's well get used to us goin' about like that."

"Oh, yes!" said Douglas bitterly. "'S easy to talk like
that when you're not goin' down to the shop."

Mr. Moss, the proprietor of the village sweet-shop,
held his sides with laughter when he saw them.

"Well, I never!" he said. "Well, I never! What boys
you are for a joke, to be sure!"

"It's not a joke," said Henry. "We're Williamcans."

Douglas had caught sight of the clock on the desk
behind the counter.

"I say!" he said. "It's only eleven o'clock."

Henry took out his watch.

"Oh, yes," he said, as if he had made a mistake when
he looked at it before.

For their midday meal the two saints purchased a large
bag of chocolate creams, another of bull's-eyes, and, to
form the more solid part of the meal, four cream buns.

Ginger and William and Jumble were sitting comfort-
ably in the old barn when the two emissaries returned.

"*We've* had a nice time!" exploded St. Henry. "All
the boys in the place runnin' after us an' shoutin' at us."

"You should've just stood still an' *preached* to 'em,"
said the founder of the order calmly.

"*Preached* to 'em!" repeated Henry. "They wun't
have listened. They was shoutin' an' throwin' things an'
running at us."

"What'd you do?"

"Run," said the gallant saint simply. "An' Douglas

has tore his robe, an' I've fallen in the mud in mine."

"Well, they've gotter last you all the rest of your life," said St. William, "so you oughter take more care of 'em," and added with more interest, "what've you got for dinner?"

They displayed their purchases and their choice was warmly and unanimously approved by the saints.

"Wish we'd thought of something to drink," said Henry.

But William, with a smile of pride, brought out from his pocket a bottle of dark liquid.

"I *thought* of that," he said, holding it out with a flourish, "have a drink of brother lik'rice water."

Not to be outdone, Douglas took up one of the bags.

"An' have a sister cream-bun," he said loudly.

When they had eaten and drunk to repletion they rested for a short time from their labours. William had meant to fill in time by preaching to Jumble, but decided instead to put Jumble through his tricks.

"I s'pose they *know* now at home that we've gone for good," said Henry with a sigh.

Ginger looked out of the little window anxiously.

"Yes. I only hope to goodness they won't come an' try to fetch us back," he said.

But he need not have troubled. Each family thought that the missing member was having lunch with one of the others, and felt no anxiety, only a great relief. And none of the notes upon the mantelpieces had been found.

"What'll we do *now?*" said William, rousing himself at last.

"*They* built a church," said Ginger.

"Crumbs!" said William, taken aback. "Well, we can't do that, can we?"

"Oh, I dunno," said Ginger vaguely, "jus' keep on putting stones on each other. It was quite a little church."

"Well, it'd take us more'n quite a little time."

"Yes, but we've gotter do *something* 'stead of goin' to school, an' we may's well do that."

"'S almost as bad as goin' to school," said William gloomily. "An' where'd they get the stones?"

"They jus' found 'em lying about."

"Well, come on," said William, rising with a resigned air and gathering the folds of his dressing-gown about him, "let's see 'f we can find any lyin' about."

They wandered down the road. They still wore their dressing-gowns, but they wore them with a sheepish air and went cautiously and furtively. Already their affection for their saintly garb was waning. Fortunately, the road was deserted. They looked up and down, then St. Ginger gave a yell of triumph and pointed up the road. The road was being mended, and there lay by the roadside, among other materials, a little heap of wooden bricks. Moreover, the bricks were unguarded and un-attended.

It was the British workman's dinner hour, and the British workman was spending it in the nearest pub.

"Crumbs!" said the Williamcans in delight.

They fell upon the wooden bricks and bore them off in triumph. Soon they had a pile of them just outside the barn where they had resolved to build the church—al-most enough, the head of the order decided, to begin on. But as they paid their last visit for bricks they met a little crowd of other children, who burst into loud jeering cries.

"Look at 'em. . . . Dear little girlies . . . wearin' nice long pinnies. . . . Oh, my! Oh, *don'* they look sweet?

Hello, little darlin's!''

William flung aside his saintly robe and closed with the leader. The other saints closed with the others. Quite an interesting fight ensued. The saints, smaller in number and size than the other side, most decidedly got the best of it, though not without many casualties. The other side took to its heels.

St. William, without much enthusiasm, picked his saintly robe up from the mud and began to put it on.

"Don' see much *sense* in wearin' these things," he said.

"You ought to have *preached* to 'em, not fought 'em," said Ginger severely.

"Well, I bet *he* wun't've preached to 'em if they'd started makin' fun of him. He'd've fought 'em all right."

"No, he wun't," said Ginger firmly, "he din't b'lieve in fightin'."

William's respect for his prototype, already on the wane, waned still farther. But he did not lightly relinquish anything he had once undertaken.

"Well, anyway," he said, "let's get a move on buildin' that church."

They returned to the field and their little pile of bricks.

But the British workman had also returned from his dinner hour at the nearest pub, and had discovered the disappearance of the larger part of his material. With lurid oaths he had tracked them down and came upon the saints just as they had laboriously laid the first row of bricks for the first wall. He burst upon them with fury.

They did not stay to argue. They fled. Henry cast aside his splendid robe of multi-coloured bath towelling into a ditch to accelerate his flight. The British workman tired first. He went back after throwing a brick at their retreating forms and informing them lustily that he knew their fathers an' he'd go an' tell them, danged if he wouldn't, and they'd find themselves in jail—saucy little 'ounds—danged if they wouldn't.

The Williamcans waited till all was clear before they emerged from their hiding places and gathered together dejectedly in the barn. William and Ginger had sustained black eyes and bleeding noses as the result of the fight with the village children. Douglas had fallen during the flight from the British workman and caught Henry on his ankle, and he limped painfully. Their faces had acquired an extraordinary amount of dirt.

They sat down and surveyed each other.

"Seems to me," said William, "it's a *wearin'* kind of life."

It was cold. It had begun to rain.

"Brother rain," remarked Ginger brightly.

"Yes, an' I should think it's about sister tea-time," said William dejectedly; "an' what we goin' to buy it—her—with? How're we goin' to get money?"

"I've got sixpence at home," said Henry. "I mean I've gotter brother sixpence at home."

But William had lost his usual optimism.

"Well, that won't keep all of us for the rest of our lives, will it?" he said; "an' I don't feel like startin' beggin' after the time I've had to-day. I haven't got much *trust* in folks."

"Henry—I mean, St. Henry—oughter give his brother sixpence to the poor," said Ginger piously. "*They* uster give all their money to the poor."

"*Give* it?" said William incredulously. "An' get nothin' back for it?"

"No—jus' give it," said Ginger.

William thought deeply for a minute.

"Well," he said at last, voicing the opinion of the whole order, "I'm jus' about sick of bein' a saint. I'd sooner be a pirate or a Red Indian any day."

The rest looked relieved.

"Yes, I've had *enough*," said William, "and let's stop callin' each other saints an' brothers an' sisters an' wearin' dressing-gowns. There's no *sense* in it. An' I'm almost dyin' of cold an' hunger an' I'm goin' home."

They set off homeward through the rain, cold and wet and bruised and very hungry. The saintly repast of cream buns and chocolate creams and bull's-eyes, though enjoyable at the time, had proved singularly unsustaining.

But their troubles were not over.

As they went through the village they stopped in front of Mr. Marsh's shop window. There in the very middle were William's father's slippers, Douglas' father's inkstand, Ginger's father's tie and Henry's father's gloves—all marked at 1/-. The hearts of the Williamcans stood still. Their fathers would probably not yet have returned from Town. The thought of their seeing their prized possessions reposing in Mr. Marsh's window marked 1/- was a horrid one. It had not seemed to matter this morning. This morning they were leaving their homes for ever. It did seem to matter this evening. This evening they were returning to their homes.

They entered the shop and demanded them. Mr. Marsh was adamant. In the end Henry fetched his sixpence, William a treasured penknife, Ginger a compass, and Douglas a broken steam engine, and their paternal possessions were handed back.

They went home dejectedly through the rain. The British workman might or might not fulfil his threat of calling on their parents. The saintly career which had looked so roseate in the distance had turned out, as William aptly described it, "wearin'." Life was full of disillusions.

William discovered with relief that his father had not yet come home. He returned the slippers, somewhat damp, to the fender box. He put his muddy dressing-gown beneath the bed. He found his note unopened and unread, still upon the mantelpiece. He tore it up. He tidied himself superficially. He went downstairs.

"Had a nice day, dear?" said his mother.

He disdained to answer the question.

"There's just an hour before tea," she went on; "hadn't you better be doing your homework, dear?"

He considered. One might as well drink of tragedy the very dregs while one was about it. It would be a rotten ending to a rotten day. Besides, there was no doubt about it—Mr. Strong was going to make himself very disagreeable indeed, if he didn't know those French verbs for Monday. He might as well—— If he'd had any idea how rotten it was being a saint he jolly well wouldn't have wasted a whole Saturday over it. He took down a French grammar and sat down moodily before it without troubling to put it right way up.

from *William—The Conqueror*

William Makes Things Hum

As William passed down the road a casual observer would merely have seen a rather dirty small boy, stockings coming down, collar bearing the impression of his own grubby fingers, cap placed awry on a shock of untidy hair, swaggering along and brandishing a stick that had obviously once formed part of the hedgerows. But William himself saw quite a different picture. He saw a tall, sinister figure, patch over one eye, coloured handkerchief round waist, brandishing a naked sword in his hands. The country lane behind him was not empty, but filled with the gallant band of buccaneers who were his followers. He had just made a shipload of his enemies walk the plank. He was now on his way to attack the stronghold of a rival company of pirates. He stopped, took a bottle from his pocket and raised it to his lips with a flourish. It was really liquorice water, but to William it was smuggled rum of a rare and potent brand. Then he pocketed it and marched along again, with so large a swagger that, turning a bend in the road, he ran full tilt into a boy who was coming from the opposite direction. He was a bigger boy than William, and even more gloriously dirty and untidy, with a shock of bright red hair. William felt an instinctive respect for him and a desire to impress him.

"Think the world belongs to you, don't you?" said the boy, recovering first from the impact.

"Huh!" said William, "it jolly nearly does anyway. I've jus' made three hundred people walk the plank, an' when I've finished conquering the pirates I'm after now, I'll be the biggest pirate chief in the world, and I bet I conquer the whole world. I've got the biggest army in the world already."

He waved his hand with an airy swagger at the empty lane behind him.

The other boy laughed.

"That's story-book stuff!" he said. "Well, would you like to known what *I've* done this afternoon?"

"Yes," said William, "I would."

"Well, first I drove all the ducks from Farmer Brewster's pond to Farmer Jenks's pond, so there'll be a nice old mess-up when they find out. Then I drove all the sheep out of his field into the lane, and I 'spect they'll be at Timbuctoo by now. Then I let his cows into the turnip stack. Then I collected all the eggs from the poultry-house and put them under the broody hen in the hedge. Then I filled my pockets from his apple loft, and now I'm going home."

"Golly!" said William, deeply impressed.

"You see, he'd annoyed me," explained the boy simply; "and when people annoy me—well, there's always something coming to them. The ole foreman chased me, but it takes more than any ole foreman to catch me."

He laughed again, and walked on down the road with a swagger that put even William's swagger to shame. William stared after him open-mouthed. His own imaginary adventures had faded into utter insignificance in the face of this convincing recital. The pirate exploits were, after all, completely impossible, but this. . . .

Suddenly he decided to adopt the red-headed boy's adventures as his own. He wasn't a pirate chief any longer. He was the boy who had driven Farmer Brewster's ducks into Farmer Jenks's pond, let out the sheep and cows, hidden his day's supply of eggs under a broody hen, and robbed his apple loft. And all because Farmer Brewster had annoyed him. He laughed—a laugh that was a faithful copy of the red-headed boy's laugh.

"When people annoy me," he said darkly, "well, there's always something coming to them."

He went on his way down the road with a new swagger, a swagger more rollicking and daredevil than his old one—the red-headed boy's swagger.

At the next bend in the lane he met a little girl. Her dark hair was cropped short, and her face was round and dimpled. She stopped and looked at him with an interest that William found irresistible. After all, what was the use of having so thrilling a story to tell if there was no one to tell it to?

"Hello," said the little girl.

"Hello," responded William, and added with the newly acquired daredevil laugh: "Would you like to know what *I've* been doing this afternoon?"

"Yes, I would," said the little girl, and turned obligingly to walk along the road with him.

William intensified his new swagger.

"Well," he said, "I drove the ducks from Farmer Brewster's pond to Farmer Jenks's pond, so there'll be a nice old mess-up when they find out. Then I drove his sheep out of their field up the lane, and they'll be at Timbuctoo by now, I expect. And then I let his cows into the turnip stack and put all his eggs under a broody hen and filled my pockets from his apple loft. His foreman ran after me, but it takes more than an ole foreman to catch me. You see," explained William, repeating the daredevil laugh, "he'd annoyed me, and when people annoy me there's always something coming to them."

Yes, the story was much more artistically satisfying than his pirate story. He enjoyed the recital immensely. He was just going to improve upon it still further and had begun: "And then after that—" when he noticed a large man in gaiters coming through a gate into the lane.

"Uncle!" called the little girl excitedly. "This is the boy—the boy what mixed up your ducks and let out the sheep and cows and took the eggs and apples. He's just told me he's the boy. . . ."

An iron grip descended upon William's neck.

"So *you're* the boy, are you?" said a voice that sent cold shivers up and down William's spine. "Well, then, you're the boy I've been looking for all morning. Come along with me."

William felt himself impelled along the road by the iron grip.

"No, please, I'm not the boy," he protested breathlessly; "I was only pretendin'. Honest, I was only pretendin'. It was another boy what did it an' he told me he'd done it an' I was pretendin' I'd done it an'—"

"Talking won't do you any good," said the ruthless voice, "so you may as well shut up."

William struggled desperately against the iron grip, but in vain. He was dragged ignominiously along the road, pitifully bereft of his swagger. Between his ineffectual struggles to escape he continued his explanation.

"You see—it was—this other—boy what did it—he told—me he'd—done it an' so—I pretended—it was me what—did it, just for fun. Please—I didn't—really do it— Please, I didn't really—"

"If I wanted to make up a tale," said the grim voice scornfully, "I'd try to make up a better one than that. Shut up and come along."

AN IRON GRIP DESCENDED ON WILLIAM'S NECK. "SO YOU'RE
THE BOY, ARE YOU?" SAID A VOICE.

The grip of iron tightened till it almost choked him,
and he was dragged through a gate into a farmyard and
towards a shed.

"I tell you what I'm going to do with you," said the
grim voice. "I'm going to shut you in this shed, and then
I'm going to fetch a policeman, and we'll see what the

magistrates have to say about your pranks."

He pushed William into the shed, turned the key, and departed.

William looked around him. There was only one small window, with a broken pane, too high up for him to reach.

He struggled with the door for some time, but it was securely bolted on the outside. Suddenly he saw the little girl at the window.

"Hello," she said, "I've climbed up a tree to have a look at you. He's gone to fetch a policeman."

"I know," said William, trying without much success to assume a nonchalant air.

"I expect you'll get put in prison."

William attempted the daredevil laugh, but it was so complete a failure that he turned it into a cough.

"I expect you'll get put in prison for years an' *years*," went on the little girl.

"I'll give you all the money I've got if you'll let me out," said William.

"How much money have you got?" said the little girl with interest.

William examined his pockets.

"I've got a halfpenny here, an' I've got threepence in my money-box. I *think* I've threepence in it. *Nearly* threepence, anyway. An' I'm goin' to start having pocket-money again when they've paid for the new landing window. That'll be threepence a week. I'll give you all my pocket-money for weeks an' *weeks* when they start givin' it me again if you'll let me out."

"You won't be able to have pocket-money in prison," said the little girl. "An' you'll only have bread an' water to eat," she went on, seeming to take a gloomy relish in the situation; "an' I expect you'll be there for years and *years*. They always send people to prison for years and *years*. Prob'ly for the rest of your life."

"You don't know anything about it," said William, but he did not sound much more confident than he felt.

"I do," persisted the little girl. "I know a *lot* about it. I once read a book about a man who was in prison for years and *years*. And then, in the end, his wife went in and changed clothes with him, and he got away in her clothes and she stayed in prison in his, but they let her out when they found it wasn't him."

"If you'll unbolt the door," said William, "I'll give you all my cigarette cards."

He had decided some time ago that cigarette card collecting was unworthy of a pirate chief.

"How many have you got?"

"A hundred."

"Oo!" said the little girl. "A *hundred*?"

"Yes."

"Will you give them me *all*?"

"Yes."

"Well"—she considered the situation, and her excitement died away—"it isn't any use, anyway, because uncle told Mr. Greg—the foreman—to keep an eye on the shed and see you didn't get away before he came back with the policeman. *Tell* you what," she went on in sudden excitement, "let's change clothes like the people did in that tale I read. That's a *jolly* good idea. I'll put on your suit and pretend I'm a boy. I've always wanted to be a boy. Then you can go out, and they'll think it's me."

William looked at her doubtfully.

"You're a good bit smaller than what I am," he said. "I don't think anyone'd think I was you."

But the little girl eagerly defended her project.

"Oh, yes, they would. I'll take off my frock and throw it down to you through the window an' I'll throw down a long stick an' you can give me your suit up on the end of it. I think it's a *lovely* idea. *Just* like the people in the book. Take off your suit, and I'll take off my frock. Then I'll come back and give you my frock, and you can give me your suit."

A few moments later a small, pink cotton frock fluttered down through the window, followed by a long stick. William took the bottle of liquorice water from his pocket, drained it lovingly, then handed up his suit on the end of the stick to the little girl, and began to struggle into the pink cotton frock.

Soon the little girl was again at the window, clad in William's well-worn tweed suit. It was far too big for her, but her face beamed with satisfaction.

"Isn't it *lovely*," she said. "Now I can pretend I'm a boy. I've always wanted to be a boy."

William, who felt that somehow his rescue was being lost sight of in her excitement over the possession of his suit, was less enthusiastic.

"It won't meet anywhere," he said still struggling with the pink cotton frock. "No one would think I was you. I can't escape in this thing. It's a rotten idea. Give me back my own suit."

But the little girl still seemed to have forgotten that the object of the change of costume was the rescue of William.

"No," she said firmly, "I *like* your suit. I'm going to keep it. It's much nicer to climb trees in than an old girl's dress."

She vanished from the window.

"Hi!" called William desperately. "Come back. Give me my suit."

But there was no answer, and the voice of the little girl, singing joyfully to herself, died away in the distance. William realised that he was in a worse plight than

ever. The pink cotton dress was so ludicrously small for
him that it would not only make escape impossible but
would considerably detract from his dignity during his
progress from the farm to prison. If he had to go to
prison for the rest of his life, at least he would like his
journey thither to be accomplished as impressively as
possible.

But the little girl had not quite forgotten him, after all.
She appeared again suddenly at the window, and began
to stuff through the hole in the pane, first a large, dark
shawl, then a battered bonnet, rakishly trimmed with
faded artificial violets.

"*Those'll* cover you all right," she said. "They're
Mrs. Hobbin's, the charwoman's. Put on the bonnet an'
tie it under your chin an' then put the shawl right round
you an' I'll open the door for you an' Mr. Greg'll think
you're Mrs. Hobbin going home because you've come
over funny. She often goes home because she's come
over funny."

William gratefully decided to give the little girl his old
whistle as well as his collection of cigarette cards. He had
long meant to give away the old whistle when he found
some worthy recipient. Though it whistled no longer, it
was large and important-looking.

The bonnet came well down over his head, and the
shawl enveloped him from neck to feet. No sooner had
he thus arrayed himself, than he heard the sound of the
latch being gently withdrawn, and the little girl peeped
in.

"Come along," she whispered. "Mr. Greg's just
gone to put the milk cans out, but he'll come back any
minute. . . ."

William gathered up his shawl and fled across the
farmyard and down the road. Finding that he was not
pursued and realising that his haste was inconsistent with

his disguise, he slackened his pace and began to walk along with an odd, lurching gait intended to combine the appearance of old age with as much speed as possible. As he went he looked anxiously about for his own suit. He soon saw it following him and stopped a minute for it to overtake him.

"Wasn't that clever of me?" said its wearer complacently.

"Let's get somewhere quick where we can change," said William; "I want to get back into my own things. I keep tumbling over the shawl and this beastly hat tickles my face."

"But I *like* wearing your suit," said the little girl firmly, "an', anyway, you're supposed to be disguised. The man in the story kept on his wife's things till he'd got into another country. You ought to go to another country."

"Well, I'm not going to," said William indignantly. "I've had enough bother over this an' it's all your fault, anyway. What did you go and *tell* him for? I was only makin' it up. I didn't do it. The other boy did it."

"You did it. You said so."

"Well, I was pretendin'. I was only jus' sayin' what the other boy had said."

"What other boy?"

"The boy what did it."

"Well, that's you. You *said* it was you."

"Oh, shut up," said William irritably. "I'm sick of arguing with you. You've got no sense. Girls never have. And let me tell you——"

He stopped abruptly. Rounding the bend in the road they had almost run into the Vicar's wife and a friend.

"Oh, here *is* Mrs. Hobbin," said the Vicar's wife, "so you can have a talk with her yourself." She gazed down the road after the figure of the little girl who had passed quickly on. "That was William Brown with you, wasn't it, Mrs Hobbin? I hope he wasn't teasing you in any way." She turned to her friend. "The little boy who's gone on down the road is a great trial to us all. My husband always calls him our village pest. Very rude and badly behaved, and a *great* nuisance in every way."

William, who had jerked his bonnet well over his eyes and drawn up his shawl well over his nose, glared ferociously at her through the narrow aperture. So the Vicar called him "our village pest", did he? He wouldn't forget that.

The Vicar's wife was looking at him with a perplexed frown. She'd broken her glasses that morning and had sent them off at once to be mended, but had not got them back yet. She hadn't realised before what a difference they made to people's sizes. Both William Brown and Mrs. Hobbin looked much smaller than when she wore her glasses. She couldn't see their features at all distinctly, of course, but that she was prepared for. What she wasn't prepared for was their looking so much smaller than they really were. Odd. Very odd. Perhaps she'd better visit her oculist again and consult him about it. It couldn't, of course, be anyone *but* Mrs. Hobbin. That violet-trimmed bonnet and all-enveloping shawl were famous in the neighbourhood. The old lady seemed to be trying to edge away, so the Vicar's wife laid a detaining hand on her arm.

"This friend of mine, dear Mrs. Hobbin," she said, "is writing a description of village characters, to be called 'Nature's Ladies and Gentlemen', and she has come over here for the day to interview some of you good old people. We were on our way to find you, as a matter of fact. . . ." She turned to her friend. "This dear old lady, Laetitia," she said, "is one of my greatest friends. She's seventy-eight, and she's never had a day's

illness in her life, have you, dear Mrs. Hobbin?"
William grimaced at her through the aperture. "She
comes regularly to our mothers' meetings and pleasant
Sunday afternoons, and takes part in all our little
outings. Now I'll leave you to have your little chat, and
I'll just go over there and rest my eyes. They seem to be
playing queer tricks with me just now."

She went over to the low wall just out of earshot and
sat on it, her eyes closed, smiling vaguely.

The visitor took out her note-book, gazing at William
in bewilderment. What a very strange old woman. One
couldn't see anything of her face at all. And how small.
Almost a dwarf. Curious that dear Elfrida hadn't mentioned that. Really not at all the sort of type she wanted
for "Nature's Ladies and Gentlemen". But still . . .

"Er—would you mind lowering your shawl a little?"
she said.

William made a hoarse noise, unmistakably indicative
of refusal. The perplexity of his interlocutor deepened.

"You—er—got a bad cold perhaps?" she suggested.

William made another hoarse noise, accepting the
suggestion.

"I expect that that's why you're so hoarse."

He croaked that it was. The authoress took her pencil.

"Now, dear Mrs. Hobbin," she said persuasively, "I
want you to tell me something about yourself. You're
seventy-eight years old, aren't you?"

William glanced up and down the road. His first
instinct had been flight from this hideous predicament,
but second thoughts counselled him to remain where he
was. Should Farmer Brewster, the policeman, or the
foreman come down the road seeking their prey they
would surely pass by this innocent little group—the
Vicar's wife seated on the wall, and, a short distance
away, her friend talking to dear old Mrs. Hobbin—

without suspicion. He decided to submit to the interview.

"How many children have you had?" said the authoress.

William tried to remember exactly how many children Mrs. Hobbin had. Certainly so many that she seemed to have peopled all the surrounding villages as well as her own.

"I've forgotten jus' how many," he croaked; "a good many."

"B-but," protested her surprised interviewer, "surely, dear Mrs. Hobbin, you remember how many children you have."

"I'm always meanin' to count 'em," croaked William, "but I keep on forgettin'."

The interviewer gaped at him helplessly. An explanation of the old lady's strange conduct suddenly occurred to her.

"Er—pardon me—Mrs. Hobbin," she said, "but—er—are you a teetotaller?"

"A what?" croaked William.

"I mean—do you *drink*—I mean, of course—er—moderately."

"Oh, yes, I drink all right," croaked William. "I drink a lot."

The interviewer laughed constrainedly.

"Fond of your glass?" she suggested faintly, with an unsuccessful attempt at a man-to-man air.

William, realising that he had no knowledge at all of Mrs. Hobbin's tastes and characteristics, decided to describe his own, considering that his own were as sensible and universal as any.

"No, not a glass," he croaked; "I like drinkin' out of a bottle best. I take a bottle in my pocket wherever I go."

The interviewer glanced beseechingly at the Vicar's wife, but the Vicar's wife was still sitting on the wall out of earshot, her eyes closed, smiling vaguely. The interviewer decided to change the subject.

"To what," she said, "do you attribute your longevity?"

"Uh?" said William.

"I mean how do you think it is that you've lived so much longer than—er—than some other people?"

"Jus' 'cause I've not died, I suppose," croaked William after deep thought.

The interviewer made a last and desperate effort.

"Now, Mrs. Hobbin," she said, "I want you to tell me something about yourself . . . your tastes and hobbies. What is your favourite food?"

"Ice-cream," croaked William promptly. "I c'n eat twenty ice-cream horns one after the other straight off."

The authoress shuddered.

"Your favourite occupation?"

"Goin' to fairs an' goin' on switchbacks an' havin' shots at Aunt Sally."

The authoress's cheeks blanched.

"Can you read?"

"Uh-huh."

"What sort of books do you like reading?"

"Plenty of fightin' an' people killin' people."

"You've had a hard life, Mrs. Hobbin?"

"Yes, I jolly well have," croaked William, thinking of his day's adventures.

"But you're at peace with the world now?"

"No, I've gotter lot of enemies."

"I'm sorry to hear that."

"I like havin' enemies," croaked William. "I like a jolly good fight. I gotter black eye only last week. But I jolly well made the other person's nose bleed all right."

The little girl had lingered for some time down the road waiting for him, but, suddenly tiring of waiting, had now set off briskly and was vanishing out of sight. William, seeing his suit disappearing, and realising that with it went his only chance of returning to ordinary life, mumbled a "'Scuse me", and set off in pursuit, repeating his attempt to combine a gait suitable to old age with as much speed as possible—an attempt that resulted in an odd, hopping step reminiscent of a kangaroo. The authoress watched him with an expression of helpless bewilderment till he was out of sight. Then she turned to her notes and read them through with shuddering horror. "Bottle in pocket." "People killin' people." "Gotter black eye last week."

What a *horrible* old woman! She considered for a moment whether to write up the notes and make from it the picture of a repulsive old battle-axe in the modern manner. But, no, that wasn't what her own particular public wanted of her, and one must give one's own particular public what one's own particular public wanted of one. She crossed out her notes and began to write again on a fresh page. "Mrs. Hobbin. This dear old lady spoke with touching affection of her many children and grandchildren, in all of whom she still takes a passionate interest. She is very abstemious in every way and is an ardent upholder of temperance, attributing her wonderful health chiefly to that. She can still do an active day's work but her chief pleasure is to sit in the porch of her little cottage, listening to the birds and watching her simple flowers. . . ."

Yes, thought the authoress with rising satisfaction, that's the sort of thing they want. Truth is, after all, the greater part of art; one must be true to what one's public wants.

The Vicar's wife rose and blinked and looked around her.

"Yes, they seem better now," she said. "They went so funny a minute ago. They made people look quite tiny. Extraordinary. I must consult my oculist about it. Mrs. Hobbin has gone, has she, dear?"

"Yes," said the friend, closing her note-book.

"A sweet old lady, isn't she?"

The friend hesitated for a moment. But already the memory of the actual interview was fading, and she saw quite vividly a dear old lady sitting in a cottage porch listening to the birds and watching her simple flowers.

"Sweet," she agreed with enthusiasm.

*   *   *

William had caught up with the little girl at the end of the lane leading to his home.

"Come along quickly into our summer-house an' give me my suit back," he said breathlessly. "I'm sick of goin' about in these things."

"But I *like* being a boy," she protested. "I want to go on being a boy. I don't want to give you back your suit. I want you to go to a foreign country like the man did in the book and let me go on wearing your suit and pretending I'm a boy."

"I've told you I'm *not* going to a foreign country," said William testily. "An' I'm sick of wearing these ole things an' ole women askin' me silly questions about liq'rice water an' ice-cream an' suchlike. Give me back my suit."

"But it's a *disguise*," persisted the little girl. "If I give you your suit back you won't be disguised any longer an' they'll take you to prison."

"Well, I don't care if they do. I'd rather go to prison than go on wearin' these ole things. Here's my house.

"COME ALONG QUICKLY INTO OUR SUMMER-HOUSE AND GIVE ME
MY SUIT BACK," SAID WILLIAM BREATHLESSLY.

Come into the summer-house an' give me my suit."

The little girl darted in at the gate and ran round the
side of the house shouting: "All right. . . . Catch me
first."

*   *   *

Mrs. Brown was entertaining a business friend of Mr. Brown's in the drawing-room. It was a business friend with whom Mr. Brown was hoping to make an advantageous business transaction, and, therefore, Mrs. Brown was doing her very best to put her visitor and his wife into a good humour. So far everything had gone well. William had not put in an appearance, for which William's mother was sincerely grateful.

"So delightful here in the country," said the visitor.

"Yes, isn't it," said Mrs. Brown. "We're all very fond of the country."

"You have a little boy, I believe?" went on the visitor.

"Yes," said Mrs. Brown.

"I love little boys. I'd love to meet him."

"I'm afraid he's out," said Mrs. Brown, aware that William was not the sort of little boy that people are thinking of when they say that they love little boys.

"Perhaps he'll come home before we go."

"I h— I mean I think not," said Mrs. Brown.

But the smile had died from her face, and a look of frozen horror had taken its place.

Out of the corner of her eye she had seen William return to the garden. She did not look at him directly because she did not wish to draw her visitor's attention to him, but the corner of her eye could not mistake that familiar grey tweed suit—originally advertised by its makers as "hard wearing", and already hard worn.

But it was not this that brought the frozen look of horror to Mrs. Brown's face. It was another familiar figure closely following the familiar figure of William. Again Mrs Brown dared not look directly at the figure for fear of drawing her visitors' attention to it, but even the corner of her eye recognised the violet-trimmed bonnet and voluminous shawl that belonged to Mrs.

Hobbin. What was Mrs. Hobbin doing here? She came as a matter of course to help with the washing on Monday morning—but this was not Monday morning. And even on Monday morning Mrs. Hobbin did not flaunt herself in the garden in this manner. What was Mrs. Hobbin doing in the garden on a Thursday afternoon? The corner of Mrs. Brown's eye answered her. She was chasing William—chasing William round and round the lawn, in and out of the flower-beds. What on earth had William been doing now? At all costs the visitors' eyes must be kept from the horrible spectacle. She rose abruptly and went to the opposite window that looked out upon the front garden.

"D-d-do look at the view from here," she said, "we—we think it so pretty."

The visitors rose and joined her at the window—gazing in a bewildered fashion at the front garden and the path by which they had come in. There was nothing in the front garden except a lawn encircled by laurel bushes. Beyond the hedge was an extremely dull stretch of country road.

"Yes, isn't it?" said the visitors dutifully but without enthusiasm, preparing to return to their seats.

"Such pretty er—bushes," went on Mrs. Brown frantically, gazing at her laurel bushes, "and the road's so pretty just here."

"Er—yes," said the visitors, glancing at her curiously.

But the corner of Mrs. Brown's eye had told her that those two strange figures had stopped chasing each other round the back garden, and she was just about to resume her seat with a sigh of relief, when she saw an equally strange company coming down the road. First came Farmer Brewster, then a policeman, then Mr. Greg, and then—Mrs. Brown put her hand to her head—yes, it *was*

Mrs. Hobbin, Mrs. Hobbin bare-headed, wearing an apron, her sleeves rolled above her elbows, Mrs. Hobbin her face set in grim, angry lines, marching to battle, arms akimbo. Two Mrs. Hobbins—one in the front garden, one in the back; one with a shawl and bonnet, one without. . . . But Mrs. Brown had no time to puzzle over the strange problem.

Farmer Brewster was opening the gate of the Brown garden. The procession entered.

"HERE'S THE BOY, CONSTABLE," SAID FARMER BREWSTER. THE POLICEMAN TOOK OUT HIS NOTE-BOOK.

"Excuse me," said Mrs. Brown faintly, "I think these people want to speak to me. . . ."

Suddenly, from nowhere as it seemed, William and a little girl appeared. He had offered her his catapult as well as the cigarette cards and whistle, and she had at last consented to return his suit. The exchange had been effected quickly in the summer-house and now William strutted about, exulting in his newly regained manhood, and the little girl drooped disconsolately in the pink cotton frock. The shawl and violet-trimmed bonnet lay discarded on the floor of the summer-house. Mrs Hobbin

"AND WHO," DEMANDED MRS. HOBBIN STRIDENTLY OF MRS. BROWN, "SENDS THEIR BOYS OUT STEALING RESPECTABLE WOMEN'S CLOTHES?"

at the front door, gazing grimly through the open garden door beyond, espied them suddenly and flung herself through the house and into the summer-house. From there she emerged wearing not only her familiar shawl and bonnet but the look of one who thirsts for vengeance. The procession had followed her into the back garden. Mrs. Brown, in helpless bewilderment, accompanied them. The visitors followed still more helplessly bewildered, thinking that somehow they must have got mixed up with a cinema show.

"Here's the boy, constable," said Farmer Brewster, once more applying the grip of iron to William's neck.

The policeman took out his note-book.

"And who," demanded Mrs. Hobbin stridently of Mrs. Brown, "sends their boys out stealing respectable women's clothes?"

"That's not the boy," said the foreman, looking at William. "That's not the boy that played those pranks on our farm. The boy that did that looked quite different. He'd got red hair for one thing."

Farmer Brewster pulled William's hair experimentally. It remained its own nondescript colour. Disappointed of his prey, he began to argue furiously with his foreman. Everyone in fact was arguing furiously with someone. The policeman was arguing with Farmer Brewster and Farmer Brewster was arguing with his foreman and his foreman was arguing with Mrs. Brown and Mrs. Brown was arguing with Mrs. Hobbin and Mrs. Hobbin was arguing with everyone else.

Under cover of this general argument, William crept quietly away.

from *William—The Rebel*

William and the Fisherman

Every June William's father went alone to a country inn for ten days' fishing. William had often begged to be allowed to accompany him, but his requests had always been met by such an uncompromising refusal that he had long since given up all hope. This year, however, to his surprise and delight Fate seemed to be on his side. He had had chicken-pox, and the doctor had decreed that a change of air was necessary before he returned to school.

His mother could not leave her housekeeping duties. The various relatives to whom (though without much real hope) she confided the problem replied kindly and sympathetically, but carefully refrained from inviting William to stay with them.

"You're going away next week, aren't you dear?" said Mrs. Brown to her husband innocently.

He looked at her suspiciously.

"If you mean will I take William," he said firmly, "I most decidedly will not."

But he felt much less firm on the point than he sounded.

If the doctor said that William must have a change of air and he was the only member of the family going away, he didn't see how he could very well refuse to take him with him. He wrote to several relatives who had not yet been approached asking them bluntly if they would care to have William for a few days. They replied as bluntly that they would not.

"Mind you," said Mr. Brown to his wife after having received the last of these replies, "if that boy comes with me, he must look after himself. I'm not going to be responsible for him in any way."

William, on learning that he was to go with his father on the fishing holiday that had been his Mecca from babyhood, could hardly contain his excitement.

He imagined himself accompanying his father and his friends upon all their fishing expeditions. He saw himself making huge catches of trout and salmon before admiring crowds of onlookers. His father seemed to be taking innumerable fishing-rods with him, and William, ever an optimist, thought that he would probably lend him the ones he was not actually using. If his father happened to be using all his rods at once, William then would use his own fishing-rod—a home-made implement consisting of a stick, a piece of string and a bent pin, with which he had distinguished himself at minnow catching in all the local streams. If it would catch minnows, there was, William decided, no reason why it should not catch trout or even salmon. . . . He set off with his father, full of hope, confidence, and excitement.

For the first day he was busy assimilating his impressions. The inn—its *clientèle* consisted entirely of angling enthusiasts—was full of large, purposeful-looking men to whom fishing was real, fishing was earnest; men who treated with silent contempt any remark that did not bear directly and intelligently upon the subject of fishing. At meal-times they sat round a large table in the dining-room in a grim silence broken only by such remarks as: "There was a good hatch of May-fly about quarter-past three," or "They were rising all right, but we couldn't find out what they were taking." Directly after breakfast they would garb themselves in all-enveloping diver-like costumes, collect their tackle and set off, still silent, grim, and purposeful, each to his favourite haunt.

They would not return till the evening and then it was the custom that each should silently and with modest pride lay his catch upon the marble-slabbed hat-stand in the hall of the inn—each catch carefully separate and apart from the others. No one talked of his catch. He merely laid it upon the hat-stand and waited for someone to ask whose it was. News of each catch spread quickly through the community. After dinner again the sportsmen sallied out, solemnly, purposefully, grimly, for the "night rise".

William watched all this with breathless interest. The thought of forming a part of such a community filled him with a fierce and burning pride.

On the first day his father asked him if he would like to come out with him in a boat, and William eagerly agreed. He found the day disappointing. His father landed him on an island in the lake with an empty tobacco box and instructions to catch May-fly in the bushes. William caught three, then became bored and began to experiment with the damming of a small stream and finally to attempt the draining of a miniature bog into which he sank to his knees. When his father returned for him, the three May-flies had escaped and his father, who immediately on reaching the fishing community had yielded to its pervading atmosphere of grim purposefulness, was coldly reproachful. The rest of the day was merely boring. The boatman would not let William try to row. His father would not let him try to fish. He got hopelessly entangled in a spare rod; he accidentally dropped overboard a box of flies that were unobtainable locally; he was bitten in the hand by a trout that he thought was dead, and thereupon gave a yell that put every other fish for miles around upon its guard.

He disgraced himself completely and finally by standing up to stretch away an attack of pins and needles, and overbalancing upon his father's rod and breaking it.

"I know one thing," said his father feelingly, "and that is that you're jolly well not coming out with me in the boat again."

William was not in any way perturbed by this sentence. It had been a boring and unsatisfactory day and he was convinced that a day spent by himself on dry land would be a much more enjoyable affair.

To his surprise and disgust, however, his father refused to lend him one of his rods. His father, it appeared, needed all his rods—either for "dapping" or "trolling" or "casting".

William considered that these people made far too complicated an affair of the simple exercise of fishing and set off alone with his home-made rod, a packet of sandwiches, and a basket lent to him for his "catch" by the landlady.

He found a suitable stream, fixed a worm on to the bent pin at the end of his line, and began to fish. His luck was amazing. He caught minnow after minnow. He worked hard all morning and all afternoon and returned in the evening with a laden basket. The other fishermen had not yet returned. The marble top of the hat-stand gleamed empty and inviting. William poured the contents of his basket upon it. They covered it completely with a shining heap of minnows. William gazed at them with fond pride. Then he got a piece of paper, wrote on it, "William Brown", and put it on the top of the silvery heap. That done, glowing with triumph, he awaited the return of the other fishermen. Not one of them had ever completely filled the marble slab with a single catch like this. He had no doubt at all that he would be the hero of the evening.

Soon he heard the sound of someone approaching and stepped back modestly into the shadow. One of the fishermen—a stalwart young man with a projecting jaw and hooked nose—entered. He looked at the minnow-filled slab, scowled angrily, swept the whole gleaming heap on to the floor with an outraged gesture, rang the bell, said to the housemaid: "Clear up that mess," then with slow deliberate care placed a row of twelve trout on the slab.

William was speechless with indignation at the affront. His first impulse was to hurl himself savagely upon the young man; his second, based upon a consideration of the young man's powerful and muscular frame, was to contain his fury as best he could till an opportunity for a suitable revenge offered itself.

Up to now the fishermen had been identical in William's eyes. They were all large, single-purposed, unsmiling men dressed in enormous waders and devoid of any ideas outside the world of fishing.

Now each detached himself from the mass, as it were, and assumed a distinct personality. There appeared to be two camps of them. The elder ones forgathered in the smoking-room. William's father, who had come to the conclusion many years ago that William was quite capable of looking after himself, and who in any case had from the beginning announced his intention of not allowing him to interfere with his holiday, belonged to the elder camp, and in order to preserve the illusion of a Williamless holiday, had from the first forbidden William to enter the smoking-room. So William, perforce, spent his time with the younger fishermen, and it was

therefore the younger fishermen whom he particularly
studied.

The leader among them was the muscular youth
addressed by his familiars as "Archie" who had swept
William's magnificent catch so contemptuously on to the
floor. Archie was the most skilful fisherman of the party.

**THE FISHERMAN SCOWLED ANGRILY, AND SWEPT THE WHOLE
HEAP ON TO THE FLOOR WITH AN OUTRAGED GESTURE.**

The others humbly asked his advice and appraised his prowess. Archie's row of trout on the hat-stand slab was always longer than that of any of the others. Archie, moreover, knew the owner of a specially prolific reach of river, and had permission to fish there. He would return from his fishing expedition in this reach laden with spoils and more blatantly pleased with himself each time.

Archie was admired, his advice was sought on all sides, but not even his dearest friends could deny that

WILLIAM WAS SPEECHLESS WITH INDIGNATION.

Archie was overbearing and conceited. It soon became evident that he disliked William as much as William disliked him. The episode of the minnows seemed to him to be a deliberate affront to his dignity, and the presence of William among the party a perpetual outrage. He found fault with William continually, pushing him out of his way whenever he met him, with such lack of ceremony that more than once he sent him sprawling to the ground. He made loud remarks in William's hearing on the unsuitability of having "kids mucking about the place".

"It's never happened before," he said, "and I hope to goodness that it'll never happen again. If it does I shall look out for another place."

William bided his time. He studied his enemy. There was no pretence about Archie's skill as a fisherman. William even followed him secretly down to his private post in the preserved reach and saw him catching trout after trout with an ease and ability that, despite his dislike, William could not help admiring.

He watched him standing in the swirling current in mid-stream up to his waist, still fishing with ease and ability. Certainly in his capacity as fisherman Archie was invulnerable. William tried to find some capacity in which he might be vulnerable, but could find none. For Archie seemed to be nothing but a fisherman. He seemed to have no instincts and desires but those of a fisherman. He seemed to function wholly and entirely upon the fishing plane.

The days passed swiftly by, and William, still enduring Archie's ceaseless snubs, almost began to give up hope of getting his own back. The last week-end of the holiday had arrived, and still Archie had revealed no weakness through which an enemy might avenge himself. His armour seemed to be jointless. Then—two days before

William and his father were to return home—there
arrived at the inn an elderly fisherman with his daughter.

The elderly fisherman was negligible enough, but the
daughter was not. Even William could see at a glance
that this was the sort of girl who made things hum. She
had dimples, and dark, curling lashes shading eyes of the
deepest blue. Her complexion was smooth and flawless.
She had a shatteringly beautiful smile. And William,
watching his enemy with ceaseless vigilance, realised at
once that Archie was smitten, utterly and uncompromisingly smitten. Smitten, as the saying is, hip and thigh.
Only the day before, Archie, after complaining for the
thousandth time of having "kids messing about the
place," had added: "But thank heaven, at least there
aren't any women this year." But now William saw his
tanned and healthy countenance deepen to a rich beet-
root immediately his eyes fell upon this latest arrival.

The girl, whose name was Claribel, while apparently
ignoring the youthful sportsmen and devoting herself
entirely to her father, was obviously fully aware of the
impression she had made. For not only Archie was
smitten, but all the other members of the younger camp
were smitten too.

It did not take long for the first shyness to wear off and
then began the competition for the damsel's notice. And
here Archie's friends, who should have rallied round
him, basely deserted him. They did not sing his praises.
They did not boost him to the skies as the world's best
fisherman. They left him to sing his own praises and
boost himself to the skies. To do him justice he was not
backward. He boosted himself well and good. He
enumerated his recent catches. He described how he
alone of all the fishing party could fish with ease when up
to his arms in a swirling torrent.

"It's partly a question of balance," he said, "and

partly that I'm—well, I'm a fairly good fisherman, of course."

And Archie stroked his microscopic moustache complacently.

At first Claribel was amused, but gradually she became impressed.

"Come out in the boat with me to-morrow," said Archie, "I'm sure you'll enjoy it. I mean I'm sure you'll find it quite interesting."

Claribel agreed, and William saw yet another triumph in store for the hated Archie. For Claribel, he realised at once, despite her affection of hauteur, belonged to the class of "soppy girls". She swam with the stream and went with the crowd. If fishing were the fashion, then Claribel bags the best fisherman. And without doubt, Archie was the best fisherman. William was very thoughtful that evening.

"Who's the kid?" he heard Claribel ask of Archie.

And Archie replied contemptuously:

"A wretched little oik someone's brought with him."

The next morning was a perfect fishing morning, and Claribel, dressed very fetchingly in pale pink organdie, set off gaily to the river with Archie. He helped her into the boat with a courteous gesture, then the boatman pushed off.

"Isn't this jolly!" William heard Claribel say gaily. "Just like a picnic."

William unobtrusively followed the progress of the boat along the bank, slipping from bush to bush. The strident voice of Archie, enumerating his fishing exploits, reached him clearly across the water.

They reached a point in the river where, only the day before, Archie had stood in mid-stream, the water up to his arm-pits, "casting" with magnificent aplomb, and catching trout after enormous trout. He lowered himself from the boat and took up his stand, a smile of proud anticipation on his lips. He took up his stand and threw his line. Claribel watched him from the boat.

"Now start catching all those fishes you talk about," she said gaily.

Archie had cast his line stylishly enough, but the complacent expression of his face was giving way to uneasiness.

He smiled a ghastly smile at her and said: "Oh, yes . . . you jolly well wait a few minutes. . . ." Then the uneasiness of his expression deepened to panic.

"Hi!" he called suddenly, dropping his rod and clutching wildly at the air. "Hi! Help!"

The boatman hastily brought the boat up to him. He clutched frenziedly at the boatside and then at Claribel. He hung dripping round Claribel's neck. "I'm drowning!" he shouted. "Take me out quick!"

The boat rocked frantically. The boatman and Claribel between them dragged Archie into it. Claribel rendered this assistance involuntarily. Archie, having clasped his arms about her neck in his first spasm of terror, refused to unclasp them, and, long before his large and struggling body was safely landed in the boat, the pale pink organdie was a sodden mass, and Claribel was weeping with fury.

"I couldn't help it," panted Archie. "I t-tell you I was going under. I'd lost my balance. I'd have d-d-drowned if I hadn't caught hold of you. My waders were flooded. I can't t-t-think how. It's a miracle I wasn't drowned. I can't think *how* I wasn't drowned."

"I wish you had been," burst out Claribel passionately. "You've ruined my dress."

"Here's the hole, sir," said the boatman, pointing to an almost imperceptible slit just above the waist of Archie's waders.

"I can't think how it came there," said Archie. "They were all right yesterday." Then to Claribel: "I couldn't help it, I tell you."

"Of *course* you could help it," stormed Claribel. "Making a fool of yourself and me like that! *Deliberately* ruining everything I've got on. I'm soaked, and my dress is *ruined*, I tell you. Take me home at once. I shall never speak to you again as long as I live."

The boatman retrieved the rod, and rowed them back to the landing-place, Archie protesting loudly, Claribel, who had had her say, now gazing over his head with an expression of icy contempt.

William did not come out of cover till they had vanished from view. Then he walked slowly homeward, tenderly fingering the penknife that had punctured Archie's waders and self-esteem.

But William never left anything to chance. He himself had an elder sister of great personal charm, and he had long studied with interest and perpetual surprise the way of a maid with a man. He had learnt that the more angry and unrelenting the maid seems at the actual moment of provocation, the sooner is she likely to relent. So that when he reached the inn he was not surprised to find Claribel and Archie on friendly terms again. Claribel had changed into a blue linen dress that was very becoming, so becoming in fact that she could not help feeling on good terms with herself and the whole world. She was even viewing the episode through a haze of glamour and looking on herself as having rescued Archie from a watery grave. Archie, with more sense than William would have given him credit for, was encouraging this view.

"I simply don't know what I'd have done if you hadn't happened to be there," he was saying.

"Well, of course," said Claribel modestly, "I always

have been considered rather fearless. I mean, I do know how to keep my head in a crisis. I just saw what to do and did it. I'm like that."

"It was wonderful of you," said Archie fervently, "simply *wonderful*. I believe that it's the first morning I've ever come in without catching a single fish. I'll go down to the river this afternoon, however, and see if I can make up for it."

"I expect you will if all I hear of your fishing is true," said Claribel sweetly.

It was very trying for William after all the trouble he had taken to see Archie resuming his old intolerable conceit and Claribel gradually softening towards him. But he had prepared for this, too. Not for nothing had he trudged yesterday into the nearest market town. Moreover, his knowledge of human nature served him well. He was sure that Claribel, after her morning's wetting, would not want to accompany Archie on his afternoon's fishing expedition.

So Archie set off alone. He was away for several hours, and when he returned he proudly laid twelve trout upon the hat-stand, and went to summon Claribel to admire.

He did not see William slip into the hall as he went out of it. When he returned to it with Claribel he saw no difference in the fish that he had laid there. It was Claribel who discovered a wet and illegible fishmonger's ticket adhering to one of them, Claribel whose small but perfect nose discovered the distinctly unpleasant odour of the thirteenth fish—unlucky enough for Archie—that William had deftly introduced into the row. It was in vain that Archie protested and pleaded, in vain that he brought proof incontrovertible that he had actually caught the fish.

Claribel's anger of the afternoon had returned redoubled.

"A nasty, mean, low-down trick to play on me!" she fumed. "A cheat, that's what you are! A nasty, common cheat! Trying to make me think you'd caught them when you'd bought every *one* of them at a fishmonger's—and one of them bad at that! First you try to drown me—yes, and nearly *did* drown me. I could get you put in prison for attempted murder for this morning. I'm sure I could. It was a plot to *murder* me. I don't believe there was a hole in your waders. Or if there was you put it there. And then when you've not been able to murder me you try to make a fool of me by pretending to have caught fish when you've been out to buy them. I hate you, and I'll never speak to you again as long as I live. I always thought fishermen were cheats and liars, and now I know they are. *And* murderers. I hate all of you. I shan't stay a minute longer in the beastly place."

Leaving Archie opening and shutting his mouth silently like one of his own expiring fish, she swept into the smoking-room, where her father sat swopping fishing yarns with some members of the elder camp. He was surprised but in no way discomposed by his daughter's sudden decision to go home. He had long ago accustomed himself to sudden changes of plans on the part of his female belongings. Moreover, he knew that she had only accompanied him on an impulse, leaving behind her several interesting "affairs" from which a good deal of kick could still be extracted. He had had a suspicion that the place would fail to supply the excitement that was necessary to a girl of Claribel's temperament, and on the whole was not sorry to hear her decision.

"All right, my dear," he said mildly, "but I'm afraid you can't leave this minute, because there isn't a train till to-morrow afternoon."

She did not come downstairs that evening. She spent it packing in her bedroom, while Archie hung about the hall, still opening and shutting his mouth silently, as if practising passionate speeches of protestation.

The next morning after breakfast Claribel directed the shattering smile at William and said: "Will you come for a walk with me this morning, William?"

William accepted the invitation with apparent eagerness, though he remained completely unshattered by the smile. He knew that Claribel had fixed on the "wretched little oik" with a true womanly intuition of what would be most galling to Archie. They spent the whole morning together. William found it intolerably boring. Claribel was the most limited human being whom he had ever met. She was wholly ignorant on the subject of pirates or smugglers or Red Indians. She was not interested in climbing trees, or damming streams, or getting through barbed-wire fences, or exploring the countryside. She was frightened of spiders, and she did not know a toad from a frog. Relations became definitely strained between them as the morning wore on, and Claribel grew more and more irritable, especially when William took her a short cut back to the inn that led directly through a bog. William persisted that the bog was now all right, as he had drained it three days before, but Claribel's dainty shoes bore ample evidence that this statement of William's erred on the side of optimism. Her resentment against the wretched Archie, however, still blazed so brightly that as soon as they came within sight of the inn she turned her shattering smile on to William again and began to talk to him with every appearance of affectionate interest.

The sight of Archie lurking morosely in the hall when they entered assured her that her efforts were not being wasted.

"WILL YOU COME FOR A WALK WITH ME THIS MORNING,
WILLIAM?" CLARIBEL ASKED.

During lunch she continued to talk brightly to William. After lunch the station bus drew up at the front door, and Claribel, attired for the journey, stepped into it. Archie sprang forward desperately.

"Listen!" he said. "Just listen! Just let me explain!"

But Claribel turned to William with the shattering smile and said:

"Good-bye, William darling, and thank you so much for being so sweet to me."

Then the bus swept her away, still waving effusively to William. Archie gave a hollow laugh, and William slipped away before Archie should try to find outlet for his feelings.

William and his father were going home the next day, so it was not difficult for William to avoid Archie's vengeance in the interval.

Failing to find William, Archie wreaked his vengeance on the fishes and brought in a phenomenal catch that he flung carelessly upon the slab, repeating the hollow laugh.

"Did you enjoy it, William dear?" asked William's mother when he reached home.

William considered the question in silence for a moment, then said:

"Yes, on the whole, I did—quite . . . especially the end part."

from *William—The Rebel*

William and the Perfect Child

William and his Outlaws wandered slowly along the road. There were only two days of the summer holiday left and they were feeling aggrieved. The longer a holiday was, they decided, the more quickly it went, which didn't seem fair. William was feeling specially aggrieved. This afternoon he had been condemned to accompany his mother to a meeting at the Vicarage. It was the housemaid's afternoon off, and the cook said that she wouldn't be left in the house again with that young limb, not if they went down on their bended knees to her, she wouldn't. She'd pack up and go, she would, sooner. She was a good cook, so Mrs. Brown promised faithfully that the young limb should not be left with her, which meant that the young limb must accompany Mrs. Brown to the meeting of the Women's Guild at the Vicarage.

Even William had to admit that the last time he and the cook had been left together in the house events had taken an unfortunate turn. While the cook was upstairs he had carried out a few experiments with the gas oven, and the resultant explosion had nearly wrecked the kitchen. The cook had had hysterics, William had narrowly escaped with his life, the kitchen window and five shillings' worth of kitchen crockery had been broken. So that he was not altogether surprised—though he pretended to be—when his passionate protests were ignored and he was condemned to accompany his mother to the meeting of the Women's Guild. All the more reason, then, to make the most of the morning, and that was what William had decided to do. And yet, as generally happens in such cases, the morning was turning out unexpectedly flat. He and the Outlaws had played at Red Indians and Highwaymen and Lion Hunters, but all the accustomed zest seemed to be lacking from these games.

The thought of the beginning of term loomed over them like a black cloud, and the games petered out finally into an aimless wandering over the fields, interspersed with such remarks as: "I 'spect ole Stinks'll be worse than ever." "There isn't even goin' to be a new master to make things a bit excitin'." "Ole Markie's always worst at the beginnin' of term." "Ole Warbeck couldn't be worse than he was last term, but he's sure to be as bad." "While as for Monkey-Face . . . "

Slower and more dejected became their progress. Suddenly they stopped. A big grey horse was trotting up to them across the field. There was a slight apprehension at their hearts as it approached. It was massive and long-haired and wild-looking. But its intentions were obviously friendly. When William daringly put up a hand to pat and stroke it, it showed every sign of gratification. They all patted and stroked it. It nozzled them affectionately. They pulled up handfuls of grass and offered them to it. It ate them obligingly.

"I say," said William excitedly, "let's get it some sugar."

"I'll go an' get some," said Douglas. "Our house is nearest."

He ran off at full speed, and the other Outlaws continued to fraternise with their new acquaintance. As they went about the field selecting the more appetising patches of grass, the horse followed them trustingly. It even rested its head affectionately on William's shoulder, and a deep emotion stirred in his breast. This was what it must feel like to have a horse. A horse of one's own. . . . Douglas returned with the sugar. He had filled his pockets with it. The horse ate it with obvious enjoyment and gratitude. At last Henry said:

"Come on. We can't stop here for ever."

Very slowly they walked towards the gate that led into the next field. The horse followed them. William opened the gate to let his band through, and the horse passed through with them. William closed the gate. After all, he reasoned with himself, he couldn't help the horse coming through the gate. He couldn't have stopped it. Well, perhaps he could if he'd shut the gate quickly enough, but—anyway, there it was, following them across the next field as closely as if determined never to let them out of its sight again. An unfounded, but thrilling, pride of possession filled William's heart. His horse . . . *his* horse. . . . He opened the next gate and again the horse accompanied the band through it. Again William assured himself that it wasn't his fault. Well, not quite his fault. You couldn't stop a horse goin' where it wanted to, could you? It was a free country, wasn't it? The next gate led into the road. Down the road . . . past the Vicarage gates . . . in at another gate . . . across two more fields . . . till they reached the old barn . . . the horse following them all the time. At the old barn they stood and gazed fondly at their new pet. Then

Douglas handed round the remainder of the sugar, and they fed him in turn.

"Let's have a ride on him," said William.

They considered this suggestion for some moments in silence, then Douglas said: "We can't ride him without reins an' stuff."

Ginger broke in eagerly.

"There's some old harness in Farmer Jenks's barn. It's a bit raggy 'cause he never uses it, but I bet it'd do all right."

He was dispatched to Farmer Jenks's barn. Fate seemed to be on their side. The barn was deserted. Ginger cautiously "borrowed" a raggy saddle and bridle and returned triumphantly with it to the Outlaws. It took some little time to attach it to their steed. Not that the steed proved in any way refractory. It was, indeed, docility itself. Only the Outlaws were unskilled in the art of harnessing, and a less phlegmatic animal would have keenly resented their amateur efforts. When, finally, after many attempts, they had adjusted both saddle and bridle right way on and right way up, they stood and gazed at their handiwork in silent pride. A horse . . . saddled and bridled . . . their horse . . . their own horse. . . .

"Well," said William at last, in a voice he strove in vain to render airy and casual, "I'll jus' have a ride on him first, shall I?"

None of them challenged his right as leader to the first ride. Instead, they clustered round, hoisting him into the large and excessively shabby saddle. After several falls he found himself firmly established there. He took the reins, said "Gee up", and—the grey horse began obediently to lumber across the field. William's feelings were beyond description. No medieval knight in gleaming armour ever bestrode a gaily caparisoned horse with feelings of greater pride and arrogance. To William, in fact, both knight and horse would have seemed shabby in comparison with his mental picture of himself. A grubby little boy, perched on a saddle from which the stuffing was oozing at all points, on a large, clumsy, untended horse of one of the less distinguished breeds, with three other little boys trotting at its heels. . . . Not so did William see himself. He was a king, surrounded by his bodyguard. His thoroughbred pranced beneath him. The gold and jewels of his crown, the scarlet ermine of his cloak, made a noble splash of colour. Massed crowds cheered him on all sides as he rode along. . . . He was a general at the head of his army. His war horse pawed the air, snorted, neighed. His armour gleamed in the sun. The enemy fled in confusion before him.

It was with the greatest reluctance that he acceded to the others' clamorous requests for their "turn." Even when he had been finally dismounted by their combined force and Ginger had been established upon the saddle, William, plodding by his side, was not really plodding by his side. He was up there instead of Ginger . . . rallying his army . . . riding in triumph through cheering crowds . . . his gallant steed curvetting beneath him. It was his turn again. He tried to leap nimbly upon his charger, but fell down ignominiously and had to be hoisted up by the others as before. The fall had brought him down to earth, metaphorically as well as literally. He was no longer a king or a general on a thoroughbred. He was William on a horse. And that was, after all, almost as much a matter for pride as the other. Why should not he lead his Outlaws about the countryside on horseback? In imagination he saw himself doing this, saw the rival gangs, Hubert Lane's in particular, fleeing at his approach, saw himself arriving at school triumphantly on horseback, the admired of all beholders. He thought that he could probably find room in the school bicycle shed for his gallant grey during school hours.

There were certain practical difficulties to be over-come, of course. He could not keep the horse at home. In fact, he would prefer his parents to remain in ignorance of it altogether. The old barn would make quite a good stable, and they could keep the steed in the corner where the rain didn't come in. Tentatively he voiced these plans to the others. They were less enthusiastic about certain aspects of it than he was. The rôle of humble followers on foot did not altogether appeal to them.

"We all found it together," protested Ginger, "an' I don't see why we shouldn't have our turns tramplin' on our enemies an' suchlike."

"All right," said William at last, generously. "We'll have it a day each, but bags me have it when anything really important's goin' on."

They conceded that. William was, after all, their leader. It was Douglas who voiced the practical objection.

"It's not our horse," he said simply.

They were slightly taken aback by the unwelcome, but undeniable, truth of it.

"I think," said William at last, slowly, "that it's a sort of wild horse. I mean, there were wild horses all over England once, and they jus' belonged to anyone who could catch 'em."

"Yes, but that was in anshunt times," objected Henry. "There aren't any wild horses now. They've all died out or been caught."

"How do you know?" William challenged him.

"How do you know they have? There's forests an' things they could hide up in. I bet this is a wild horse that's been hidin' up in forests an' things, an' now it's come out an' we've caught it."

"It doesn't *seem* very wild," said Douglas.

"'Course it does," persisted William. "Look at it. All long hair an' suchlike."

"Yes, but it doesn't *act* wild."

"Well, I bet they don't all act wild. I bet there's some of 'em born sort of quiet. Same as schoolmasters. Most of 'em act wild, but some of 'em act quite quiet. It's jus' the way they're born. It's the same with wild horses."

"It's got horseshoes on," said Douglas.

"Well," began William slowly, obviously trying to reconcile this with a state of wildness, but Ginger interposed before he had found a satisfactory explanation.

"Seems to me more like it belonged to someone who's dead," said Ginger. "That's what I think, anyway. The man it belonged to's dead, an' it was tryin' to find someone else to belong to. It acted jus' like that, din't it? An'—well, look at it. It's not had its hair cut or its face washed or anythin' for ever so long. Stands to reason it mus' belong to someone who's dead. If he'd been alive he'd have looked after it—washed its face an' so on. Well, if the man it belonged to's dead, then it belongs to anyone that finds it. Stands to reason."

"I don't know if that's the lor," said Henry doubtfully.

"I bet it is," persisted Ginger. "Stands to reason it is."

"Well, anyway," said Douglas with the air of one who offers the complete solution of a mystery, "even if it doesn't belong to someone who's dead, it mus' be a stray horse. It was sort of wanderin' about the field as if it didn't know what to do. An' so we oughter take care of it till we find out who it belongs to."

"Yes," agreed William, "an' we've not time to start findin' out to-day, 'cause I've gotter go to that thing at the Vicarage this afternoon. Anyway, I've always wanted to have a horse, 'cause there's a thing in my penknife for takin' stones out of their shoes."

"We could ask people if they know whose it is," suggested Douglas tentatively. Douglas's conscience was always a little more tender than that of the other three.

"No, we couldn't," said William firmly. "We'd only get thieves comin' tryin' to steal it once people knew we'd got it. No, we'll jus' keep it till we've got time to start findin' out who it belongs to. We'll put it away in the ole barn now 'cause it's lunch time, an' we'll come back to it this afternoon. Gosh! I wish I hadn't got to go to that ole thing this afternoon. I'll come as soon as I can, anyway."

They led their unresisting steed into the barn, took off saddle and bridle, fetched a bucket of water, several armfulls of grass, and a whole pound of sugar, which Ginger had shamelessly filched from his mother's store-cupboard, and left it surveying its surroundings with an air of detached interest.

William allowed himself to be garnished and burnished for the afternoon with unusual meekness.

After all, there would be all the evening and all the next day to ride the horse. The next day he might do something really spectacular. If he could get hold of a banner he'd like to ride through the village streets with it, his Outlaws following behind. Or he'd like to put on his helmet and breastplate (he had an old saucepan and tray that filled these rôles) and charge Hubert Lane and his gang, pursuing them over the countryside and finally taking them prisoners. The only drawback was that any such public and spectacular appearance might attract the attention of the horse's missing owner, and William had quite decided that it would be foolish to do that. All in good time. No use rushing things. More haste less speed. There were, in fact, quite a lot of copy-book maxims to support his decision.

"I do hope, dear," Mrs. Brown was saying, "that you'll sit very quietly through the speech."

"What's it going to be about?" said William.

"I really don't know, dear," said Mrs. Brown. "I suppose I must have had a notice." She burrowed among the papers on her writing-desk. "Oh, here it is! The Upbringing of Children, by Mrs. Gladhill."

"Gosh!" said William. "Who's she?"

"I don't know, dear. I believe she's written books and things. I expect she hasn't got any children. They generally haven't." She sighed. "It's so much easier to know how to bring them up, if you haven't got any."

But it turned out that Mrs. Gladhill had. Or rather she had one—a dainty, docile, beautifully mannered little girl of seven called Frances Mary. And Frances Mary was at the Vicarage with her mother. It would have been foolish indeed of her mother to leave her behind, for Frances Mary was a living, breathing, moving testimony to the success of the methods advocated by her mother. She was, as it were, her stock in trade, for Mrs. Gladhill made quite a good thing out of her lectures and books. *The Mothers' Vade Mecum* was in its sixth edition, and *Frances Mary and Her Mother*, published last month, had been sold out before publication. Frances Mary herself was quite a cult among childless elderly ladies, and many a mother had copied the large butterfly bow that adorned Frances Mary's golden curls. There were those who called her "smug" and "priggish," and even used such hard words as "impossible" and "intolerable," but perfection always has its detractors.

The two had arrived at the Vicarage for lunch, a meal at which Frances Mary had displayed, with much unction, the table manners for which she was justly famous, and at which Mrs. Gladhill had carefully pointed out to the rest of the company any of the more attractive traits of the child that might otherwise have escaped notice. Soon after lunch the members of the Women's Guild began to arrive. As the day was warm and sunny, the meeting was to be held on the lawn. Mrs. Gladhill went out to her audience accompanied by the Perfect Child. She introduced the Perfect Child to them, then said: "And now, Frances Mary, go back to the drawing-room and stay there quietly. Mrs. Monks will kindly let you look at her photograph albums." She flashed her brilliant smile at her audience. "I never let Frances Mary listen to my lectures. A child's brain should not be over-strained."

Frances Mary smiled sweetly at the gathering, then trotted off into the house. The accustomed murmur of admiration followed her. Mrs. Gladhill threw a benign glance around, cleared her throat, and began majestically: "Fellow mothers . . ."

She was well under way when Mrs. Brown and William arrived. There had been a slight hitch in their preparations, owing to William's having been discovered to be wearing odd shoes—both for the same foot—when they were half-way there. William protested passionately that it didn't matter, that he never kept his shoes for special feet, anyway, that he always wore any shoe on any foot, and both shoes and feet were used to it.

He said that no one would notice the fact that they were of different pattern unless they were balmy, and then it didn't matter what they thought. But Mrs. Brown was determined that for once in his life William should do her credit. So, by the time they had returned home, found the missing shoe, put it on, and made their way again to the Vicarage, Mrs. Gladhill was just beginning the exposition of her third rule for the upbringing of the Perfect Child.

There was an unusually large attendance of members, most of whom had come in a spirit of curiosity in order to see the much advertised Perfect Child at close quarters. It had even been rumoured that she would recite a poem of her own composition after tea.

Fortunately, however, there were two empty seats, one in the back row and the other in the middle. William hastily claimed the one in the back row, and Mrs. Brown, throwing him an anxious glance, but feeling assured that there was no possibility of his getting into mischief, hemmed in as he was on one side by the churchwarden's wife and on the other by the postmistress, made her way to the other seat. William sat for two minutes, giving his whole attention to the speech, before he came to the conclusion that it wasn't worth it. He looked round furtively and began to consider the possibilities of a large bush that grew just behind his chair. The possibilities were, he decided, more worthy of his attention than the speech. Slowly, and by degrees, he edged his chair back towards it. Whenever he did this his neighbours turned to look at him, but always when they did so he was sitting motionless, his eyes fixed earnestly on the speaker. At last he had edged it back so far as to be practically outside their range of vision. And then, quite suddenly, he vanished. When next his neighbours turned to look at him, he wasn't there. Without sound, without movement, as it seemed, he had disappeared—disappeared as completely as if the earth had swallowed him up. They were slightly puzzled, then dismissed the subject from their minds and gave their attention once more to the lecture. He wasn't their business, and the lecture was. They'd paid for their tickets and they meant to get their money's worth, boy or no boy.

William emerged from the shrubbery at the other side of the Vicarage and heaved a sigh of relief. He couldn't have gone on listening to that awful stuff a moment longer. It would be all right. He'd be back in his place by the time she'd finished, and his mother would never know he'd been away. He might even have time to slip over to the old barn and see how the horse was getting on. Ginger and Douglas and Henry would be having rides on it. It was jolly hard lines on him, not being able to be there, too. Well, it wouldn't do any harm to go and watch them just for a minute or two and then come back. He wouldn't stay long. Suddenly, he became aware of a little girl watching him from an open French window. She was a definitely attractive little girl, with golden hair, blue eyes, and rosy cheeks. She looked at him with interest and distinct favour. Though not of prepossessing appearance, William, fresh from his mother's hands, was radiantly neat and clean, his hair sleeked back, his collar shining, his tie in place, his stockings well gartered, his shoes decorously tied and a-gleam with polish. Definitely a nice little boy, such as her mother had no objection to her knowing.

"Hello," she said.

"Hello," he replied with an ingratiating smile.

"What's your name?"

"William. What's yours?"

"Frances Mary. . . . What are you doing here?"

"Me?" he said vaguely. "Oh, I'm jus' sort of walkin' round a bit."

"Have you come to the meeting?" she asked.

"Oh, yes . . . yes. I've been to the meeting. I've jus' come from it."

"Why've you come from it?" said the little girl. "It's not over, is it?"

"I'VE GOTTER GO AND HAVE A LOOK AT A HORSE OF MINE,"
SAID WILLIAM PROUDLY.

"No, it's not over," admitted William, "but I've gotter go an' have a look at a horse of mine."

The little girl stared at him, obviously impressed.

"Have you got a horse?" she said.

"Me?" said William. "Oh, yes, I've got a horse all right." He gave a short laugh implying that the idea of his not having a horse was ludicrous in the extreme. "Course I've gotter horse."

"Of your very own?" said the little girl, still in an awestruck voice.

"Course," said William, momentarily disallowing the claims of Ginger, Douglas and Henry to their joint property. "Like to come and have a look at it?"

"I'd love to," said the little girl, "but I don't think mother would like me to."

"Oh, yes, she would," persisted William, "I'm sure she would. Why shouldn't she? She likes you havin' a good time, doesn't she?"

"Oh, yes, but—I've got to go out there and have tea with them all as soon as she's finished speaking. I'm going to recite, too. Something I've made up myself."

She spoke with pride, but there was a certain undercurrent of humility. After all, even the reciting of a piece of one's own composition paled before the possession of a real live horse.

"Oh, well, I've gotter be back for tea, too," said William. "It won't take two minutes to go an' look at this horse of mine. It's only across a field. We'll be back long before it's time for tea."

The little girl obviously weakened.

"Well, I could just come and *look* at it, anyway," she said. "After all, it's natural history—isn't it?—and mother thinks that's very important."

"Oh, yes, it's that all right," said William.

"Yes, I'll come," said the little girl. "P'raps I'll be able to make up a poem about it afterwards."

"Oh, yes, I bet you will," said William. "It's a jolly good horse."

She came out of the French windows and walked sedately with William across the lawn to the gates. In the distance could be heard the clipped emphatic tones of the speaker.

"She can speak for a whole hour without stopping, except to take drinks of water," said the little girl proudly.

"This horse of mine," said William, "can run for hours and hours without drinks of water at all."

"She's been to America," went on the little girl.

"This horse of mine's been everywhere," said William.

They had reached the old barn now. The big horse was ambling good-naturedly across the field with Ginger on his back. Douglas and Henry walked proudly on either side, holding the bridle.

William stopped.

"That's my horse," he said casually.

Frances Mary was impressed.

"What a *lovely* one!" she said. "Isn't it big! Who are those boys?"

"Oh, they're jus' friends of mine," said William. "I said they could ride on my horse while I was away. I say"—he turned to her—"would you like a ride?"

Her eyes shone.

"Oo, I'd love it."

"All right," he said generously. "You have one. You have as many as you like. Hi, Ginger! Get off my horse."

They stared at him, so much impressed by his

immaculate appearance and the beauty and daintiness of his escort, that they did not even dispute his claim of sole ownership.

William introduced his new friend with an airy wave of his hand.

"She's called Frances Mary, an' she wants a ride."

Ginger scrambled down obediently, and they stood round Frances Mary, looking from her to the horse.

"How's she goin' to get up?" said Douglas.

"Oh, we'll push her up," said William. "Come on!"

Willing hands pushed the excited Frances Mary on to the saddle. She held on for one ecstatic moment, then, as soon as the horse took a step forward, fell off on the other side. The fall did not hurt her, as the ground was soft and muddy, but it altered her appearance to a considerable extent.

She got up laughing.

"Again! Again!" she cried. "Help me up again!"

Again willing hands pushed her up on to the saddle. Again, at the first step forward of the grey horse, she rolled off on the other side. Again she leapt up, muddy and laughing.

"Isn't it *fun*?" she said. "Do it again."

The Outlaws' admiration for her increased. They called her a sport. They hoisted her up again and again. Again and again she fell off. Her frock was torn and grimy, her hair ribbon came off, her hair fell about her face, her face was covered with mud. She was laughing and shouting in a way in which the Perfect Child had never laughed and shouted in her life before.

After the tenth fall, they hoisted her up yet again.

Now the horse was an amiable animal, but he was getting bored. These young creatures had been climbing on and off him nearly all day. He had followed them originally for sugar, not for donkey work. It occurred to him suddenly that he was fed-up, and that he'd like to go back to his field for a spot of peace and quietness. No sooner had he formed this decision than he acted on it, setting off at a determined canter, careless of the fact that Frances Mary had just been hoisted up on his back for the eleventh time. Frances Mary clawed the air wildly then lurched forward on to his neck, to which she clung with both arms. Shouts of delight came from her.

"I'm staying on, William. Look! I'm staying on."

The grey horse went at a quick trot towards the open gate that led into the next field. The Outlaws, alarmed, called to it to stop. It quickened its pace. Frances Mary still clung on, shrieking with delight. The horse kept determinedly in front of the Outlaws. When they ran to try to catch him up, he ran too. When they walked, he walked. And all the time Frances Mary clung on, shrieking with delight. All semblance to the Perfect Child had gone. She was transformed into a little savage with no thought for anything but the glorious exhilaration of the moment. The grey horse reached the road and cantered along it with its hilarious burden, the Outlaws running behind, imploring it to stop. Ginger even threw a piece of sugar at it, but it was beyond the seductions of sugar. It would be satisfied now with nothing short of home and liberty. The road back to its own field led past the Vicarage gates. It was just passing these gates when a large traction engine appeared, coming from the opposite direction. The grey horse did not like traction engines. It stopped, snorted, then galloped in at the Vicarage gates.

Mrs. Gladhill was drawing to the close of her lecture. She had described the method of bringing up children in much detail and emphasised its success in the case of her

own child. "Several of you have remarked to me to-
day," she said, "on the beautiful manners and behaviour of my own little girl. They are not some freak of
nature, but merely the result of correct upbringing."
She then invited questions. A woman in a purple hat in
the second row got up and, with a side glance at Mrs.
Brown, asked how one could counteract the contaminat-
ing influence of other children. She went on to say that
certain children in the village had a most pernicious
influence over other children. Again she glanced at Mrs.
Brown. Mrs. Brown assumed an air of lofty detachment.
At least, she assured herself, no one could have anything
against William this afternoon, because she'd seen him
herself, nicely settled in a chair in the back row, looking
the picture of cleanliness and good behaviour. No, no
one could have anything against William this afternoon,
at any rate. Patiently, Mrs. Gladhill replied that it was all
a question of the right method. Any child brought up on
the right method would be an influence for good among
other children. "I could trust my little girl," she ended
with a bright smile, "among any children."

It was at this moment that the grey horse entered the
garden and galloped clumsily across the lawn, upsetting
several of the tables laid for tea. He was ridden by a
crumpled, torn, dirty little girl who yelled and screamed
with delight. "It's running! It's running! And I'm staying on!"

She had by now accustomed herself to the horse's
motion, and was sitting more or less upright, and using
the reins. But suddenly the horse recognised his own
field across the hedge of the Vicarage. He leapt forward,
shooting the little girl off his back, and, cantering
through the side gate that someone had obligingly left
open, disappeared from view.

"FRANCES MARY, WHAT *HAVE* YOU BEEN DOING?"

The little girl sat, still laughing, on the lawn, where he had thrown her, the centre of a horrified group. She was, indeed, hardly recognisable as the Perfect Child. But her mother knew her. Her mother gazed at her, growing paler and paler as she took in each detail of her dishevelment.

"Frances Mary," she faltered at last, "what *have* you been doing?"

THEY HARDLY RECOGNISED HER AS THE PERFECT CHILD.

Frances Mary laughed up at her through her mask of mud and tangled curls.

"I've been having a simply *lovely* time," she said.

Mrs. Brown glanced round fearfully for some trace of William.

The empty seat in the back row was all she could find.

from *Sweet William*

William and the Eastern Curse

William had not, however, really expected to enjoy his visit to Aunt Jane's, and on arriving he found things exactly as he had known they would be. The house was depressingly clean and tidy. Everything in it had its own place and was not to be moved or touched. Even the Pekinese in the opposite house had, it turned out, died of overeating the month before. Aunt Jane was tall and prim and what she called "house proud". She winced at the passage of William's boots over her parquet floors even when he did not attempt to slide on them. She met all his suggestions for the employment of his time with an unfailing: "No, William, *certainly* not." She did not want him to play in her garden, because he spoilt the flower-beds ("It isn't as if you kept to the grass, dear, and even the grass, with those heavy shoes——"). She did not want him to play out of her garden, because he always came home so dirty and untidy. She did not want him to play in the house, because he made a noise. She found a friend for him, a nice quiet boy whose interests centred entirely in the study of geography and the making of maps. After one meeting William announced to his aunt that he would not go out with that boy again, not if he was to be put to death by torture for it.

"I thought you'd find him so *interesting*, dear,". she said wistfully. "I thought he'd do you *good*."

"Well, he hasn't done," said William firmly.

His aunt looked at him in pathetic bewilderment.

"I simply can't understand you, dear," she said. "I've always thought him such a *nice* boy."

She had plenty of suggestions in answer to William's demands as to what there was for him to do.

"Well, dear, there's a lot for you to do. You can sit quietly in the morning-room and read. I've got a complete set of the *Encyclopædia Britannica*, and I'm sure you'd find it interesting. One sees quite young children reading it in the advertisements. And, when you're tired of reading, you could go for a nice walk. There's a very interesting church in the village. Part of it Early Perpendicular. I'm sure you'd find that *most* interesting. You could spend a few hours looking round it, and then you could come home and read the article on Architecture in the *Encyclopædia Britannica*. Then in the afternoon you could go out with a notebook and make notes of all the wild flowers you see—keeping to the roads, of course, because the grass is always apt to be damp—and then you could spend the evening reading the article on Botany in the *Encyclopædia Britannica*. And you could make a little collection of pressed wild flowers. I think that you would find the time pass very quickly and happily in that way."

William surveyed this programme morosely, and finally consented to set off on what his aunt called a "botanical stroll", armed with a small tin in which to put his specimens.

He returned (late for lunch) covered with mud, and with his suit torn in several places. The only wild flowers that he had to show for his "walk" were a daisy and a dandelion, which, suddenly remembering the mission on which he was supposed to have gone, he had gathered in haste from the roadside just outside his aunt's gate. He had lost the tin. He explained that this was not his fault. He had been using it to dam a stream, and a farmer had come and chased him away before he could recover it. It was a farmer, too, he explained, who was solely responsible for his torn suit.

"I can get through a barbed-wire fence without tearing anything," said William. "I often have done. If he'd not been running after me and shouting at me, I'd 've got through it all right."

Aunt Jane raised her hand to her head with the expression of one who suffers acute mental anguish.

"But I said keep to the *road*, William," she said.

"Yes," said William unabashed, "I remember now that you said that. But I forgot it this morning. I've got a very poor memory."

Aunt Jane made him change into his best suit and sent his torn one into the kitchen for Molly, the maid, to mend. Aunt Jane also decreed that William must not set foot out of the house in his best suit, and, to make sure of this, sat with him in the drawing room reading the *Encyclopædia Britannica* article on Architecture to him aloud.

Neither Aunt Jane's mind nor William's was really concentrated upon the *Encyclopædia Britannica* article on Architecture. Both, in fact, contained one single thought, and the single thought was that it was high time that this visit of William's came to an end. Both of them, however, felt a certain delicacy about suggesting it.

Aunt Jane's eyelids began to droop. In the excitement of William's late return she had missed her afternoon nap.

AUNT JANE RAISED HER HAND TO HER HEAD WITH THE EXPRESSION OF ONE WHO SUFFERS ACUTE MENTAL ANGUISH. "I SAID KEEP TO THE *ROAD*, WILLIAM," SHE SAID.

"I'm just going up to my bedroom to write a few letters, my boy," she said to William. "You might go into the kitchen and see if Molly has finished mending your other suit."

So William went into the kitchen where Molly, a pretty, rosy-cheeked girl, sat by the window drawing together the edges of one of William's famous three-cornered tears. She greeted him with a friendly wink.

"Well, you young monkey," she said, "I bet the old girl's read you a proper lecture."

William had not given any attention to Molly till now, but suddenly he realised her as a person worth cultivating. The smile, the grin, the wink, and the friendly greeting, warmed his heart. They belonged to a world in which the *Encyclopædia Britannica* did not exist.

"It's the devil an' all to mend," she went on, half admiringly; "me own brother never made such a one, an' he was as big a scamp as you every bit. Anyway, come and sit down and tell me all about yourself while I finish it off."

So William sat down and told her all about himself, and when he had finished she told him all about herself. She was, it appeared, wooed by two suitors, and she did not know which to choose. One was the chauffeur-coachman next door, and the other was the baker's man. William, who knew them both, was deeply interested in the problem.

"James looks a treat in his uniform," said Molly, "an' he's smarter an' he's better off. But there—I always had a soft corner for George. I've tossed up over an' over again, but it always comes different. I tell you, I don't know *what* to do. It fair keeps me awake at nights."

"I like George best," said William.

She sighed.

"I dare say you do, but a boy's nothing to go by. I mean, the one you like best mightn't make me the best husband."

"I don't think James would make a good husband," said William.

She sighed again.

"That's just because George can blow smoke-rings and yodel," she said. "Boys always like him. But smoke-rings and yodelling isn't much good to a wife."

William knew both James and George more thoroughly than Molly realised. He was, in fact, deeply involved in hostilities with James. He had greeted both James and George with a challenging grimace on his first meeting. George had replied by a grimace that was unquestionably superior and had asked him if he would like a ride round the village in his baker's cart. During the ride he had yodelled for him and blown smoke-rings and at the end had let him help unharness Daisy, the horse. In William's eyes George was a demi-god. His relations with James were different. James, who was out with the car when they first met, had replied to his grimace by deliberately driving through a puddle so as to drench William in muddy water, and the next morning when out with the trap had given him a stinging flick of the whip. Thenceforward, whenever James met William in his capacity of chauffeur, he drove his car so near him as to precipitate him into the ditch, and, whenever he met him in his capacity of coachman, he flicked him neatly but painfully with his whip. James was one of those men who believe that small boys exist to be teased. But William possessed a grown-up sister, and he knew that women are incalculable in their attitude to admirers of the opposite sex. With Ethel, the fact that William disliked a particular suitor generally predisposed Ethel in that particular suitor's favour. So he said little to Molly about the rival merits of James and George, confining himself to discussing with her ways and means of choosing between them. The ways they tried were numerous and intriguing. They threw apple peel over their shoulders to see what initial it formed. It formed unmistakably the letter S, but, as Molly knew no one whose name began with that letter, the experiment carried them no further. They made spills of the same length, one with the name James written upon it and the other George, lit them at the same second, and watched to see which should burn the longer. They burnt out at the identical second. They wrote their names on paper, put them in a hat, shook them up, and let Molly draw one out. She drew four times. Twice she drew James and twice George. She wrote their names yet again on small pieces of paper and put them beneath her pillow to see which she would dream of. She dreamed of the pig that had shared her home in her childhood. It was a handsome, friendly pig, but did not even remotely suggest either George or James.

William, in a conscientious desire to help her, cultivated the acquaintance of her suitors yet further. He went to the next door garage, and in all good faith offered to help James clean the car. James playfully directed the full stream of the hose upon him. After that William confined his attention to George, who let him harness and unharness Daisy and spent many patient hours trying to teach him to yodel.

Aunt Jane was engaged in preparing an address on "The New Thought" for the "New Era Society", of which she was vice-president, and she was glad that William should spend his time quietly anywhere and with anyone as long as he did not disturb her. She found his yodel-practising inexpressibly painful, but tried to combat it with the exercise of the New Thought. As she sat at her little desk, trying to write her address, while William, going to bed above her, filled the house with horrible and raucous strains that changed with nerve-shattering suddenness from bass to tenor, she addressed her mind over and over again with the words: "You are poised and in harmony. No outside disharmony can disturb you."

Her mind, however, had quite different ideas on the subject, and persisted in being disturbed by the outside disharmony of William's yodelling. William, when remonstrated with, was profusely apologetic.

"I'm sorry," he would say, "I thought I was doing it low so as you wouldn't hear. I keep forgettin' that you don't like music."

William, in his self-appointed capacity of umpire, liked to be present at the frequent conversations that Molly held with her suitors at the kitchen gate. Though he was an unqualified supporter of George, he had to admit that James was the better conversationalist. Moreover, James always had the local news and gossip at his finger-ends.

"Old Marlow's dead," he said solemnly one evening leaning over the kitchen gate. "Ill-wished that man was."

"Ill-wished!" jeered Molly; "you don't believe in them things surely!"

But it appeared that James did believe in them things.

"Why, I've known of cases—well, you'd hardly believe them," he ended feebly.

"You tell me an' see if I'll believe them," challenged Molly.

"Well, of course," he admitted, "things like that aren't so common in England. It's in the East they happen most. I knew a man once that had lived in the East, and the things he told me——"

The silence was made eloquent by James's solemnly rounded eyes.

"Go on," said Molly still incredulous, "tell us some

of the things he told you."

James, seeing William standing within reach, seized his arm and twisted it half mechanically, then relapsed into solemnity.

"Well," he said, "it's true. This man who told me vouched for its truth. I can tell you I think twice before I ever annoy anyone from the East. They can put curses on you."

Molly was impressed despite herself.

"What sort of curses?" she said. "Go on! Tell us a bit more."

"They can put a curse of animals or insects onto people," said James slowly. "Well, honestly, you'd hardly believe it. They can put—say—a cat curse onto you, so that wherever you go there's cats. Cats everywhere, and you can't get rid of them, because, if you harm them in any way, it's you that's hurt, just as if someone had made you in wax and stuck pins in. And they generally put in the curse that one of them—say, the tenth you see—is fatal. And it always is. This man told me of some awful curses like that. Snakes one man had, and the seventh snake bit him and killed him, though it wasn't a real snake at all. The man that put the curse on him had told him that the seventh snake would kill him, and it did."

Molly threw back her head and laughed.

"I never heard such nonsense," she said.

James stared at her gloomily.

"You wouldn't call it nonsense if you knew some of the things this man told me," he said.

"Go on!" laughed Molly, her dark eyes sparkling. "Can't you find anything more interesting to talk to a girl about?"

James moved nearer her, and, replying to the challenge

of her eyes, found something more interesting to talk to a girl about.

That evening Molly grew still more confidential to William.

"It's no good me goin' on like this an' not being able to make up my mind," she said. "I must give them a test same as people do in books."

"What sort of a test?" said William.

Molly wrinkled her brow.

"Well, that's what I've got to make up my mind about," she said. "The test the girl in the last book I read gave, was pretending that she'd lost all her money, then the one that wasn't really worthy of her chucked her, and the other one stuck to her. And he was rewarded, of course, because she hadn't really lost her money."

"Well, you do that," said William with interest. "Tell them you've lost your money."

"They know I've not got any money, so it wouldn't make any difference," said Molly. "But I've made up my mind to give them a test, and I'm going to think hard what test to give them."

"Yes, an' I'll think hard too," said William helpfully, "we'll both think hard all to-morrow, an' to-morrow night we'll decide."

The next evening he joined Molly in the kitchen as usual. Aunt Jane was now wrestling with an address on "The World of Nature". "The New Thought" had got so far beyond her that she had had to give it up in favour of something on which the *Encyclopædia Britannica* was more explicit.

"I've thought of a ripping test," said William excitedly. "Have the one that can make the best ducks and drakes on a pond. I bet anyone that can make good ducks and drakes must be nice."

George, William knew, was the best maker of ducks and drakes for miles around. But his deep plot for making George the winning candidate did not succeed. Molly shook her head.

"No," she said. "I've thought of something much better than that. It was in a book I was reading last night after you went to bed, and in it the man was out walking with the girl, and they came to a place that was under water, and the girl said that she wanted to go to the other side, and the man just picked her up and carried her across, and didn't care how wet he got. Well, I think it was beautiful, don't you?"

"No, I don't," said William, "I think it was silly. I bet I wouldn't do that. Not for anyone."

"Yes, but you aren't in love," said Molly. "I think it's beautiful, and that's what I'm going to do. I'm going to go out for a walk with the two of them together on Sunday afternoon, and I'm going to take them down to Forster's meadow where it's flooded, and I'm going to see which will carry me over."

"But you could go round by the path," objected William. "The path isn't flooded."

"Yes, but I'll say I don't want to go round by the path," said Molly firmly, "I'll say I want to go to Mereham over the meadow. And I'll see which will carry me over. . . ."

William considered the situation gloomily. There was something flamboyant and theatrical about James. He would quite probably offer to carry her across, even if he punished her for it afterwards. George, on the other hand, was simple, and endowed with a large fund of common sense. If she could get to Mereham as well by the path, George would naturally object to wading over his knees through a flood. George would be kind but firm. George would not see any point in making a fool of himself. George, in short, would fail in the "test".

"I think it's a rotten test," said William. "If I were you I'd make it yodelling. I think it would be jolly nice to have a husband who could yodel."

"No," said Molly firmly, "I've made up my mind, and that's the test I'm going to have. And you've got to *promise* not to tell either of them."

Reluctantly William promised. He felt gloomy and apprehensive. He wanted George to marry Molly. He was convinced that Molly was too good for James. And it would be James, he was certain. who would triumphantly pass the "test".

That evening he sat on the fence, dangling his feet and wondering how, short of breaking his promise to Molly, he could make George pass the "test". George let him help unharness his horse every evening. George coached him kindly and painstakingly in his not-yet-successful efforts at yodelling. George even gave him an occasional bun left over from his "round". While James——

Suddenly the next-door car, driven by James, came into sight. The road was narrow and deeply pitted, and the pits were filled with water from the recent rain. A man was walking along the road, his head buried deep on his chest, his hat pulled low over his eyes. James, grinning, performed his favourite trick, driving his car as near to the pedestrian as possible and splashing him from head to foot with water. Then he turned round, still grinning, to enjoy his victim's discomforture. His victim had lifted his head angrily, revealing a black face and white, furiously rolling eyes. He shouted some words they could not hear, shook his fist, then turned and resumed his walk.

James's mouth had dropped open, his face had paled. He drew up, and, forgetting to twist William's arm or push him off his perch, said: "Did you hear what he said?"

"No," said William.

"He—he was an Eastern, wasn't he?"

"Oh, yes," said William, "he was an Eastern all right."

"Cripes!" said James aghast, "I wish I'd heard what he said."

"It sounded like a curse," said William, enjoying James's dismay.

James's face turned from white to yellow. His eyes bulged and his hands trembled so much that, continuing on his way, he nearly took the gate off its hinges as he re-entered his employer's home.

William's spirits brightened. James would live in terror of a curse for many days to come. William felt avenged for the ills he had received at the hands of James. Then his spirits clouded again. James would still pass the test triumphantly to-morrow.

Then he completely forgot everything about James and George and Molly. For down the road was coming a familiar figure . . . a small, pied dog with a head too big for its body and a strange and unexpected tail. It was William's mongrel, Jumble. It had found life at home dull without him and had followed him to Aunt Jane's. It was travel-stained from its long journey, but it greeted William with ecstatic and uproarious delight. William, as deeply touched at the reunion as Jumble, gathered him into his arms with affectionate congratulation.

"Well done, old chap. You're a jolly clever dog, aren't you, coming all this way. Good old Jumble! Good old boy! I bet you're hungry. Come along———"

Dismay settled on his face again. Aunt Jane disliked dogs.

She would not let Jumble stay there. She would insist on Jumble's being sent home at once.

Very cautiously, very slowly, William led Jumble to the little shed at the bottom of Aunt Jane's garden and tied him up. Then he went indoors to consult Molly. Molly was sympathetic. Molly, it appeared, had a weakness for mongrels. "I had one at home. No breed at all, it wasn't, but as faithful and loving as any dog ever made. An' the first thing I'm going to do when I'm married is to set up a dog."

Together they took food down to Jumble. Jumble won her heart at once by sitting up to beg despite his weariness. Together they watched him eat the meaty bones and the biscuits that they had brought down for him.

"She'll send him back," said Molly. "She'll send him back sure as Fate. She can't abear 'em, says they mess up the place. She'll tell the gardener to take him back by train to-morrow. Sure as Fate she will."

William was silent for a few seconds then gave a sudden gasp.

"*Tell* you what! I've got an idea. Let's keep him here. She won't know he's here. She never comes out here. I can sneak out with him sometimes through the hedge to take him for a walk. An' we can bring food to him down here. It's a *fine* idea."

Molly hesitated, and finally yielded. The prospect of an impending engagement to either James or George according to the results of the "test", made her feel independent and inclined to a gesture of defiance.

"Sure, my soul's my own," she said, "an' I've a right to give shelter to a fellow-creature if I like. An' if she finds it an' gives me notice she's welcome to. I'll be glad to shake the dust of her off my feet, the old fool."

At this moment Aunt Jane called William indoors and gave him some letters to post. William, after due consideration, decided not to take Jumble. For one thing, Jumble was tired. For another, he did not wish to risk detection the first night of Jumble's stay. Instead he took a ball with which he was in process of perfecting a trick. The trick consisted in throwing it over his left shoulder from behind and catching it in front. William had only begun to practise it yesterday, and he was very much pleased with the progress he had made. He had already almost decided to be an acrobat when he grew up. As soon as Jumble was rested, he would start training Jumble for their joint career. He had gratifying visions of himself, clothed in tights, balancing Jumble (standing on one paw) on one hand, and with the other throwing a swift succession of balls over his left shoulder from behind and catching them again in front.

Just as he was passing the next door gate the ball slipped from his hand and flew over the gate, landing at the feet of James, who stood idly watching a garden fire. Grinning at William, James picked up the ball, held it tantalisingly aloft, then dropped it into the flames. William walked on, scowling angrily. Then he stopped suddenly as if struck by an idea. The scowl cleared from his face, and a beatific smile took its place.

*   *   *

James, spick and span, in his Sunday best, lounged elegantly at the back gate of Aunt Jane's house, completely ignoring George, who, less elegant though also in his Sunday best, lounged there also. They were both waiting for Molly. The arrangement was an unusual one.

Generally she went out with them on alternate Sundays, but this Sunday, though neither James nor George yet knew it, was the Sunday of the "test". After a few minutes Molly, flushed and pretty and demure, joined them.

"I thought you wouldn't mind us all three going out together," she said brightly. "I'd like to go over Mereham way if it's all the same to you."

Evidently it was all the same to them. The three set off towards Mereham. Molly's bright eyes sparkled. She enjoyed the situation to the full. She did most of the talking. George was generally rather silent. James, on the other hand, was generally a fluent talker, but to-day a constrained silence held him too. A close observer would have noticed that he was nervous. He threw quick, apprehensive glances about him as he walked. He was distinctly white about the gills. He kept one hand in his pocket, tightly clutching a note. It was an anonymous note, and he had received it last night. It began without any form of address:

"I have put the curse of dogs upon you. If you harm any of these dogs the harm will come back to you. The fifth dog will be fatal.

The Eastern you splashed this afternoon."

James had tried to make light of this to himself, but he had passed an uneasy night. This morning he had not even tried to make light of it. For the curse had taken effect. He was a doomed man. As he walked by Molly, glancing nervously about him and fingering the fateful note, his mind went over the events of that morning. On going down to the garage he had heard a strange noise from the car. He had opened the door, and to his horror a dog had jumped out. He had remembered the contents of the note just in time to restrain himself from throwing anything after it as it ran off, but it had taken him a long time to recover from the shock sufficiently to rub up the brasswork of the car, as was his custom on Sunday mornings. He had then gone to the woodshed to chop some firewood for the cook—one of his daily duties. Immediately on his opening the door a dog shot out and past him. He then faced the horrible truth. He was a man under a dog curse. He took a much longer time than usual to chop the firewood, then went to the greenhouse to water the chrysanthemums—another of his Sunday duties, as the gardener did not come on that day. This time the dog almost knocked him down in its frantic exit. He watched its vanishing figure with bulging eyes, and then took out a handkerchief to mop his brow. That was the third dog (all exactly alike—they were alike in these curses of course). The fifth was the fatal one.

Feeling shaken, he decided to go to his room over the garage and rest. He opened his door with the glad feeling of one who goes to a familiar refuge where danger cannot penetrate, but the feeling was short-lived. A dog—exactly like the other three dogs—shot out, tumbled head over heels down the stairs and vanished from sight. And so it was that James walked with less than his accustomed swagger, and glanced furtively from side to side. Molly, taking his silence for the embarrassment of one who suffers the pangs of love, was not displeased by it. She chattered gaily to both of her suitors impartially. The road turned a sharp corner, and there in front of them lay the flooded meadows. The trio stopped, and Molly looked from one to the other beneath demurely lowered lashes.

"I want to get across," she murmured. "What shall I do?"

"The other path isn't under water," said George reasonably, "we can go round by that."

"I don't want to go by the other path," said Molly, "I want to go by the path through the meadows."

There was a silence.

"Can't—can't either of you think of a way?" said Molly, smiling bewitchingly at James.

But James did not return the smile. His face was grey, and he was staring with a gaze of petrified horror at the fifth dog, that sat just beyond the strip of water. William lay at ease in the shadow of the hedge. Jumble sat in the sunlight, watching the water with friendly and enquiring interest. William had had a tiring day. First of all he had had to elicit from Molly a detailed account of James's Sunday activities. He had done it very cunningly, pretending that he was thinking of becoming a chauffeur himself when he grew up. The rest of the business had been much more difficult, requiring on William's part the utmost finesse and dexterity. To glide unseen under cover of the bushes with Jumble in his arms, to slip Jumble into James's next objective, retrieve him still unseen on his escape, and put him ready to be re-discovered, had needed all William's resource. Fortunately Jumble and William had often played Red Indians together, and therefore the whole proceeding was less startling to Jumble than it might otherwise have been. The only part of it he really objected to was being shut up in strange places without William, but Jumble was a sensible dog and knew that it was all part of the game, and that in that particular game he wasn't supposed to bark. He had unlimited faith in William, and was convinced that it would all come right in the end. It had been a brilliant inspiration of William's to make the fourth appearance of Jumble take place in

James's own bedroom. He had guessed that by that time James would want to go somewhere to think the situation over quietly.

Suddenly Jumble noticed that one of the three people on the other side of the water was the Girl, the nice Girl, the Girl who had welcomed and fed him last night. He gave a shrill bark of excited recognition, and, plunging into the water, began to swim in her direction. With a wild cry James turned and fled, fled with such alacrity that in a few seconds he had completely vanished from the landscape.

Molly looked after him with tears of discomfiture in her eyes. George's manly heart was stirred by her distress.

"What is it, honey?" he said.

"I thought—I thought one of you would carry me over," said Molly forlornly.

Without a word George picked her up and carried her across to the waiting William.

*   *   *

William went into the drawing-room where his aunt was talking to the lady next door, and sat down patiently to wait till her visit should be over. He hoped that the sight of him would bring her visit to a premature conclusion. He had often noticed with secret gratification that his entry cleared his mother's drawing-room of guests.

"*So* annoying," William's aunt was saying, "I don't mean that she isn't far from perfect. In some ways she's *hopeless*. But I'd taken a lot of trouble training her, and *just* when I've begun to get her into my ways she tells me she's going to marry the baker's man next month. *Most* tiresome!"

"They're *all* tiresome," said the lady next door. Her tone showed more concern for her own troubles than for Aunt Jane's. "There's James now. I've always found him *most* satisfactory, and all of a sudden he turns peculiar."

"How 'peculiar'?" said William's aunt with perfunctory interest. She thought that Mrs. Bellews might have shown a little more sympathy about Molly.

"Well, I get a complaint from Mr. Jones at The Hawthorns that when he was coming home from the rehearsal at the Village Hall—he and some others are doing a sort of minstrel show with blacked faces in aid of the Organ Fund. I'm surprised at the Vicar for allowing it. I shan't go. I always find that sort of minstrel show vulgar. Anyway, he says that when he was coming back from the rehearsal James passed him in the car and deliberately drove into a puddle to splash him. It's *quite* ridiculous, of course. James is always *most* careful. It must have been some other chauffeur. He couldn't *possibly* recognise anyone with his face covered with that revolting black stuff anyway. But I sent for James and questioned him just as a matter of form, and he behaved most peculiarly."

"In what way?" said Aunt Jane, interested despite herself.

"Stared at me in the wildest fashion, his mouth wide open and his eyes nearly starting out of his head. And gave a *dreadful* sort of laugh. I told him to go and lie down till he felt better. It may be just the heat or, of course, it may be the beginning of insanity. I once had a housemaid——"

She caught William's eye fixed upon her with a stony glare, and decided to put off the story of the housemaid till another time. One never knew how much children understood nor what they would repeat. She rose and took her leave, patting William vaguely upon the head and thinking what a very unattractive-looking child he was.

As soon as she had gone William turned to his aunt and said abruptly: "My dog's come."

"Your what, dear?" said Aunt Jane bewildered.

"My dog's come," repeated William impatiently, "an' I 'spect you don't want him here."

"*Certainly* not, dear," said Aunt Jane firmly, "the animal must be sent home at once."

"Well, you see," said William slowly, "it wouldn't go back with anyone but me. It would bite anyone but me, so that they'd prob'ly get hydrophobia. So I'd better take him back. An'" (he fixed her with an unblinking eye), "it's not worth while me coming back here to finish up my visit once I've gone home, is it? I'd better stay there, hadn't I?"

Aunt Jane brightened visibly. She badly wanted a few quiet days with her address. She'd given up "The World of Nature" as being too crude and had begun to write an address on "The Duty of Happiness". But she wanted quiet for concentration, and it was curious how disturbing William's presence was, even when he was comparatively silent.

"Yes, dear," she said, "I shall be sorry to lose you, but I think it's an *excellent* idea."

from *William—The Pirate*

William the Persian

William was mildly interested when he heard that Miss Cliff of Lilac Cottage and Mrs. Nichol of The Elms were going to exchange houses for a month because Miss Cliff wanted a larger house and Mrs. Nichol a smaller one. Mrs. Nichol's mother, who generally lived with her, was going away for a change, and Miss Cliff's aunt was coming to her while her own companion took a much needed holiday. The aunt was a bedridden invalid of the more exacting type, who insisted on a room with plenty of space, facing south; and as there was no such bedroom in Miss Cliff's cottage and as Mrs. Nichol's mother's bedroom in The Elms fulfilled all the requirements and as Mrs. Nichol was notoriously mean and ready for any excuse to save a penny (the rent of Lilac Cottage was, of course, far smaller than that of The Elms), the exchange was quickly effected. William was interested, because so far the situation was unique in his experience. He had, of course, known people to remove from the village or to the village, with all the accompanying paraphernalia of vans and packing-cases and picnic meals on grand pianos in the garden, but he had never before known two people just walk out of their own houses into each other's, only a few yards away, and proceed to live in them.

It was like a new sort of game, and he at once decided

to join in it. He arranged with Ginger that they should go to bed in each other's houses one night, just in order to enjoy the novel experience, but the plan was discovered and foiled by their parents before it could be put into execution. So interested, however, was William in this new idea that he hung round the gate of Lilac Cottage for a whole morning, trying to catch a glimpse of Mrs. Nichol moving about in Miss Cliff's surroundings. The situation seemed to open whole vistas of possibilities. It would, thought William, add considerably to the zest of life if everyone in the world had to move on one each year and go to live in the next-door house. Other people's things were always more interesting than your own. By degrees, if you moved on every year, you'd travel all over England, and, if you lived long enough, all over the world. Perhaps it would be better to move on every day, so as to get along more quickly. Then—and this was a cheering thought—you'd soon be out of reach of your own school, and you'd have to go to another for a week or two, and then to another, and then to another. You'd be going to a different school nearly every week. The possibilities of the situation became more and more entrancing as William considered them. A new school every week. One new master was fun enough but a whole school full of new masters . . . and every week!

He decided to put the plan into effect immediately on becoming dictator of England—a post he intended to occupy as soon as he left school. He wondered that no one had thought of it before.

But, though he hung about the gate of Lilac Cottage for nearly half an hour, he could see no signs of Mrs. Nichol inside it. On a sudden impulse he walked up to the front door and knocked. Mrs. Nichol opened it.

"Well?" she said.

For a few minutes William enjoyed the spectacle of Mrs. Nichol in Miss Cliff's hall, opening Miss Cliff's front door. He didn't know why it was such a satisfying spectacle, but it was. It varied the monotony of life, and William liked anything that varied the monotony of life.

"What do you want?" said Mrs. Nichol. Her tone was impatient. She was busy "settling in" and, anyway, she disliked William.

William collected his forces and assumed an ingratiating expression.

"I came to see if I could help you any way," he said.

She looked at him in silence. He was, for him, comparatively tidy, and he wore the expression that always made people feel that they had misjudged him. And as a matter of fact there were several things that he could do for her.

"Er—thank you," she said, a little less distantly. "Yes, there are one or two things you could do. Come in and wipe your shoes."

William came in and wiped his shoes, then proceeded to make himself useful in a way that would have drawn cynical comments from his own home circle. He chopped wood, he carried in coal, he moved furniture, he cleaned brasses. And he enjoyed the spectacle of Mrs. Nichol moving about in Miss Cliff's house among Miss Cliff's possessions. As he prepared to go he noticed that Mrs. Nichol was looking at him thoughtfully.

"William," she said at last, "I wonder—er—were you going by Miss Cliff's by any chance?"

"Well——" began William guardedly. (He had been meaning to pay a visit to Miss Cliff in order to enjoy the spectacle of Miss Cliff moving about among Mrs. Nichol's possessions.)

"Because if you *are*, William," she interrupted, "I'd

be so grateful if you'd just look in at the drawing-room and make sure that she hasn't got the piano standing in a draught. I know she was going to alter the furniture round a bit, and I said she could, but I don't want the piano in a draught. I'd be so glad if you'd see whether she's moved it. It should be against the wall next to the fireplace. Don't tell her I sent you to find out, of course, but if you *are* going there for anything else, I'd like you to find out. I'll give you a penny if you come back and tell me just where the piano is."

William set off briskly in the direction of Miss Cliff's. He saw an ample source of revenue in the situation if skilfully handled.

Miss Cliff, small and harassed looking, opened the door and looked at him questioningly. Once more William assumed his ingratiating expression.

"I've come to see if I can help you any way," he said.

"Oh, that's very kind of you, William," she said, opening the door wider to admit him. She'd had rather a trying morning with the bedridden aunt and welcomed a diversion of any sort. Moreover, as in the case of Mrs. Nichol, there were several small jobs about the house that a boy could do very usefully. Tentatively she suggested some of these, and William promptly set to work, ascertaining incidentally that the piano duly stood against the wall next to the fireplace in the drawing-room. As he was about to take his departure, Miss Cliff looked at him hesitatingly and said:

"I wonder if you're going past my house on your way home, William?"

"Oh, yes," admitted William. "Oh, yes, I think I'm goin' past your house."

"I wonder if you could just—just look in at the drawing-room as you pass and see whether Mrs. Nichol has got my fern-stand *right* in the window. The ferns get no sun at all unless they're *right* in the window. If you'll just look, and then come back and tell me, I'll give you a penny, William."

Thereafter began a busy and lucrative existence for William. He visited each house as the spy of its owner and brought back regular reports. Mrs. Nichol wanted to know whether Miss Cliff was using her Worcester tea service ("I asked her not to, but one never knows"). Miss Cliff wanted to know whether Mrs. Nichol was watering her ferns regularly ("I asked her to, William, but she didn't seem a bit interested in ferns"). Mrs. Nichol wanted to know whether Miss Cliff was keeping her dining-room curtains drawn at midday ("The sun pours right in and takes the colour out of everything if you don't"). Miss Cliff wanted to know whether Mrs. Nichol was using a precious Chinese bowl for flowers or sugar or any other secular purpose ("I told her it was valuable, William, but I don't know whether she quite realised. . . . It belonged to my grandfather. I never used to allow anyone but myself even to touch it").

Neither, of course, knew that he was acting as the emissary of the other, and each admired the tact and dexterity that he must have used to gain access to the other's house, little dreaming that whenever he went to gain any information for her he took some valuable information from her at the same time.

There was an element of intrigue in the situation that appealed to William's romantic soul. He could pretend that the houses were different kingdoms. He could people the stretch of road between them with innumerable dangers. He could imagine the pieces of information he gleaned to be matters of far higher import than the watering of plants and the drawing of window curtains and the uses of Chinese bowls.

But, though he continued to serve two mistresses, he soon began to have a strong sense of partisanship. Miss Cliff, he decided, was very much nicer than Mrs. Nichol. Mrs. Nichol sneered at Miss Cliff's little house and domestic arrangements and soon began to show herself overbearing and imperious in her dealings with William. Moreover, she was so mean that she generally made some excuse for not giving him the penny she had promised him. Miss Cliff, on the other hand, though everyone knew she was very badly off, was kind and generous, always very grateful for William's help, lavish of pennies and slabs of cake, and loyally appreciative of the amenities of Mrs. Nichol's house. Also she was unfailingly cheerful, though the bedridden aunt was the type of bedridden aunt who delights in tyrannising over an entire household and summoned her upstairs a dozen times an hour merely for the pleasure of summoning her upstairs.

Even before the incident of the silver spoons William had begun to feel compunction at the thought of spying upon Miss Cliff, and indeed the only reason he continued to do so was that it gave him an opportunity of keeping an eye upon Miss Cliff's possessions for her, and surreptitiously watering the ferns, which Mrs. Nichol was flagrantly neglecting.

But the episode of the silver spoons made him wholly the champion of Miss Cliff; for Mrs. Nichol asked him to look into the sideboard drawer in the dining-room at The Elms, and see if her silver spoons were still there, and to make sure that Miss Cliff was not using them, as they were an heirloom and she had distinctly told Miss Cliff that they were not to be used. William indignantly refused the commission, so Mrs. Nichol wrote a note to

Miss Cliff, reminding her that the silver spoons in the sideboard drawer were not to be taken into use. William agreed to take the note, because he wanted to be there when Miss Cliff received it, in order to give what comfort he could, should its brusqueness cause that gentle soul any alarm. And, as things turned out, he was glad that he was there. Miss Cliff turned pale with anxiety as she read.

"Oh, dear!" she said. "Yes, I remember she did mention the spoons. I haven't used them. I've not even noticed them in the drawer, as a matter of fact, but of course they must be there."

She scurried to the sideboard drawer, was called upstairs by an imperious summons from the bedridden aunt, scurried down again when she found that the bedridden aunt didn't want anything, and began a feverish and prolonged search for the spoons in the sideboard drawer, her face growing paler and paler as the search failed to reveal them.

"They *must* be here!" she cried desperately, turning over tablecloths and doilies and table-mats and table-centres and the usual odds and ends that mysteriously congregate in such drawers.

"William, they aren't here!" she said wildly.

William joined in the search. Tablecloths, table-mats, table-napkins, table-centres, cascaded on to the floor as he burrowed among them like a terrier after a rat. But even this chaotic hunt failed to reveal the spoons. Together they searched through the sideboard cupboard and in every nook and cranny in the dining-room. The spoons were not there. Miss Cliff was almost in tears.

"What shall I do, William?" she said. "It's *terrible*. I've never even seen them, but she hasn't got them, so they must be somewhere here."

"WHAT SHALL I DO, WILLIAM?" ASKED MISS CLIFF, ALMOST IN TEARS.

But they weren't anywhere there, and finally Miss Cliff sat down to write a distraught note to Mrs. Nichol, begging her to make quite sure that she hadn't taken the spoons with her. William carried the note to Mrs. Nichol. Mrs. Nichol looked grim as she read it.

"What appalling carelessness!" she said, with a disagreeable sniff. "Well, if she can't find them, she must just pay for them, that's all, and she won't find *that* very cheap."

She conveyed this information to Miss Cliff in a terse note, over which Miss Cliff wept.

"William, I simply don't know *how* I can find the money to pay for them if they're really lost. They'll be *terribly* expensive. Heirlooms are, you know."

William searched indefatigably in the greenhouse and tool shed (he had a theory that all lost property finally turns up in such places), but without result. The news spread through the village, and the village constable came to visit Mrs. Nichol's house in hopes of finding proofs of a burglary. He had longed for a burglary ever since he joined the force, but so far had met with nothing more exciting than two motorists who had failed to produce a driving licence, both of whom duly produced it the next day. A thorough examination of the premises assured him that there had been no burglary from outside, and Miss Cliff's distress increased.

"You see, William, I can't help feeling that I'm under suspicion, as it were. It isn't even as if I had a maid or a charwoman. If anyone's taken them it must be me. I didn't, of course, but I can't help feeling that that's what people must be thinking. . . ."

Poor little Miss Cliff spent all her time hunting for the silver spoons, except when she was flying up- and downstairs at the bidding of the querulous aunt. She was too anxious even to eat and was growing visibly thinner.

Therefore William was very glad of the diversion of the Persian boy.

The Persian boy was a real flesh-and-blood Persian boy who was in England on a visit and was coming to spend a day at the Vicarage, because the Vicar knew a man who knew a man who knew a man who had met the boy's father in Persia. The Vicar happened to meet Miss Cliff in the village on the day on which he had heard the boy was coming, and Miss Cliff asked him to bring the boy to tea. He said that he himself had to attend a meeting in Hadley that day, but that the boy could come to tea with her alone. At this Miss Cliff was so much excited that she almost forgot the silver spoons and began to take an interest in her food once more, even complaining to the local butcher about a tough piece of steak (the butcher had been presuming on the silver spoons and the querulous aunt). Her pleasure was not in any way lessened when she heard that Mrs. Nichol had also asked the Persian boy to tea, but that the Vicar had said he was only being there for one day and had already accepted Miss Cliff's invitation. Mrs. Nichol was annoyed and went about muttering of silver spoons and some people's inadequate domestic arrangements. But Miss Cliff had regained her old cheerfulness. She asked William to come to tea to help entertain the Persian boy, and she consulted him in detail about the tea itself. On his advice she ordered largely of doughnuts and iced cakes and cream buns and chocolate biscuits. She made a jelly and a trifle. She spent much time arranging the room as she thought a Persian boy would like it.

"I'm afraid the carpet's Axminster, William, dear," she said. "I hope it won't annoy him. Of course, a Persian one would have been nicer. Do you think he'll sit on the floor, William? Ought the tea-table to face the east? I believe that's an Oriental custom. If he doesn't sit on the floor, I wonder if he'll object to a leather chair? Or is that Hindoos?"

In the end she arranged several cushions on the floor, in case the Persian boy wished to sit there, and a basket-chair facing the east at the tea-table, in case he didn't.

The fact that Mrs. Nichol, who had tried unsuccessfully to get the Persian boy to tea at her home and who had been so very disagreeable about the silver spoons, would be able to watch his arrival at Miss Cliff's from her drawing-room window, added considerably to her pleasure though she tried conscientiously not to let it. Miss Cliff wasn't worrying about the silver spoons at all now. She was far too much excited about the Persian boy. She meant to worry extra hard afterwards to make up. . . . .

She was so much excited the night before the tea-party that she hardly slept at all. As she lay awake brilliant ideas occurred to her—such as procuring a Persian flag and hanging it out of the window or getting a gramophone record of the Persian national anthem and borrowing a gramophone for the afternoon to play it on—all of which seemed less inspired in the cold light of day.

She spent the morning making jellies and trifles and scones and sponge-cakes and a mixture of bananas, strawberry jam and cream that William strongly recommended.

She had asked William to come early and so William, interpreting the word "early" in a fairly wide sense, set out from home, cleaned and brushed and spruced, soon after two o'clock. Conventional hours of social intercourse meant little to William.

Near Miss Cliff's gate he met the Vicar hurrying along and looking at his watch, like the White Rabbit. He hailed William as soon as he saw him.

"William, my boy, will you do something for me?"

"WILLIAM, MY BOY, WILL YOU GO TO MISS CLIFF'S FOR ME AND GIVE HER A MESSAGE?"

William murmured a guarded acquiescence.

"Will you go to Miss Cliff's for me and give her a message? I'm afraid I shall miss the 'bus into Hadley if I call on her myself, and I've got a very important meeting. I thought it was earlier than it is. My clock must be slow. Will you tell her that I'm very sorry but I'm afraid that Hassan won't be able to come to tea this afternoon. He's had to go back directly after lunch. It seems that his friends had made other arrangements for him for the afternoon. I didn't realise that. Please convey my apologies to Miss Cliff for the unfortunate misunderstanding and tell her how very sorry I am. I only hope that she made no special preparations."

With that he hurried on in the direction of the 'bus terminus. William stood motionless, considering this piece of news. "Hoped she'd made no special preparations" indeed! She'd been doing nothing else for days. She'd thought of nothing else for days. The Persian boy had bounded her whole horizon, ousting even the silver spoons. This stroke of fate seemed so cruel as to be almost incredible. He imagined the bitterness of her disappointment, the ruthlessness with which the silver spoons would return to dominate her horizon once more. From exaltation her spirits would drop to the very depth of depression. And—Mrs. Nichol, noting the non-arrival of the Persian boy from behind her window curtains, would crow triumphantly over her neighbour. It was the last consideration that finally decided William. A plan formed itself quickly in his mind. He walked briskly up the little garden path and knocked on the door. Miss Cliff opened it. She looked somewhat surprised to see him at this hour but stood aside to let him enter, smiling a welcome.

"I'm so glad to see you, William," she began, but

William interrupted her.

"I've jus' come to say that I'm very sorry that I can't come to tea, but my mother wants me to help her this afternoon. She's not feeling well an' cook's goin' out an' the housemaid's in bed an' my mother wants me to stay in to answer the door an' suchlike. She tol' me to tell you she was very sorry."

Miss Cliff's face fell.

"I'm so sorry, William. I shall miss you so much, but I *quite* understand. Of course you must stay and help your mother."

"An'," said William, his face becoming quite expressionless, "I met the Vicar jus' outside. He tol' me to tell you that that boy'll be here about four, but that he'll have to wear his native costume—veil an' suchlike. He has to wear it when he goes out to tea always. He promised his mother."

Miss Cliff looked slightly taken aback.

"Oh, dear! I hadn't realised that. A veil, did you say, William?"

"Yes, same as what boys wear in Persia," said William.

"Oh, yes, of course," said Miss Cliff vaguely. "I hadn't quite realised . . ."

"He's promised his mother to wear it whenever he goes out to tea."

"Of course he must, then, dear. I quite understand. By the way, I was taking for granted . . . I suppose he does speak English, doesn't he?"

William shook his head.

"Not much," he said. "Jus' a little, but not much. An' he's very shy. He often doesn't speak at all when he goes out to tea." He felt that he must prepare for all contingencies. "Sometimes he jus' speaks a little an' sometimes he doesn't speak at all. He doesn't know much English, but he does jus' know one or two words. An' he can understand English when people speak it to him." He felt that he was showing a suspicious familiarity with the guest's habits and added hastily: "Least, that's what I heard the Vicar say."

"I *do* wish you were coming, dear, but you're quite right to stay and help your mother. I'll tell you all about it to-morrow. And you must come to tea to-morrow and finish up the trifle and jelly and the cakes he doesn't eat."

"Thanks," said William, and added: "He eats quite a lot. Least, that's what I heard the Vicar say."

"Perhaps you'll find time to pop in this evening, dear, and hear all about it. . . ."

"Yes," said William thoughtfully. "Yes, perhaps I might. Thanks very much. Well, p'raps I'd better be gettin' home now to help my mother."

He went home quickly and set to work at once on his simple preparations. Fortunately, his sister Ethel was out for the day, and so he could rummage undisturbed among her possessions. An embroidered shawl was draped about his person. Over his head and face he hung a large *crêpe de Chine* square, securing it by a round embroidery frame that fitted his head like a crown. Thus garbed, his figure, though small, looked fairly impressive. He could only just see through the *crêpe de Chine* square, and this necessitated a slow and dignified gait that suited the impressiveness of his appearance. He managed to escape from his own home without being seen, made his way in the shadows of the hedge to the Vicarage gate, then walked from the Vicarage gate to Miss Cliff's house, followed by one or two small children who thought that he had come from a neighbouring circus.

He saw Mrs. Nichol watching him from her window as he opened Miss Cliff's gate, saw her look of jealous fury as her eyes took in his stately and ornate figure and felt that the whole adventure was already a glorious success. Miss Cliff received him with a beaming smile of welcome and conducted him into the drawing-room, waving one hand questioningly to the cushions on the floor and the other to the chair facing the east. William, with a courteous bow, took the chair facing the east.

"This is such a pleasure, my dear boy," said Miss Cliff as she fluttered excitedly about him. "*Such* a pleasure. I've been looking forward to it for so long. I had asked another boy to meet you, a very dear little friend of mine. Such a nice boy. I'm sure you'd have liked him. So kind and helpful and companionable." William smirked self-consciously behind his veil. "But he had to stay at home to help his mother this afternoon. I'm sure you'll understand. I'm sure you'd have done the same in his place, wouldn't you?"

William made a little assenting sound under the veil.

"You can understand English, dear boy, I hear, but not speak it very well?"

William made another little assenting sound behind his veil.

"Well, dear boy, I don't want you to bother to talk to me because I know how difficult it is trying to talk in an unfamiliar language. I went to Germany once and found it almost impossible to make myself understood, though I had learnt German at school. As an extra. With a man teacher who had excellent qualifications and had spent several months in Heidelberg. But the fact remains that I found the language an insuperable difficulty, and it quite spoilt my enjoyment of the holiday. So don't try to talk to me, dear boy. Just enjoy your tea. You'll please me far more by making a good tea than if you talked the most beautiful English in the world."

She laughed at her little joke, and William chuckled dutifully behind his veil.

"That's right, dear. So nice to hear you laugh. Now how about a little jelly and whipped cream to begin with?"

William made a sound expressive of assent and set to work with zest. He managed remarkably well, holding his veil clear of his face with one hand and conducting food to his mouth with the other. Jelly, trifle, cream buns, iced cakes, chocolate biscuits, all disappeared under the veil like magic. At intervals he made little sounds expressive of appreciation and gratitude. Miss Cliff was delighted. After tea she took him round the garden, watched with tense jealousy by Mrs. Nichol from behind her window curtains. Then she led him back into the drawing-room, where the *pièce de résistance* of the entertainment took place. She had, after all, managed to borrow a gramophone, and she had also borrowed a record of "In a Persian Market." She beamed with delight as she put it on.

"There, dear boy!" she said. "That takes you to your dear home far away beyond the seas, doesn't it?"

William listened to it, making appreciative sounds at intervals. The whole thing had gone off better than he had dared to hope. It was now time to end it. He rose, pointed to the clock, which stood at half-past five, and made little deprecating sounds as of someone compelled reluctantly to take his departure. While he was thus engaged, there was a knock at the front door, and Miss Cliff hastened to it, to admit Miss Milton, a middle-aged lady with whom William lived in a state of perpetual enmity, owing to the fact that William's dog, Jumble, was in the habit of chasing her obese and cherished Pom and that she rightly suspected William of being an accessory before, during, and after the fact.

Miss Cliff introduced William to her proudly as "Hassan".

"This is Miss Milton, Hassan. And this, Miss Milton, is Hassan, the little Persian boy."

"Oh, yes," said Miss Milton, looking at William. "I met him at the Vicarage this morning. He wasn't dressed like that then, though. He was wearing an ordinary suit."

"This is his national costume," explained Miss Cliff. "I think it's so charming, don't you?"

"Y-yes," agreed Miss Milton doubtfully.

"He has to wear it when he goes out to tea. He promised his mother." She smiled fondly at the veiled figure. "He can't talk English, you know."

"I know," said Miss Milton. "At least, not fluently. But he talks French beautifully. He and I had quite a long conversation in French at the Vicarage to-day, *n'est-ce pas*, Hassan?"

She proceeded to pour out a flood of fluent French upon the unhappy William, at the end of which she obviously asked him some question and waited for the answer. William was seized with a sudden violent paroxysm of coughing. He had perfected this art by long practice for use in tight corners in school and had acquired a hollow "churchyard" ring that was harrowing in the extreme. The two ladies gazed at him in concern.

"What a dreadful cough!" said Miss Milton.

"Yes," agreed Miss Cliff anxiously. "I hope he didn't take cold in the garden. He hasn't coughed at all before. It's come on quite suddenly."

"They do sometimes," said Miss Milton, and added in a sinister tone of voice: "Sounds lungy to me."

She then addressed to William in French what was evidently an enquiry about his health. This brought on a fresh spasm more heartrending than the last.

Miss Cliff began to pat him on the back in a way that endangered his somewhat precarious headgear. Miss Milton said: "Water, quick!" and William, suspecting that it might be difficult to drink water at such close quarters without revealing his features, hastily recovered from the cough and instead began to gasp for breath in a manner that obviously precluded speech. It was at this point that there came another knock at the front door. William welcomed the diversion till he heard the Vicar's voice in the hall.

"I'm so sorry that Hassan couldn't come, Miss Cliff. You got my message, didn't you? He had to go back directly after lunch. He was most disappointed."

"B-b-b-but he's here," stammered Miss Cliff. "He's in the drawing-room."

"Impossible," said the Vicar, flinging open the door.

William felt that there was no time to be lost. He leapt through the open window, knocking over an occasional table and two chairs. His shawl fell from him. His headdress caught on a bush just outside the window. Hassan vanished, and the figure of William Brown was seen in full flight towards the gate.

He crept round miserably to Miss Cliff's later in the evening to apologise. To his surprise Miss Cliff was beaming with smiles. She received him with every manifestation of delight and gratitude.

"Oh, William," she said, "of course it was naughty of you, but I know you only did it to save me disappointment, and—oh, the most wonderful thing has happened, and it would never have happened if it hadn't been for you."

From the somewhat incoherent story that followed, William gathered that the table he had overturned in his headlong flight from the room was a small antique table that contained a secret drawer in which Mrs. Nichol kept the few pieces of good jewellery that she possessed. Before she left her house she had added the silver spoons to the collection, and then had completely forgotten having done so. The fall had loosened the secret spring, and a diamond brooch, some rings, a gold bracelet, and the silver spoons had rolled out over the floor. Miss Cliff had sent the spoons round to Mrs. Nichol with a letter from which she could not keep a certain note of triumph and reproach.

Mrs. Nichol had come round herself to apologise. She had grovelled uncompromisingly. Miss Cliff had been very sweet and forgiving and had enjoyed every minute of it.

"So I don't mind a bit about Hassan, dear. I understand why you did it, and I'm grateful to you. And now, dear, I'm sure you're hungry. Let's finish up Hassan's tea."

from *William—The Detective*

William—The Good

The Christmas holidays had arrived at last and were being celebrated by the Brown family in various ways.

Ethel and her friends were celebrating it by getting up a play which was to be acted before the village on Christmas Eve. Mrs. Brown was celebrating it by having a whist drive, and William was celebrating it by having influenza.

Though William is my hero, I will not pretend that he made a good invalid. On the contrary he made a very bad one. He possessed none of those virtues of patience, forbearance, and resignation necessary to a good invalid. William, suffering from influenza, was in a state of violent rebellion against fate. And he was even worse when the virulence of the attack had waned and he could sit up in bed and partake of nourishment.

There was, he bitterly complained, nothing to do.

Kind friends brought him in jig-saw puzzles, but, as he informed those about him incessantly, he didn't see what people *saw* in jig-saw puzzles. He didn't like doing them and he didn't see any good in them when they were done. As an occupation, they were, he gave his family to understand, beneath his contempt. His family offered him other occupations. One of his aunts kindly sent him a scrap album, and another kindly sent him a book of general knowledge questions. He grew more morose and bitter every day. No, he didn't want to do any of those things. He wanted to get up. Well, why not? Well, to-morrow then? Well, WHY NOT?

Well, he'd always said that the doctor wasn't any use.

He'd said so ever since he wouldn't let him stay in bed when he felt really ill—that day last term when he hadn't done any of his homework. And now, now that it was holidays, he made him stay in bed. He simply couldn't think why they went on having a man like that for a doctor, a man who simply did everything he could to annoy people. That was all the doctoring he knew, doing everything he could to annoy people. It was a wonder they weren't all dead with a doctor like that. No, he didn't want to do cross-word puzzles.

What did he want to do then?

He wanted to get up and go out. He wanted to go and play Red Indians with Ginger and Douglas and Henry. He wanted to go to the old barn and play Lions and Tamers. He wanted to go and be an Outlaw in the woods. That was what he wanted to do. Well, then, if he couldn't do anything he wanted to do what did they keep asking him what he wanted to do for?

In disgust he turned over on his side, took up a book which a great-aunt had sent him the day before and began to read it.

Now it was a book which in ordinary circumstances would not have appealed to William at all. It was a book in the "Ministering Children" tradition with a hero as unlike William as could possibly be imagined. William merely took it up to prove to the whole world how miserably, unutterably bored he was. But he read it. And because he was so bored, the story began to grip him. He read it chapter by chapter, even receiving his mid-morning cup of beef tea without his usual execrations.

It was perhaps because of his weakened condition that the story gripped him. The hero was a boy about William's age, whose angelic character made him the sunshine of his home. He had a beautiful sister who, he discovered, was a secret drinker. He pleaded with her to give up the fatal habit. That was a very beautiful scene. It had, however, little effect upon the sister. She became a thief. The youthful hero saw her steal a valuable piece of old silver in a friend's house. At great risk of being himself suspected of the crime he took it back and replaced it in the friend's house. The sister was so deeply touched by this that she gave up her habits of drink and theft and the story ended with a youthful hero, his halo gleaming more brightly than ever, setting out to rescue other criminals from their lives of crime.

"Gosh!" said William as he closed the book, "an' only eleven, same as me."

At once, William ceased to long to play Red Indians with Ginger and Henry and Douglas. Instead he began to long to rescue those around him from lives of crime.

* * *

Downstairs, Ethel and her mother were talking. "Have you settled the parts for your play yet, dear?" said Mrs. Brown.

"N-no," said Ethel, "it's all rather annoying. Mrs. Hawkins has taken up the whole thing, and is managing everything. Of course, we can't stop her, because, after all, she's going to finance the whole show, and have footlights put up and make it awfully posh, but still —she's insisting on our doing scenes from 'As You Like It'. She *would* want Shakespeare. She's so deadly dull herself."

"And you'll be Rosalind, I suppose?" said Mrs. Brown quite placidly.

Ethel was always the heroine of any play she acted in. But Ethel's face grew slightly overcast.

"Well," she said, "that's the question. Mrs. Hawkins is having a sort of trial at her house. It lies between me and Dolly Morton and Blanche Jones. She wants to hear us all read the part. She's going to have all the committee at her house on Tuesday to hear us all read the part. It *does* seem rather silly, doesn't it? I mean, making such a fuss about it. However——"

"Well, darling," said Mrs. Brown, "when you are at the Hawkins' I wish you'd ask them if they can let us have one bon-bon dish. I haven't quite enough for all the tables at the whist drive, and Mrs. Hawkins kindly said she'd lend me as many as I liked."

"Very well," said Ethel absently. "I shall feel *mad* if she gives the part to Dolly Morton or Blanche Jones. I've had much more experience and after all——"

After all, Ethel's silence said, she was far and away the prettiest girl in the village. She heaved a sigh.

Mrs. Brown, as if infected with the general melancholy, also heaved a sigh.

"The doctor says that William can get up tomorrow," she said.

Ethel groaned.

"Well," said her mother wearily, "he *can't* be worse up than he's been in bed the last few days."

"Oh, *can't* he?" said Ethel meaningly.

"But he's been quite good this afternoon," admitted Mrs. Brown in a voice almost of awe, "reading a book quietly all the time."

"Then he'll be awful to-morrow," prophesied Ethel, gloomily, and with the suspicion of a nasal intonation.

Mrs. Brown looked at her suspiciously. "You haven't got a cold, have you, Ethel?" she said.

"No," said Ethel hastily.

"Because if you have," said Mrs. Brown, "it's probably influenza, and you must go to bed the minute you feel it coming on."

*   *   *

William was downstairs. He did not, strangely enough, want to go out and play Red Indians with Henry, Douglas and Ginger. That lassitude which is always the after effect of influenza was heavy upon him. William, however, did not know that this was the cause. He mistook it for a change of heart. He believed his character to be completely altered. He did not want to be a rough boy ranging over the countryside any longer. He wanted to be a boy wearing a halo and rescuing those around him from lives of crime. He watched Ethel meditatively where she sat on the other side of the room reading a newspaper. She looked irritatingly virtuous.

William found it difficult to imagine her drinking in secret or stealing pieces of silver from a neighbour's drawing-room. It was, he reflected, just his luck to have a sister who was as irritating a sister as could be, and yet who would afford him no opportunity of rescuing her from a life of crime. His expression grew more and more morose as he watched her. There she sat with no thought in her mind but her silly magazine, resolutely refusing either to drink or steal.

As a matter of fact, Ethel had other thoughts in her mind than the magazine upon which she was apparently so intent. Ethel was afraid. There was no doubt at all that a cold was developing in Ethel's head, and Ethel knew that, should her mother guess it, she would be summarily despatched to bed and would not be able to attend Mrs. Hawkins' meeting, and that the result would be that either Dolly Morton or Blanche Jones would be Rosalind in the play.

Now, Ethel had set her heart upon being Rosalind. She felt that she would die of shame if Dolly Morton or Blanche Jones were chosen as Rosalind in her stead. And, therefore, the peculiar feeling of muzziness, the difficulty of enunciating certain consonants that she was at present experiencing, filled her with apprehension. A cold was coming on. There was no doubt of it at all. If only it could escape her mother's notice till after to-day!

After to-day, when she was chosen as Rosalind, Ethel was willing to retire to bed and stay there as long as her mother wanted, but not till then. Hence she was silent and avoided her mother as much as possible. She might, of course, take something to stave it off (though she knew that that was generally impossible), but her mother had the keys of the medicine cupboard, and to ask for anything would arouse suspicion.

The muzziness was growing muzzier every minute, and she had a horrible suspicion that her nose was red.

Suddenly she remembered that when William's cold began, her mother had bought a bottle of "Cold Cure," and given it to him after meals for the first day before the cold changed to influenza and he had to go to bed. She believed that it was still in the sideboard cupboard in the dining-room. She'd sneak it upstairs and take some. It might just stave it off till to-night.

She looked up and met William's earnest gaze. What was he looking at her like that for? He'd probably noticed that she'd got a cold and he'd go and tell her mother. It would be just like him. He'd blurt out, "Mother, Ethel's got a cold," and she'd be packed off to bed and not be able to go to Mrs. Hawkins', and Dolly Morton or Blanche Jones would be Rosalind and she'd die of shame. She stared at him very haughtily, and then went off to the dining-room for the bottle of "Cold Cure."

But her manner had attracted William's attention. He moved his seat so that he could see her through the crack of the door. She went across the hall to the dining-room. She looked about her furtively. She tiptoed to the hall again and looked up and down to make sure that no one saw her. Then very furtively she went back into the dining-room. She opened the sideboard cupboard and with a quick guilty movement took out a bottle and hid it under her jumper. *A bottle!* William gaped. His eyes bulged. *A bottle!* Still looking furtively around her she went upstairs. William followed just as furtively. He heard her bolt her bedroom door. He put his eye to the keyhole and there he saw her raise the bottle to her lips. He was amazed, but he had to believe the evidence of his eyes. She was a secret drinker. Ethel was a secret drinker!

His spirits rose. He must set about the work of reforming her at once. The first thing to do was to plead with her. That in the book had been a very moving and beautiful scene.

* * *

He was waiting for her in the morning-room when she came down. Yes, she did look like a secret drinker now that he came to look at her more particularly. She'd got a red nose. They always had red noses. She threw him a haughty glance, took up her magazine and began to read it. Then suddenly she was shaken by an enormous sneeze. It came upon her unawares, before she could stop it. As a matter of fact, it wasn't the sort of sneeze you could stop. It was the sort that proclaimed to all the world that you have a cold, perhaps influenza, and that you ought to be in bed.

Thank heaven, thought Ethel, her mother was in the village shopping. William, however, was gazing at her

WILLIAM MOVED HIS SEAT SO THAT HE COULD SEE HIS
SISTER THROUGH THE CRACK OF THE DOOR.

ETHEL WENT ACROSS THE HALL TO THE DINING-ROOM.
SHE LOOKED ABOUT HER FURTIVELY.

reproachfully. He was, she supposed, wondering bitterly why she was allowed to go about with a cold when he'd been went to bed at once. She gazed at him defiantly. William, as a matter of fact, had not noticed the sneeze at all. His mind was so taken up by the problem of how to plead with her to give up her habit of secret drinking.

He began rather sternly.

"Ethel, I know all about it."

"Whatever do you mean?" said Ethel feebly, "all about it! Why, I'm perfectly all right. *Perfectly* all right. Anyone can do it once. Once is nothing. It—it's *good* for you to do it once."

Of course, she'd say that, thought William. In his book the sister had said that it was the first time —— "Have you only done it once, Ethel?" he said earnestly.

"*Of course*," she snapped, "that was the first time."

She must have known that he'd seen her through the keyhole. He couldn't think what to say next. He'd quite forgotten what the boy in the book had said, but he remembered suddenly Ethel's pride in her personal appearance.

"It's making you look awful," he said.

"It *isn't*," snapped Ethel; "my nose *is* a tiny bit red, but it's not due to that at all."

"I bet it *is*," said William.

"It *isn't*," said Ethel. "Anyway"—and she became almost humble in her pleading—"anyway—you won't say anything to mother about it, will you? Promise."

"Very well," said William.

He promised quite willingly, because he didn't want his mother interfering in it any more than Ethel did. He wanted to have the sole glory of saving Ethel from her life of crime, and if their mother knew, of course, she'd take the whole thing out of his hands.

*   *   *

"Ethel," said Mrs. Brown tentatively, "I wonder—I'd be so much obliged if you'd take William with you to Mrs. Hawkins'. He's getting so restless indoors, and I daren't let him go out and play, because you know what he is. He'd be walking in the ditch and getting his feet wet and getting pneumonia or something. But if he goes with you it will be a nice little change for him, and you can keep an eye on him, and—well"—vaguely—"it'll be about Shakespeare, and that's improving. His last school report was awful. And, as I say, it will be a nice little change for him."

Ethel knew that her mother was thinking about a nice little change for herself, rather than for William, but, chiefly lest her pronunciation of certain consonants should betray her, she acquiesced.

"Then I can get on with the preparations for the whist drive," said Mrs. Brown, "and you won't forget to ask for the bon-bon dish, will you, dear?"

Ethel said "No" (or rather "Do"), and felt grateful to the whist drive because she knew that it was pre-occupation with it that prevented her mother from recognising the symptoms of a cold in the head which were becoming more and more pronounced every minute.

William showed unexpected docility when ordered to accompany Ethel to Mrs. Hawkins'. He felt that he had not so far acquitted himself with any conspicuous success in his rôle of reformer of Ethel. He could not flatter himself that anything he had said would have saved her from drink. He might get another chance during the afternoon.

There was quite a large gathering at Mrs. Hawkins'.

There was Mrs. Hawkins and her daughter Betty. There was the Committee of the Dramatic Society. There were Dolly Morton, brought by Mrs. Morton, and Blanche Jones, brought by Mrs. Jones. They were first of all given tea by Mrs. Hawkins in the morning-room. "And then we'll have our little reading," she added.

She accepted William's presence with resignation and without enthusiasm.

"Of course, dear," she said to Ethel, "I *quite* understand. I know they're trying, especially when they've been ill. Yes, it's a *joy* to have him. You'll be very quiet, won't you, my little man, because this is a very serious occasion. Very serious indeed."

Ethel sat down next to Betty Hawkins, and a great depression stole over her. She knew perfectly well that she could not be chosen as Rosalind in competition with Dolly Morton or Blanche Jones, or indeed with anyone at all.

She was feeling muzzier and muzzier every minute. Her eyes were watery. Her nose was red. She knew that with the best will in the world she was incapable of giving full value to the beauty of Rosalind's lines.

"*I show bore birth than I am bistress of*," she quoted softly to herself, "*and would you yet I were berrier?*"

No, it was quite hopeless. Moreover, Mrs. Morton and Mrs. Jones were both very wealthy, and fairly recently additions to the neighbourhood, and she had a suspicion that Mrs. Hawkins was trying to ingratiate herself with them. Yet she felt that she simply couldn't go on living if she didn't get the part of Rosalind. Mrs. Hawkins handed her a cup of tea. William had wandered away. He had gone over to the bay window where Mrs. Morton sat alone. Mrs. Morton was inclined to be superior and wasn't quite sure whether or no she were compromising herself in any way by allowing herself to be drawn into Mrs. Hawkins' circle. So she sat as far aloof from it as she could. Of course, she wanted Dolly to be chosen as Rosalind. On the other hand, it was never wise to be too friendly with people till you knew exactly where they stood.

William sat down on the window-seat next to her, watching Ethel morosely. Everyone must know that she'd been drinking. Her nose was as red as anything now.

Suddenly, Mrs. Morton said to him:

"Your sister doesn't look very well."

"Oh, she's all right," said William absently. "I mean, she's all right in one way. She's not ill or anything." Then he added casually: "It's only that she drinks."

"*W-what?*" said Mrs. Morton, putting her cup down hastily upon an occasional table, because she felt too unnerved to hold it any longer.

"She drinks," said William more clearly and with a certain irritation at having to repeat himself. "Din't you hear what I said? I said she drinks. She keeps a bottle of it in her room and locks the door an' drinks it. It's that what makes her look like that."

"B-but," gasped Mrs. Morton, "how terrible."

"Yes," asserted William carelessly, "it's terrible all right. She takes it up to her bedroom, in a bottle an' locks the door and drinks it there, an' then comes out lookin' like that."

Mrs. Morton's worst fears were justified. Whatever sort of people had she let herself be drawn among? She rose, summoned her daughter with a regal gesture, and turning to Mrs. Hawkins said with magnificent hauteur:

"I'm sorry, Mrs. Hawkins, but I've just remembered a most important engagement, and I'm afraid I must go at once."

And she swept out, followed by the meek Dolly.

"OH, ETHEL'S NOT ILL OR ANYTHING!" SAID WILLIAM.
"IT'S ONLY THAT SHE DRINKS."
"W-WHAT?" SAID MRS. MORTON.

Gradually Mrs. Hawkins recovered from her paralysis.
"Well," she gasped, "what simply extraordinary
behaviour! I never *heard*—— Well, I wouldn't have her
daughter now for Rosalind not for a thousand pounds."
William, left high and dry on his window seat, continued thoughtfully to consume cakes. Perhaps he
oughtn't to have told her that. It had seemed to upset
her. Well, he wouldn't tell anyone else, though he did
rather want people to know about the noble work he was
doing in reforming Ethel. What was the use of reforming
anyone if people didn't know you were doing it?

"William, dear," said Mrs. Hawkins sweetly, "would you like to go into the dining-room and see if you can find anything you'd like to read on the shelves there?"

William went, and conversation became general.

"Oh, I nearly forgot," said Ethel to Betty Hawkins. "Mother asked me to ask you to lend us a bon-bon dish for the whist drive. We find we won't have *quite* enough after all."

"Oh, rather. I'll get one for you."

"Don't bother. Tell me where to get it."

"Well, there's one on the silver table in the drawing-room. I'll get it and wrap it up for you."

"No, don't bother. I can slip it into my bag. I can get out much more easily than you can."

Thus it was that William, returning from the dining-room to inform the company that he hadn't been able to find anything interesting to read, was met by the sight of his sister creeping out of the morning-room where everyone was assembled and going alone into the empty drawing-room.

William glued his eye to the crack in the door and watched her.

She took a piece of silver from a table and slipped it into her hand-bag and then returned to the drawing-room, without noticing him. He stood for a minute motionless, amazed. Crumbs! *Crumbs!* She was like the girl in the book. She stole as well as being a secret drinker. He must do something at once. He must get the thing she'd stolen and put it back in its place again. That was what the boy in the book had done.

He returned to the morning-room. They hadn't begun the trial reading yet: they were all talking at once. They were discussing recent social happenings in the village. Mrs. Jones, as a newcomer, was feeling slightly out of it, and Mrs. Jones had a lively sense of her own importance and did not like feeling out of it. She had previously, of course, been kept in countenance by Mrs. Morton, and she was still wondering what had made Mrs. Morton go off like that. But there was no doubt at all that people weren't making enough fuss of her, so she rose and said with an air of great dignity:

"Mrs. Hawkins, I am suffering from a headache. May I go into your drawing-room and lie down?"

She had often found that that focused the attention of everyone upon her. It did in this instance. They all leapt to their feet solicitously, fussed about her, escorted her to the drawing-room, drew down the blinds and left her well pleased with the stir she had made.

This, she thought, ought to assure the part of Rosalind for Blanche. They wouldn't surely risk making her headache worse by giving the part to anyone else. Meanwhile, William was seated upon the floor between Betty Hawkins and Ethel. His whole attention was focused upon Ethel's bag which she had carelessly deposited upon the floor. Very slowly, very furtively, inch by inch, William was drawing it towards him. At last he was able to draw it behind him. No one had seen. Betty and Ethel were talking about the play.

"Do, I don't really bind what I ab," Ethel was saying, untruthfully.

Very skilfully, William took the silver dish out of the bag, slipped it into his pocket and put back the bag where it had been before. Then, murmuring something about going to look at the books again, he slipped from the room and went back to the drawing-room to replace it. He had quite forgotten Mrs. Jones, but just as he was furtively replacing the dish upon the table, her stern, accusing voice came from the dark corner of the room where the couch stood.

"What are you doing, boy?"

William jumped violently.

"I—I—I'm putting this back," he explained.

"What did you take it away for?" said Mrs. Jones still more sternly. William hastened to excuse himself.

"I din' take it," he said. "Ethel took it," then, hastening to excuse Ethel. "She—she sort of can't help taking things. I always," he added virtuously, "try'n put back the things she's took."

Mrs. Jones raised herself, tall and dignified, from her couch.

"Do you mean to say," she said, "that your sister *stole* it."

"Yes," said William. "She does steal things. We always try'n put them back when we find things she's stole. I found this just now in her bag."

"A kleptomaniac," exclaimed Mrs. Jones, "and I am expected to allow my daughter to associate with such people!"

Quivering with indignation, she returned to the morning-room. William followed her.

"Feeling better?" said Mrs. Hawkins brightly, "because if you are, I think we might begin the reading."

"I find," said Mrs. Jones icily, "that I cannot, after all, stay for the reading. I must be getting home at once. Come, Blanche!"

When she'd gone, Mrs. Hawkins looked about her in helpless amazement.

"Isn't it *extraordinary?*" she said. "I simply can't understand it. It's an absolute mystery to me what's come over them. Now, have I said a single thing that could have annoyed them?"

They assured her that she hadn't.

"Well," she said, "it's just as well to have no dealings with people as unaccountable as that, so, Ethel dear, you'd better take Rosalind after all."

"Thag you so buch," said Ethel gratefully.

"You've got a little cold, haven't you?"

"Yes, I hab," admitted Ethel, "perhaps I'd better go hobe dow. Bother asked me to ask you kidly to led her a bod-bod dish as Betty kidly let me hab this frob the drawing-roob."

She opened her bag.

"It's god," she gasped.

William was looking very inscrutable, but his mind was working hard. There was more in this, he decided, than had met his eye.

Betty had gone into the drawing-room and now returned with the bon-bon dish.

"You never took it," she said.

"But I did," persisted Ethel. "I dow I did. It's bost bysterious."

"You'd better get home to bed, my dear," said Mrs. Hawkins.

"Yes. I'm *awfully* glad I'b goig to be Rosalid. Cub od, Williab."

William did not speak till they'd reached the road. Then he said slowly:

"She'd *lent* you that silver thing Ethel?"

"Of course," said Ethel shortly.

"An—an' you've—you've got a bad cold?" he continued.

Ethel did not consider this worth an answer, so they walked on in silence.

"Well, dear?" said Mrs. Brown when they reached home.

"I'b goig to be Rosalid," said Ethel, "but I've got a bit of co'd, so I think I'll go to bed." In her relief at having been chosen as Rosalind, she became expansive and confidential. "I knew I'd god a co'd this borning, an' I sneaked up that boddle of co'd cure ad drank sobe id my bed roob, but it didn't do any good."

William blinked.

"Was it—was it the cold cure stuff you were drinkin' in your room, Ethel?"

"You'd better go to bed, too, William," said his mother. "The doctor said that you were to go to bed early this week."

"All right," said William with unexpected meakness. "I don't mind going to bed."

Still looking very thoughtful, William went to bed.

"Was he all right at Mrs. Hawkins?" said his mother anxiously to Ethel.

"Oh, yes," said Ethel, "he was quite good."

"I'm so glad," said Mrs. Brown, relieved, "because you know he sometimes does such extraordinary things when he goes out."

"Oh, no," said Ethel, preparing to follow William up to bed, "he was quite all right." She was silent for a minute, as she remembered the abrupt departures of Mrs. Morton and Mrs. Jones, and the mysterious disappearance of the bon-bon dish from her bag.

"Sobe rather fuddy things did happed," she said, "but Williab couldn't possibly have beed respodsible for any of theb."

from *William—The Good*

William Adopts
an Orphan

The Outlaws sat on their usual seat at the back of the school hall and surreptitiously played marbles while the lecturer on the school platform poured forth his spate of eloquence over their unresisting heads. They had not the slightest idea what he was talking about nor did they wish to have the slightest idea what he was talking about. To the Outlaws a lecture was merely a blessed respite from lessons, an oasis in the desert of a school morning, an hour when they could sit, screening themselves from the eye of Authority with an art born of long practice, and indulge in various recreations suitable to the occasion—such as racing the caterpillars they always carried on their persons, playing a game of cricket invented by William, in which a ruler took the place of a bat and a ball of blotting-paper the ball, or marbles. These were not, of course, all the diversions at their command. There was no end to the diversions at the command of the Outlaws during the hour of a school lecture. The idea that a lecturer had anything to say that could possibly be of any interest to anyone would have surprised them. A lecturer was to them simply a man who stood on a platform and talked. It did not matter what he said. You did not listen to him. He was not meant to be listened to.

His sole function was to provide an hour's relaxation in the middle of the morning. Had they been told after a lecture that it had been delivered in the Arabic language they would not have been in the least surprised. It might have been given in any language under the sun for all the Outlaws, deeply engrossed in caterpillar racing, ruler-and-blotting-paper-cricket, marbles and other pursuits, ever knew of it.

A marble dispatched with undue energy by Ginger rolled with a sudden re-echoing noise against the wall. A master rose from the front bench and walked slowly down the room. When he reached the back bench he found the four Outlaws sitting in rigid immobility, their eyes fixed with tense earnestness upon the lecturer. There were no traces of marbles, or caterpillars or anything but a burning interest in the lecturer and his lecture. The master was not for a minute deceived, but there was nothing to go on, so he returned to his seat.

After the short interval dictated by caution, the Outlaws relaxed the rigidity of their pose and the earnestness of their expressions, took out the ruler and balls of blotting-paper and began to play cricket. William bowled, Ginger batted, and Douglas and Henry fielded. The game proceeded uneventfully till an unguarded "swipe" on Ginger's part sent the ball high into the air. It travelled the length of the hall before it descended upon the head of the master who had already visited them. He rose from his chair and once more made his way slowly down to the back of the room. Again he found four boys in attitudes of frozen rigidity, gazing with rapt concentration at the lecturer. Again they appeared to be so deeply absorbed in the lecture as not even to notice his approach. He took up his position, leaning idly against the wall, watching them. The Outlaws, keeping the corners of their eyes upon him,

realised with a sinking of their hearts, that he meant to
stay there till the end of the lecture. In sheer self-defence
they began to listen to what the lecturer was saying.

He was talking about orphans.

He represented an Orphanage to which the school
evidently sent an annual contribution. He was pleading
for an increase in the contributions. He was urging them
to "adopt" an orphan, that is, to pay for its maintenance
each year. He had just reached the climax of his speech.

"Those of you who are well fed, well clothed, well
looked after,"—William's eye stole round. The master
was still watching him. He stiffened to attention
again—"owe a duty to those who are less well clothed
and fed and looked after. You owe a debt to them. Good
things are given to you in order that you may pass them
on to others. It's your social duty. Some people, of
course, take an orphan into their homes and give it all
the blessings of home life. And I may say that prosperity
always visits those homes. If every family in England
adopted an orphan we could close down our Institutions.
That, of course, is impossible, but I hope, dear boys,
that you will all give of your best this year so that we may
inscribe the name of your school in our book of honour
as wholly maintaining an orphan each year."

He sat down amidst deafening applause.

The headmaster, who had been growing more and
more restive, because the lecturer had overstepped his
time and encroached upon the headmaster's Latin Prose
class, arose and, with one eye upon the clock, said how
much they all had enjoyed the lecture and how sorry
they were that it had come to an end, and that he hoped
that the annual Sale of Work would double their
subscription, and as time was getting on would the boys
go straight to their class rooms, please. Frenzied
applause broke out again, prolonged to its utmost limits

by the headmaster's Latin Prose class, who had been watching the clock with emotions as deep as the headmaster's, though of a different nature.

The master, who had appointed himself guardian angel of the Outlaws, gave them one last long, meaning glance and went to join his colleagues.

The Outlaws filed out with the others and went to an Algebra class. William could generally be trusted to hold up the Algebra class indefinitely by not understanding. William had a very plausible way of not understanding, and the Mathematical master was so new to teaching that he had not yet seen through it. He was a very conscientious young man and it was a matter of principle with him never to go on to the next step till everyone in the class fully understood the first one. He took William's expression of earnest endeavour at its face value. He thought that William was slow but well meaning and deeply interested in Algebra. And so, provided that William was in good form, no second step in any lesson was ever reached.

But William was distrait this morning. He let slip every opportunity of not understanding and did not even notice the reproachful glances and exhortatory nudges of his classmates. Various others of them tried to take his place but they lacked his skill. The master simply explained their difficulties and passed on. They could not, like William, think of another difficulty while he was explaining the first. The lesson progressed with unwonted speed and the master began to think that he was really making headway with them at last.

The Outlaws streamed out of school at the end of the morning with the others. They scuffled in and out of the ditch as usual on their homeward way, but William scuffled half-heartedly. Obviously his thoughts were still elsewhere.

"I say, we were jolly lucky," Ginger was saying, "I thought old Stinks was going to keep us in."

"Jus' like you," said Douglas disgustedly, "sendin' it right on to his head."

"It was jolly clever," said Ginger proudly, "I bet you couldn't have done it if you'd tried."

"No, neither could you if you'd tried," said Douglas.

William awoke from his reverie.

"Did you hear what he said about it bein' everyone's juty to adopt a norphan?" he asked.

"He *didn't*," said Ginger.

"He did," said William. "I know, 'cause I was listenin'. He said that everyone ought to adopt a norphan. He said that if everyone adopted a norphan all the orphan places would shut up."

"I wish *you'd* shut up."

"All right," encouraged William. "Come on. Shut me up."

Ginger closed with him, and they wrestled till the arrival of a motor car sent them both into the ditch. They found a frog in it, and after another fight that was to decide the ownership of the frog (during which the frog disappeared), climbed out, much invigorated and having completely forgotten what both fights were about.

"What'll we do this afternoon?" said Douglas (it was a half-holiday). "I votes we go to the stream."

"He said," put in William suddenly, "that *everyone* oughter adopt a norphan. He said it brought you luck."

"He didn't," said Ginger again.

"You're thinking of horse shoes," said Douglas, "they bring you luck."

"I'm not," said William doggedly, "I'm thinking of orphans. He said that everyone ought to adopt a norphan. You weren't listening. He said that it brought them luck. He din' say it in jus' those words. He said it in the sort of langwidge letcherers talk in. But it meant that it brought them luck."

"He din' say *everyone* ought to adopt one."

"He did. He said it was a sociable juty. He said that everyone what had clothes ought to adopt a norphan. You weren't listenin'. I was. Ole Stinks was starin' at me so's I'd *got* to listen, 'cause with him starin' at me I'd gotter look somewhere else, so I looked at *him*, an' when you look at a person you've got to listen to what they're sayin', even if you don't want to. An' he was sayin' that it was everyone's sociable juty to adopt a norphan 'cause it brought 'em good luck. He said all about them havin' no home an' how we ought to adopt 'em so's to give 'em a home. He said it was a sociable juty."

"What *is* a sociable juty?" said Ginger.

"Dunno," said William vaguely, "but it's what he said."

"Well, anyway," said Ginger, "we can't adopt a norphan, so let's talk about what we're goin' to do this afternoon. I don' want to go fishin'. I'd rather play Red Indians."

"We can ask our parents to, can't we?" said William. "He said *everyone* ought to."

"He didn't. I votes we play Red Indians in Croombe Woods."

"He did. You weren't listening. I was. I listened all the time after old Stinks came to stare at us. He said that if you'd got clothes you ought to take a norphan into your home to give it blessings. He said it was a sociable juty, and I'm going to ask my mother to adopt one, anyway. I'm goin' to tell her what he said."

But there were William's favourite dishes for lunch —baked potatoes and roast chicken, followed by trifle—and he completely forgot the morning's lecture till an aunt, who was lunching with them, fixed her eyes on him grimly and said: "I hope you realise how fortunate you are, William, to have such a good dinner, and I hope that you remember how many little boys there are who haven't got a good home like yours."

This reminded William. He swallowed half a potato and said:

"Mother, may we adopt a norphan!"

"*What!*" gasped his mother.

"I said may we adopt a norphan," repeated William rather impatiently.

"Why?" said his mother.

"A man came round to school this morning and said we'd got to," said William, "he said they brought you luck."

"*What?*"

"That's what he *said*," said William calmly, and with an air of one who disclaims all responsibility.

"*William!* I'm *sure* he never said that."

"He did," William assured her, "you weren't there. I was listening 'cause of old Stinks. He said it in lecturing sort of langwidge, but that was what it meant."

"I never heard such nonsense."

"Aren't you goin' to, then?" said William, disappointed.

"Going to what?" said Mrs. Brown.

"Adopt a norphan?"

"Of *course* not, William."

"Well," said William darkly, "if you don't get good luck now after this, don't blame me. You take a lot of trouble throwin' salt over your shoulder when you spill it and touching wood and that sort of thing, and yet you won't do a little thing like adoptin' a norphan. It isn't as if you'd have to pay anything for one. They *give* them free. And you needn't buy new clothes for it. It could wear mine. It could wear my Sunday suit while I was wearing my weekday one, and my weekday suit while I was wearing my Sunday suit. And it could sleep with me and have half my food at meals. It needn't be any trouble or expense at all, and this man said——"

"William, *will* you get on with your lunch and stop talking."

"When I was young," said the aunt, "children were seen and not heard."

William finished his meal in gloomy silence and then went out to meet the other Outlaws.

"Well, I asked mine," he said disconsolately, "and she wouldn't. Did you ask yours?"

It appeared that Douglas had mentioned it tentatively, but that his mother had rejected the idea as summarily as William's.

"Well, then, let's go an' play Red Indians," said Ginger impatiently.

But once William had formed a project it was never easy to induce him to abandon it.

"Why shun't *we* adopt one?" he said slowly.

They stared at him open-mouthed with amazement.

"We *couldn't*," gasped Ginger.

"I don't see why not," said William aggressively. "Why couldn't we as well as anyone else?"

"They wouldn't let us," said Douglas.

"They needn't know," said William. "We could keep it in the old barn while we were at school an' it could go about with us after school and we could get food for it from home. Surely if all of us got a bit at each meal it would be enough for one orphan. It could sleep with us in turns. I guess we could easily get him up the stairs without anyone seeing if we're careful. And he could get under the bed when they come to call us in the morning

so that no one'd know he'd been sleeping there at all.
And we could get him up something to eat for breakfast
and then get him down to the barn while we go to school,
without anyone knowing. Just keep a look out till no
one's about and then jus' get him quickly downstairs. I
bet it would be fun. Jus' like hiding a fugitive. I've
always wanted to live in the days when they went in for
hidin' fugitives. An' he'll be so grateful to us for givin'
him a home that he'll do everything we tell him. He'll
field balls for us when we play cricket an' make arrows
for us an' be the squaw when we're playing Red
Indians."

"But—but what about him not going to school?"
objected Henry. "There's a lor that everyone's got to go
to school. If they find you don't know anythin' when you
grow up 'cause of not havin' been to school they put you
in prison."

"I wish he could go to school 'stead of me," said
William in a heartfelt tone, then suddenly his whole face
lit up. "I *say!* I *know* what I'm goin' to do. I'm goin' to
try'n' get one that looks like me an' let him go to school
'stead of me an' I'll stay away."

"Yes, an' then when you grow up an' they find you
don't know anythin' they'll put you in prison," Henry
warned him darkly. "There's a lor about it."

"I shan't care," said William. "I bet it'll 've been
worth it. . . . An' he might get on better at school than
me, too. He might get me a good report. My father's
promised me five shillings if ever I get a good report. If
he got me one I'd give him half."

"You'd never get anyone that looked jus' like you,
William," said Ginger gazing at William's homely
freckled countenance with its scowl of aggressive
determination, and shock of wiry hair. "I don't s'pose
that there *is* anyone else that looks like you."

"Why not?" challenged William threateningly, scenting a personal insult in the words.

Ginger, who had intended a personal insult, hastily withdrew from his position at William's tone and said:

"Well, I mean that we're all made jus' a bit different. It's a lor of nature. And they know your face so well at school that they'd know at once if anyone came without your face pretendin' to be you. An' then it'd spoil everything."

Despite themselves the Outlaws were becoming interested in the orphan scheme. William could always make the most outrageous schemes sound reasonable.

"How're you goin' to get one?" said Douglas.

"Well, how *do* they get them?" said William.

"I think they advertise," said Henry.

"All right," said William, "we'll advertise."

* * *

The notice was written and pinned up outside the old barn. Though short, it had caused the Outlaws much searching of heart. None of them was widely read, and it so happened that none of them remembered ever having seen the word "orphan" in print.

At first its spelling suggested no difficulties to them, and William wrote:

"Wanted an orfun," with no misgivings at all except for the blots that his crossed nib (William's nibs were always crossed) had deposited on it. It was Douglas who cast the first doubt upon it. Douglas felt it his duty to sustain his reputation as a master of the intricacies of spelling.

"I don't think that's the way you spell it," he said.

"It *must* be," said William firmly, "it couldn't be any other way. It couldn't possibly. How *could* it? Orfun.

Well, you spell or O-R—don't you?—and you spell fun
F-U-N. So orphan must be ORFUN."

"Well, what about words like awful," said Douglas,
"you spell or A-W then. It might be that sort of an or. It
might be AWFUN."

"Well, we'll put it both ways then," said William
firmly. "I shun't like one to come along an' not know we
want one 'cause of it not being spelt right. We'll put it
both ways."

But Douglas was still pondering the problem and the
more he pondered it the more beset with difficulties did
it appear.

"Then there's the —un," he said, "it might be O-N,
not U-N. You know, like lesson. You say it lessun but
you write it lesson, O-N."

The subject was becoming too complicated for
William.

"Well, let's spell it all the ways it could be spelt, so's if
one comes it'll know we want one."

Douglas therefore drew up a fresh notice whose final
form was:

Wanted an	orfun
	awfun
	orfon
	awfon

They fixed it on the barn door and gazed at it proudly.

"Well, one's more likely to come along if we aren't
here, waiting for it to come," said William. "Things
never happen when you're waiting for them to happen. I
votes we go out to look for one and then I bet you
anything that when we come back we'll find one waiting
for us here."

The Outlaws recognised the sound sense of this and

set off. As they were setting off Ginger looked doubtfully back at the notice.

"I bet he won't think much of us not knowin' how to
spell it," he said.

Douglas returned and wrote slowly and carefully at
the foot of the notice:

"we gnow whitch is wright."

*   *   *

Clarence Mapleton stood at the gate of his aunt's
garden and looked gloomily about him. He had been
told not to go into the road and so, in order to assert his
independence, he went into the road and walked up and
down it several times, although the procedure did not
afford him much pleasure, as the garden was far more
interesting in every way. He then returned to the gate
and stood leaning against it in an attitude of dejection.
Though nearly eight years old, he still wore his hair in a
mop of curls and he was still dressed in a tunic suit with
microscopic knickers from which long bare legs emerged
to end in baby socks and strap-over shoes. Despite
appearances, however, there beat within Clarence
Mapleton's breast a manly heart and he felt deeply the
ignominy of his appearance. Nor were the curls and
tunic suit all. Besides the obnoxious name of Clarence
he possessed the name of John, and yet no one called
him by it. They called him Clarence because his aunt
with whom he lived loved the name of Clarence and
disliked the name of John.

He was the apple of his aunt's eye. She worshipped
him from his curly head to his strap-over shoes. She
called him her "little Prince Charming." When he
pleaded for more manly attire, she said: "Oh no, no,
darling. Not yet. You're not old enough for those horrid

boys' suits yet. He's his auntie's darling baby boy. . . ."
And other yet more revolting epithets.

She didn't even let him go to a proper boys' school.
He still had a governess.

"No, sweetheart," she said. "Auntie doesn't want
her darling to go with all those horrid rough boys yet."

Considering the limitations of his circumstances,
however, Clarence had not done badly. He had undertaken his own education to the best of his ability under
the general directorship of the butcher's boy, and the
result was on the whole quite creditable.. Despite his
curls and tunic suit he could hold his own in single
combat against the butcher's boy, who was several
inches taller and of a fierce disposition. He could walk
on his hands and he could distort his angelic features
into a mask so horrible that strong men blenched
at it. Moreover, though his devoted aunt should
wash him and change his suit and brush up his golden
curls a dozen times a day,—a dozen times a day he could
conscientiously dishevel himself in order to assert his
manhood.

Lolling against the gate post, his hands in the little
pockets of his saxe blue suit, he was devising various
dramatic means of freeing himself from his ignominious
position. In his imagination strange and wonderful
things were happening.

A band of robbers descended upon the house and
were going to kill his aunt, and he told her that he would
save her if she would let him go to school, give him a
proper boy's suit and call him John. She promised, and
he killed all the robbers. His aunt, despite her many
failings, always kept her promise.

The house was surrounded by Indians who were going
to burn it down. He told his aunt that he would drive
them off if she would promise to let him go to school,

give him a proper boy's suit and call him John. She promised, and he went out and drove off the Indians.

He and his aunt were going through a wood and a pack of wolves surrounded them. They were just going to spring upon his aunt and he told her that he would save her if she would promise to let him go to school, give him a proper suit and call him John. She promised, and he killed the wolves.

Cannibals had captured them and—

He awoke from his dreams with a start.

Four boys were coming down the road—four dirty, untidy boys, in battered tweed school suits, the sort of boys with whom his aunt would not let him play. He watched them in wistful envy. They were talking to each other. They glanced at him as they passed and went on talking to each other. It was that glance that stung Clarence into action. It seemed to say that he was unworthy even of their scorn. He pulled his face at them. They swung round and stared at him with sudden interest. William accepted the challenge and pulled his face back. Clarence, still leaning nonchalantly against the gate, replied by pulling his face again.

"How d'you do it?" said William. Clarence did it once more.

"Mine's a better one," said William, with an inner conviction that it wasn't, for though a masterpiece in its way he realised that it lacked the finish of Clarence's. The butcher boy, who had taught Clarence, was an artist in faces.

Without answering Clarence turned a somersault and then walked across the road on his hands.

William could stand on his hands, but he could never walk on them without overbalancing.

"I c'n do that too," said William, but in a tone of voice that betrayed that he couldn't.

Clarence walked back across the road on his hands, reversed himself lightly and leant nonchalantly against the gate post again. William, feeling that he was not showing up well in this competition of accomplishments, put a finger into each corner of his mouth and emitted a piercing whistle. Immediately Clarence did the same. The horrible echoes died away. William, listening, had an uncomfortable suspicion that Clarence's were the more horrible of the two.

The Outlaws had gathered round Clarence and were looking at him with interest.

"How old are you?" said William at last.

"Eight," said Clarence, mentally adding a month or two on to his age.

"Why does your mother dress you like that?"

"Not got no mother," said Clarence with a swagger.

He had early learnt that his lack of parents conferred distinction upon him.

"Why does your father, then?"

"Not got a father either," said Clarence, with an exaggeration of the swagger.

William stared at him open-mouthed, open-eyed.

"Not got—You're a *norphan*?" he shouted excitedly.

"Yes," said Clarence gratified by the sensation his news had caused. "I'm a norphan."

For a moment William's emotion was too strong for speech. Then he turned to the others, and, pointing to Clarence, said still more excitedly: "D'you hear that? He's a *norphan*."

They all stared at Clarence.

"Well," said Clarence rather distrustfully, feeling that their surprise was a little overdone, and suspecting ridicule behind it. "Why shun't I be?"

"B-b-but we're *lookin'* for a norphan," said William, still breathless with excitement.

"Why?" said Clarence.

"'Cause we want to adopt one."

"What's that?" said Clarence.

"We want to take one to live with us."

"Take *me* to live with *you?*" said Clarence eagerly.

"Yes," said William.

"An'—an' give me clothes like what you're wearing, an' let me play with you?"

"Yes," said William. "We'd fetch one of our Sunday suits for you, 'an' you could wear one of our weekday suits on Sundays. Will you?"

Clarence looked at them. Four dirty, rough, untidy, scuffling boys—four boys after his own heart. His face was shining.

"I should jus' think I *will*," he said.

"All right," said William. "Come on then."

They escorted him in proud proprietorship down the road.

"What's your name?" said William.

"John," said Clarence happily.

At the bend of the road William plunged suddenly into the grass and brought out a frog.

He glanced affectionately at his orphan.

"I *knew* he'd bring us luck," he said.

* * *

They were in the old barn. The afternoon had been a busy one. William had gone home at once to fetch his Sunday suit, and Ginger had gone home to fetch a pair of scissors as the orphan had peremptorily insisted on having his hair cut and being dressed in a school suit before any further proceedings took place. William had done the thing properly, bringing his best boots and stockings, and collar and tie as well as his Sunday suit.

"You can let me have them on Saturday night ready

for Sunday," he explained carelessly, "an' I'll let you have my weekday ones then, so it'll be all right. I bet they won't find out they're gone."

The outfit was far too large for Clarence, and Ginger's cropping of his curls was as unscientific as it was thorough, but words cannot convey the pride that swelled at Clarence's heart, as he swaggered about the barn, passing his hand every now and then with a complacent smile over his unevenly cropped head.

The Outlaws looked at him with some misgivings. He certainly didn't look as they'd meant him to look.

"He's all right, I think," said William doubtfully, "don't you?"

"Yes, I think he looks all right," said Ginger with unconvinced optimism, "anyway, whatever he looks like he looks better than he did in the other things."

"You won't mind stayin' here while we're at school, will you?" said William to Clarence.

"I should jolly well think *not*," said Clarence enthusiastically.

"You see you'll sleep with us in turns an' get under the bed in the morning when they come to call us so's no one'll know, an' then go out when no one's lookin'. An' you can stay here while we're in school an' play games by yourself, an' we'll bring you food an' things, an' you can play with us when we're not in school an' wear our clothes in turn. See?"

He looked at Clarence anxiously, hoping that this *ménage* would meet with his approval. It was evident that it did. It was evident that Clarence accepted the prospect of this strange existence, not only with equanimity, but with exultation.

"Can I *really!*" he said gratefully.

He was certainly an orphan after the Outlaws' own

hearts. But it was after tea-time, and reluctantly they took their leave of him.

"We'll come back soon," William assured him, "and bring you some tea. We'll all get a bit from our homes. You don' mind us goin' just for a bit to get tea, do you?"

"No," his orphan assured him cheerfully, and glancing down at his person, added with pride, "it fits me jolly well, doesn't it?"

When they had gone the orphan amused himself by practising the accomplishments that had won him this proud position. He whistled, pulled his face, and walked round the barn on his hands, and when he was tired of doing that, stroked his unevenly-cropped head and admired his suit, the sleeves of which had to be rolled up almost to their elbows.

The Outlaws returned long before he had exhausted his resources of self-amusement.

They brought with them a large if somewhat varied meal. Ginger had managed to abstract a pot of jam from the larder, Henry had brought a tin of sardines that he had obtained in the same way, Douglas had brought an orange, and William a carton of cream. The orphan hailed the meal with delight and consumed it zestfully.

"It's the nicest tea I've ever had," he announced blissfully as he scraped out the last spoonful of jam and put the last sardine into his mouth.

They watched him with wistful envy. It was certainly a more exciting meal than the ones they'd had at home. And they'd not only brought him the tea. They'd put together what money they had, and been into the village to buy him sweets and toys. They'd bought him a bag of bulls' eyes, a whistle, a pistol and a stick of liquorice. They'd spent their last penny on him. They took their duty as his guardians and protectors very seriously.

"Then there's supper to think of," said William

slowly, as they stood round their orphan watching him consume the remnants of his tea.

There was a shade of anxiety over his face. He realised that their orphan was going to be a drain on their slender resources.

"There's his pocket money, too," he went on still more slowly. "I vote we each give him a penny out of ours every week in turns."

"I don't think he'll *need* pocket money," said Douglas tentatively, but he was over-ruled by the others. When the Outlaws did anything they did it properly.

"Have you ever *heard* of anyone adoptin' a norphan an' not givin' him pocket money?" said William indignantly.

As Douglas had never heard of anyone adopting an orphan at all till that morning he retired from the argument. There was no doubt at all that the orphan appreciated their attentions. He was happily engaged in sucking his stick of liquorice and playing with his pistol. He had handed round his bulls' eyes and lent Ginger his whistle.

He looked up suddenly and said anxiously: "I *am* goin' to stay here with you always, aren't I?"

"Yes," said William firmly.

The way of adopters of orphans might be beset by unexpected difficulties, but William was of the stuff that having adopted an orphan holds him against the world.

"Sure?" said the orphan.

"Yes," said William.

"Golly!" murmured the orphan, ecstatically putting another bulls' eye into his mouth. "Golly . . . Jus' *think* of it."

"Well, he's had his tea," said Ginger restively, "let's go out an' play till bedtime."

So they went out to play. They played Red Indians. The orphan climbed trees and fences, scrambled through hedges and dived into ditches with the best of them. He took falls and knocks without a murmur. William watched him with delight.

"He's a jolly fine orphan, isn't he?" he said to Ginger proudly.

His delight in his protégé was, however, tempered by a slight anxiety about his Sunday suit, that increased as the evening wore on, and the passage of hedges and ditches and the bark of trees left their marks more and more thickly upon it.

To Clarence it was like a wonderful dream—the tweed suit, the stockings, the boots (all many sizes too big for him, but he didn't mind that), the shouting and running and scuffling and scrambling over the countryside with these heroic beings who treated him with such flattering consideration. It seemed far too good to be true. Once or twice indeed he wondered if he'd died and gone to Heaven.

They ended their game at a house that was being built just outside the village. The Outlaws always paid it a visit in the evening when the workmen had gone home. It was, as it were, the Mecca of their day. Its attractions included scaffolding, planks, ladders, half-built walls, perilous chasms and dizzy heights, shavings, sawdust, cement, bricks, and various builders' tools.

An added zest was imparted to the proceedings by the fact that occasionally an irate householder from the neighbourhood, who was to be the inhabitant of the house, would descend upon them in fury to drive them away.

Clarence enjoyed it even more than he'd enjoyed the game of Red Indians. He climbed the scaffolding, walked along the top of half-built walls, slid down planks

and joined in a sawdust battle with a zest and fearless-
ness that made William's heart swell with pride.

"He's a *jolly* fine orphan," he said again to Ginger,
"we couldn't 've got a better one however long we'd
looked for one."

They were standing on the top of a half-built wall.
Opposite it was another half-built wall at a distance of
about two yards. They were of equal height, and the
space between them was spanned by a narrow plank.

"I bet I could walk across there on my hands," said
Clarence, whose orgy of emancipation was going to his
head.

"I bet you couldn't," said William.

"I bet I could," persisted Clarence.

"All right," said William. "Go on. Do it."

Without a moment's hesitation Clarence sprang upon
his hands, and in a breathless silence began to walk the
plank. He got half-way, then overbalanced and fell into
the yawning chasm beneath. The Outlaws peered down
anxiously.

"Hello," called William. "Are you all right?"

A heap of cement at the bottom stirred, convulsed,
and finally gave forth what seemed to be the plaster cast
of a boy miraculously imbued with life.

"Yes," said a muffled voice, "I'm all right. I fell into
the stuff an' din' hurt myself at all. It tastes funny,
though."

The Outlaws scrambled down from the wall to meet
their protégé on the ground. He was completely encased
in cement from head to foot.

William looked anxiously at the point where, according to the rules of anatomy, his Sunday suit must be, then
his unfailing optimism came to his aid.

"I 'spect it'll brush off," he said.

"We can't take him home like that," said Ginger,

"an' it's getting too dark to see. So it must be bed-time."

Again the responsibilities of their position cast a cloud over their spirits. Only Clarence had no misgivings. He gazed at them happily, trustingly, through his covering of cement.

"I got half-way, anyway, din' I?" he said cheer-fully. "It was a jolly fine sort of feeling, falling into that stuff."

"We can't take him home like that," said Ginger again.

"Tell you what," said William, "let him go'n' rub himself on the grass on the side of the ditch. I bet that'll take it off."

"A' right," said Clarence, and trotted out in the gathering dusk to the road.

Almost immediately he returned.

"I *say*!" he gasped, "Annie—she's my aunt's maid —was jus' passing. She saw me. I say, let me hide! Quick!"

He leapt into the kitchen floor and disappeared into the bowels of the earth. The Outlaws quickly sought similar hiding places. But after a few minutes it was evident that no one was looking for them and they emerged.

William went cautiously into the road to reconnoitre. He could dimly see a figure fleeing down the road in the distance. Faint moans reached him.

He returned.

"'S all right," he said. "No one's there 'cept some ole luny a long way off. Come on."

They walked home rather thoughtfully. The cement-clad figure was the only really cheerful one. It walked jauntily. It had no thought for the morrow. It trusted its adopters entirely.

"It's your night to have him first, isn't it, William?" said Ginger.

"Yes," said William without enthusiasm.

They had reached William's home.

"Well, good night," said the other Outlaws.

"I say," said William pleadingly, but they were already disappearing.

They felt that after all it was at William's suggestion that they had saddled themselves with this lifelong responsibility, and that it was only fair that he should bear the first brunt of it.

William, left alone with his white-clad protégé in the gathering dusk at his garden gate, gazed about him with a sinking heart.

"Isn't it *fun?*" said Clarence enthusiastically. "What shall we do now?"

"I've gotter get you up to bed now," said William.

This proved easier than William had thought, for Clarence scaled the pear tree by which William always entered his bedroom in emergencies almost as easily as William himself. He stood in William's bedroom, cement dropping all around him, and said placidly: "And now do I go to bed?"

"Yes," said William with a harassed glance at the carpet. "I'd better give that suit a bit of a brush. An' we'll have to try and get it off the carpet somehow, too."

"I say," said his orphan, as if making a sudden discovery. "I'm hungry."

William's expression grew yet more harassed.

"I'll see if I c'n get anything," he said, "you be gettin' undressed. You'll find pyjamas in that drawer. An' get under the bed if you hear anyone coming."

"All right," said the orphan happily. "I'm jolly sleepy. I've had a lovely day. What're we goin' to do to-morrow?"

"Dunno," said William rather shortly, as he descended to the garden by way of the pear tree, and then entered the house noisily by the side door.

Voices from the drawing-room told him that his mother had a visitor. That reassured him, and he went into the dining-room where his supper was laid. Having eaten it, he looked about for something for his orphan. All he could find was a pot of jam in the sideboard cupboard and half a pine-apple that was on the sideboard. He would, of course, be called to account for the disappearance of the pine-apple, but he had no thought just then for anything but his orphan, who must be fed at all costs. He took both upstairs, hoping that his Sunday suit and bedroom carpet weren't really as bad as he'd thought.

He opened the bedroom door to find that they were far, far worse. The situation was in fact beginning to assume the proportions of a nightmare.

The orphan himself was nowhere to be seen, having dived beneath the bed on William's approach, but everything in the room was covered with a thick, white powder. It seemed inconceivable that the human form could accommodate such large quantities of cement.

The orphan emerged when William entered and gazed with gleaming eyes at his supper.

"How *scrummy!*" he said. "It's ever so much nicer than the things I used to have—blancmange and rice pudding and silly things like that."

"Let's hurry up and get into bed," said William anxiously, "someone'll be coming."

The orphan hastily finished his supper, and was in bed in a few minutes—jam and cement and all.

"Your mother doesn't come in to see you in bed like my aunt, does she?" he said anxiously.

"No," said William, "not if we pretend to be asleep.

CLARENCE EMERGED AND GAZED WITH GLEAMING EYES AT HIS SUPPER. "HOW *SCRUMMY!*" HE SAID.

She'll open the door, and if I don't say anything she'll think I'm asleep and go away.''

But the orphan was asleep already.

William lay awake for a few minutes, trying to grapple with the problems that confronted him. There was breakfast to-morrow to think of, there was dinner, tea and supper. There were four meals to provide every day. There was his Sunday suit. . . . Anyway it was Ginger's turn to have him to-morrow night. . . .

He'd had a very tiring day. He fell asleep. . . .

*   *   *

Mrs. Brown went to the garden gate to look up and down the road. It was getting dark. Time that boy came home. She hoped that he wasn't in any mischief. . . .

A figure was coming down the road, but it wasn't William. It was the figure of a maid servant, apron and streamers flying in the wind. She was moaning as she ran.

"He's dead . . . he's dead. . . . I've seen his gho-o-o-ost . . . he's de-e-e-ead."

"Who's dead?" said Mrs. Brown.

"Clarence," wailed the maid. "I've seen his ghost. I've seen his gho-o-o-o-ost. Oo-o-o-o. I'm goin' to faint in a minute."

Mrs. Brown led her into the house, installed her in an arm-chair in the drawing-room and gave her some sal volatile.

"Now tell me all about it," said Mrs. Brown.

The maid took a deep breath and, still unsteadily, began her tale.

"Clarence . . ." she sobbed. "He was lorst. We couldn't find him nowhere in the house nor garding. Such a beautiful little chap 'e was, with 'is golden curls," she began to sob again, so Mrs. Brown said:

"Yes, yes. I'm sure he was. Well, and what happened?"

"I keep tellin' you," moaned the maid. "'E got lorst. Disappeared clean. Couldn't be found nowhere. Lured away to 'is death 'e must've been," she showed symptoms of another spasm but collected herself, "an' the mistress sent me out to look for him down this 'ere road while she rang up police stations and," her voice rose again to a wail, "I sor his gho-o-o-ost. He's de-e-e-ead."

"Nonsense!" said Mrs. Brown in a tone that succeeded in quelling an incipient attack of hysterics. "Nonsense! You must have seen a-a tree or a-a shadow or something. There aren't such things as ghosts."

"There are. I seed 'im with my eyes," said the maid solemnly, "not as 'e looked in life. All white an' shinin' 'e was. I seed 'im as plain as I see you now, 'm. 'E didn't look the same as 'e looked in life. 'Is 'ead was different an' 'e wore different clothes. All white an' shinin'. It was 'is ghost. 'E's de-e-e-ead."

The hysterics gathered force again. With relief Mrs. Brown heard her husband's key in the lock.

"Wait a minute," she said. "I'll ask my husband to come to you."

She went out and returned in a few moments with an obviously reluctant Mr. Brown.

"But I say," he murmured, "I can't do anything. I don't——"

"Tell this gentleman what you saw," said Mrs. Brown to the maid.

The maid, who was secretly beginning to enjoy her position as purveyor of news from the spirit world, burst again into her description: . . . "and there I seed 'im . . . there 'e stood all white an' shining. Not the same as he looked in life. 'Is 'ead was different. 'E'd got one of the white things round his 'ead. What d'you call them, 'm?"

"A halo?" suggested Mrs. Brown.

"Yes, a hello round his 'ead an' white robes same as the angels an' there he stood lookin' at me with a wonderful white light coming from him like what you see in pictures of 'em. 'E'd come back to me to give me some message but I was all of a jelly same as you'd have been yourself, sir, an' came runnin' down the road all of a jingle an' this lady'll tell you, sir, that I'd've been dead by now if she hadn't of give me some stuff to drink."

Mrs. Brown looked anxiously at her husband, but it was evident that there was little hope of help from him. He was already looking at his watch and edging towards the door.

"Yes," he said. "Well . . ." he turned to his wife and with a heartless "I'll be back for dinner, dear," vanished.

Mrs. Brown looked helplessly at her visitor.

"Don't you think you'd better go home now?" she said.

"I couldn't," said the visitor earnestly. "I couldn't walk down that road again—what 'is blessed spirit 'aunts—not to save my life, 'm. I never was one for ghosts. I'm still all of a jingle in my inside. I can still hear my ribs knockin' against each other. It's a miracle I'm not dead."

"You came out to look for him and left your mistress at home?" said Mrs. Brown.

"Yes, I came to look for that pore little child what has been lured to his death, an' there when I got to the corner of the road I sor——"

"Yes, yes," said Mrs. Brown hastily. "I'd better ring your mistress up and let her know that you're here, hadn't I?"

"All of the jiggers," said the maid. "I c'n still hear my bones knockin' against each other as plain as plain. There he stood, a white light shinin' from him an' a hello round his head same as in the Bible an'——"

"Yes, yes," said Mrs. Brown again. "I'll ring her up and tell her what's happened."

She was feeling relieved, as she'd heard William come

"I COULDN'T WALK DOWN THAT ROAD AGAIN," SAID THE
MAID. "I NEVER WAS ONE FOR GHOSTS."

in by the side door and go into the dining-room for his
supper. She always felt relieved when William came
home for the night.

She meant to go up to see him as soon as she'd
communicated with Clarence's aunt, but Annie, feeling

that her due position as centre of the stage was not being accorded her, made a bold bid for it by a fainting fit for which a glass of brandy had to be administered. She was only just emerging from it when Clarence's aunt appeared.

Annie, fortified by the brandy, leapt again into her narrative.

"Oh, mum, I was comin' along the road lookin' for him when suddenly 'is spirit appeared to me out of the darkness—all shinin' bright. 'E'd got a little hello round his head same as what they have up there an' long white robes an' beautiful wings. An' he looked at me an' he said:

" 'Give 'er my love,' 'e said, 'an' tell 'er I'm 'appy.' "

At this point Annie was so deeply moved by her narrative that she broke down again. Clarence's aunt broke down too, and they sobbed together.

"Lured to 'is death," sobbed Annie.

"And I loved him so," sobbed Clarence's aunt.

"Shinin' so bright it almost blinded you to look at him."

"The apple of my eye."

" 'Give 'er my love,' 'e said, 'an' tell 'er that I'm 'appy with the hangels.' "

"If only I'd let him have his darling hair cut off."

"Flowin' bright robes an' a narp in his 'and."

As another attack of hysterics seemed to be threatening, Mrs. Brown hastily led Annie across the hall to the kitchen and gave her into the care of her cook and housemaid who enjoyed hysterics and were skilled in the treatment of them.

Then Mrs. Brown returned to Clarence's aunt, composing on the way various little sarcasms with which she would greet her husband on his return.

Clarence's aunt was by now a little calmer.

"Of course I don't really believe that she saw his ghost but it's so *dreadful*," she sobbed. "I'm simply *distracted* by anxiety. I've communicated with all the police stations for miles around. If only I haven't driven him to anything desperate. He wanted to wear those Rugby suits and have his beautiful hair cut off and go to a rough boys' school and be called John and I wouldn't let him. . . . Oh, if only I could get him back safe and sound I'd let him. I *swear* I'd let him. Have you got a little boy?"

"Yes," said William's mother.

"Then you know how they *twine* themselves round your heart?"

"Y-yes," said William's mother rather doubtfully.

"Is your little boy in bed now?"

"Yes," said William's mother, whose listening ear had noted the cessation of bangs and bumps from William's bedroom that meant that he was at rest.

"Will he be asleep now?"

"I expect so."

"Do you go and *gaze* upon him when he's asleep?"

"Not generally."

"I do at Clarence. . . . Do let me go with you and look at your little boy asleep. It will—it will *lull* my anxiety. Let me go and try to imagine my own little Clarence's head upon the pillow, too."

"Very well," said Mrs. Brown rather reluctantly.

They went upstairs. The sound of Annie's voice came from the kitchen. "There 'e stood all bright an' shinin' . . ."

Mrs. Brown opened the door of William's bedroom and they entered on tiptoe.

Upon the pillow lay William's and Clarence's heads side by side. William had not thought of washing his orphan and upon Clarence's cheek a large circle of jam outlined itself vividly against a background of cement. His unevenly cropped hair was quite white. . . .

He smiled happily in his sleep.

William's Birthday

It was William's birthday, but, in spite of that, his spirit was gloomy and overcast. His birthday, in fact, seemed to contribute to his gloom instead of lightening it. For one thing, he hadn't got Jumble, his beloved mongrel, and a birthday without Jumble was, in William's eyes, a hollow mockery of a birthday.

Jumble had hurt his foot in a rabbit trap, and had been treated for it at home, till William's well-meaning but mistaken ministrations had caused the vet. to advise Jumble's removal to his own establishment. William had indignantly protested.

"*Why*'s he got to go away? *Me?* I've been *curin'* him, I tell you. Well, a gipsy boy told me about that. He said, tie beech leaves round it. Well, he started chewin' off his bandage himself. I din' tell him to. Well, I wanted to try splints. I read in a book about how to put a dog's legs into splints. An' he *liked* it. He liked it better'n what he liked the bandage. . . . Well, he'll prob'ly die now without me to look after him, an' it'll be your fault."

His fury increased when his visits to the vet.'s establishment were forbidden. The vet. explained quite politely that William's presence there was having a deleterious effect upon his nerves and business.

"I din' do any harm," said William indignantly. "I cun't help upsettin' that jar of goldfishes an' I din' reely start those two dogs fightin'. I bet they'd done it even if I'd not been there. An' I din' mean that white rat to get out of my pocket an' get 'em all excited. An' I din' bother him for food or anythin' when dinner-time came. I jus' ate dog biscuits an' ant eggs an' any stuff I found about."

William's family, however, was adamant. William was not to visit the veterinary surgeon's establishment again.

"All right, he'll die," said William with gloomy conviction, referring not to the vet., whose death would have left him unmoved, but to Jumble, "an' it'll be all your faults, an' I hope you'll always remember that you killed my dog."

So annoyed was he with them that, in order to punish them, he lost his voice. This, of course, alone, would have been a reward rather than a punishment, but he insisted on writing all he had to say (which was a lot) on a slate with a squeaky slate-pencil that went through everyone's head. They gave him paper and pencil, and he deliberately broke the point on the first word, and then returned to his squeaky slate-pencil to explain and apologise at agonising length. Finally, in despair, they sent over to the doctor for some medicine which proved so nauseous that William's voice returned.

This episode increased the tension between William and his family, and, when the question of his birthday celebration was broached, feeling was still high on both sides.

"I'd like a dog for my birthday present," said William.

"You've got a dog," said his mother.

"I shan't have when you an' that man have killed it between you," said William. "I've seen him stickin' his fingers down their throats fit to choke 'em, givin' 'em pills an' things. An' he puts on their bandages so tight that their calculations stop flowin' an' that's jus' the same as stranglin' 'em."

"Nonsense, William!"

"Then why'd he stop me goin' to see 'em?" went on William dramatically. " 'Cause he knew that I saw he was killin' 'em, chokin' 'em with givin' 'em pills an' puttin' tight bandages on 'em stoppin' their calculations flowin'. I've a good mind to go to the police. He ought to be done something to by lor."

"You're talking a lot of nonsense, William."

"Anyway, I want a dog for my birthday present. I'm sick of not havin' a dog. I've not had a dog for nearly three days now. Well, even if he doesn't kill Jumble—an' he's tryin' jolly hard—an' what dog can live when he's bein' choked an' strangled all day for nearly three days—well, even if he doesn't kill him, I want another dog. I want two more dogs," he added shamelessly, knowing that his family wouldn't give him another dog, and feeling that if he were going to have a grievance against them, he might as well have it for two dogs as one.

"Nonsense! Of course you can't have another dog."

"I said two more dogs."

"Well, you can't have two more dogs."

"I'm going to give you a bottle of throat mixture for my present," said Ethel, who had suffered more than anyone through the squeaky slate-pencil because she had been deputed to attend on him.

William glared at her.

"Yes," he said darkly, "you needn't think I don't know that you're trying to kill me as well as Jumble. Poisonin' *me* an' chokin' an' stranglin' *him*."

"Would you like a party for your birthday, William?" said his mother, vaguely propitiating.

William considered this offer for a moment in silence. His mother's idea of giving a party consisted in asking back all the people who had asked him to their parties, and William knew from experience that it was impossible to move her from this attitude. He assembled in a mental review all the people who had asked him to their parties that year, and the result was a depressing one.

"I'd like a party," he said, "if you'll let me ask——" There followed a list of the more rowdy members of the juvenile male population of the neighbourhood. Mrs. Brown paled.

"Oh, but William," she said, "they're so rough, and if we give a party at all we *must* have little Susie Chambers and Clarence Medlow and all the people who've asked you——"

"Then I won't have one," said William, "anyone'd think it was a funeral treat you were tryin' to give me, not a birthday treat. It's not my *funeral*."

"No, it's more likely to be ours," said Ethel. "I can still hear the noise of that slate-pencil."

"I don't see how you can when it's stopped," said William, the matter-of-fact. "You can't hear things that aren't there to hear. At least not if you're not balmy."

He was evidently going to elaborate this theme in relation to Ethel, but Mrs. Brown stopped him with a hasty "That will do, William," and William returned to a mournful contemplation of his birthday.

"You can have Ginger and Henry and Douglas to tea," said his mother, but it appeared that William didn't want Ginger and Henry and Douglas to tea. He explained that she always stopped them playing any interesting games when they *did* come to tea, and he'd rather go out with them and play interesting games in the fields or woods than have them to tea and get stopped every time they started an interesting game.

"Well, anyway," he said at last, brightening, "I needn't go to the dancing-class on my birthday afternoon."

The dancing-class was at present the bane of William's life. He had been dismissed from one dancing-class some years ago as a hopeless subject, but Mrs. Brown, in whose breast hope sprang eternal, had lately entered him for another that was held in a girls' school in the neighbourhood. It took place on Wednesday afternoon, William's half-holiday, and it was an ever-present and burning grievance to him. He was looking forward to his birthday chiefly because he took for granted that he would be given a holiday from the dancing-class. But it turned out that there, too, Fate was against him. Of course he must go to the dancing-class, said Mrs. Brown. It was only an hour, and it was a most expensive course, and she'd promised that he shouldn't miss a single lesson, because Mrs. Beauchamp said that he was very slow and clumsy, and she really hadn't wanted to take him. William, stung by these personal reflections, indignantly retorted that he *wasn't* slow and clumsy, and, anyway, he *liked* being slow and clumsy. And as for her not wanting to take him, he bet she was jolly glad to get him and he could dance as well as any of them if he wanted to, but he didn't believe in dancing and he never had and he never would, and so he didn't see the sense of making him go to a dancing-class, especially on his birthday. He added sarcastically that he noticed anyway that *she* (meaning Mrs. Brown) took jolly good care not to go to a dancing-class on *her* birthday.

Mrs. Brown was quietly adamant. She was paying a guinea for the course, she said, and she'd promised that he shouldn't miss any of it.

To William, wallowing with a certain gloomy relish in his ill-fortune, it seemed the worst that could possibly

happen to him. But it wasn't. When he heard that
Ethel's admirer, Mr. Dewar, was coming to tea on his
birthday, his indignation rose to boiling point.

"But it's my birthday," he protested. "I don't want
him here on my birthday."

William had a more deeply-rooted objection to Mr.
Dewar than to any of Ethel's other admirers. Mr. Dewar
had an off-hand facetious manner, which William had
disliked from his first meeting with him. But lately the
dislike had deepened, till William's happiest dreams
now took the form of shooting Mr. Dewar through the
heart with his bow and arrow, or impaling him on a fence
with his penknife or handing him over to the imaginary
wild beasts who obeyed William's slightest behest.

For in the very early days of their acquaintance Mr.
Dwar had once come upon William, dressed in his Red
Indian suit, cooking an experimental mixture of treacle
and lemonade in an old sardine tin over a smoking fire in
the shrubbery, and since then he had never met William,
without making some playful reference to the affair.
"Here comes the great chief Wild Head. Hast thou yet
finished yon pale face thou wast cooking, friend?"

Or he would refer to William as "the great chief Dark
Ears," "the great chief Sans Soap" or "the great chief
Black Collar." Or he would say with heavy sarcasm:
"How the flames of thy fire leapt up to the sky, great
Chief! I still feel the heat of it upon my face."

William did not consider his character of Indian Chief
to be a subject for jesting, but his black looks, in Mr.
Dewar's eyes, only added to the fun.

And this hated creature was coming to tea on his
birthday, and would probably insinuate himself so much
into Ethel's good graces that he would be coming now
every day afterwards to darken William's life by his
insults.

"But, William," said his mother, "you wouldn't have a party or anyone to tea, so you can't complain."

"You don't want us all to go into a nunnery because it's your birthday, do you?" said Ethel.

William wasn't quite sure what a nunnery was, but it sounded vaguely like a "monkery," so he muttered bitterly, "You'd suit one all right," and went out of the room so that Ethel could not continue the conversation.

* * *

He awoke on the morning of his birthday, still in a mood of unmelting resentment. He dressed slowly and his thoughts were a sort of refrain of his grievances. A dancing-class and that man to tea on his birthday. On his *birthday*. A dancing-class and that man to tea on his *birthday*. A dancing-class and that man to *tea* on his birthday. *A dancing*-class. On his *birthday*. . . .

He went downstairs morosely to receive his presents.

Ethel, of course, had not dared to give him a bottle of throat mixture. She would have liked to, because she still felt very strongly about the slate pencil, but she had learnt by experience that it was wiser not to embark upon a course of retaliation with William, because you never knew where it would lead you. So she had bought for him instead a note-book and pencil, which was as nearly an insult as she dared offer him. She assumed a very kindly expression as she presented it, and William's gloom of spirit deepened, because he had a suspicion that she meant it as an insult, and yet he wasn't sure, and it would be as galling to his pride to accept it with gratitude when she meant it as an insult, as it would be to accept it as an insult when she meant it kindly. He kept a suspicious eye upon her while he thanked her, but she showed no signs of guilt. His mother's present to him was a dozen new handkerchiefs with his initials upon each, his father's a new leather pencil-case. William thanked them with a manner of cynical aloofness of which he was rather proud.

During morning school he took a gloomy satisfaction in initiating one of his new handkerchief's into its new life. In the course of the morning it was used to staunch the blood from William's nose after a fight in the playground, to wipe the mud from William's knees after a fall in a puddle, to mop up a pool of ink from William's desk, to swaddle the white rat that that William had brought to school with him, and as a receptable for the two pennyworth of Liquorice All Sorts that had been Ginger's present to him. At the end of the morning its eleven spotless brothers would have passed it by unrecognised.

"Now, William," said his mother anxiously at lunch, "you'll go to the dancing-class nicely this afternoon, won't you?"

"I'll go the way I gen'rally go to things. I've only got one way of goin' anywhere. I don't know whether it's nice or not."

This brilliant repartee cheered him considerably, and he felt that a life in which one could display such sarcasm and wit was after all to a certain degree worth living. But still—no Jumble. A dancing-class. That man to tea. Gloom closed over him again. Mrs. Brown was still looking at him anxiously. She had an uneasy suspicion that he meant to play truant from the dancing-class.

When she saw him in his hat and coat after lunch she said again: "William, you *are* going to the dancing-class, aren't you?"

William walked past her with a short laugh that was wild and reckless and dare-devil and bitter and sardonic. It was, in short, a very good laugh, and he was proud of it.

Then he swaggered down the drive, and very osten-
tatiously turned off in the opposite direction to the
direction of his dancing-class. The knowledge that his
mother's anxiety had deepened at the sight of this, was
balm to his sore spirit. He did not really intend to play
truant from the dancing-class. The consequences would
be unpleasant, and life was, he considered, quite complicated enough without adding that. He walked on slowly
for some time with an elaborate swagger, and then
turned and retraced his steps in the direction of the
dancing-class with furtive swiftness. To do so he had to
pass the gate of his home, but he meant to do this in the
ditch so that his mother, who might be still anxiously
watching the road for the reassuring sight of his return,
should be denied the satisfaction of it.

He could not resist, however, peeping cautiously out
of the ditch when he reached the gate, to see if she were
watching for him. There was no sign of her at door or
windows, but—there was something else that made
William rise to his feet, his eyes and mouth wide open
with amazement. There, tied to a tree in the drive near
the front door, were two young collies, little more than
pups. Two dogs. He'd asked his family for two dogs and
here they were. Two dogs. He could hardly believe his
eyes. He stared at them, and shook himself to make sure
that he was awake. They were still there. They weren't
part of a dream. His heart swelled with gratitude and
affection for his family. How he'd misjudged them! How
terribly he'd misjudged them! Thinking they didn't care
two pins about his birthday, and here they'd got him the
two dogs he'd asked for as a surprise, without saying
anything to him about it. Just put them there for him to
find. His heart still swelling with love and gratitude, he
went up the drive. As he went the church clock struck
the hour. He'd only just be in time for the dancing-class

now, even if he ran all the way. His mother had wanted him to be in time for the dancing-class, and the sight of the two dogs had touched his heart so deeply that he wanted to do something in return to please his mother. He'd hurry off to the dancing-class at once, and wait till he came back to thank them for the dogs. He was sure that his mother would rather he was in time for the dancing-class than that he went in now to thank her for the dogs.

He stooped down, undid the two leads from the tree, and ran off again down the drive, the two dogs leaping joyfully beside him. In the road he found the leads rather a nuisance. The two dogs ran in front of him and behind him, leapt up at him, circled round him, and finally tripped him up so that he fell sprawling full length upon the ground. When this had happened several times it occurred to him to take off their leads. They still leapt and gambolled joyfully about him as he ran, evidently recognising him as their new owner. One was slightly bigger and darker than the other, but both were very young and very lively and very lovable. Soon he grew out of breath, and began to walk. The collies began to walk, too, but had evidently preferred running. The smaller one began to direct his energies to burrowing in the ditches, and the larger one to squeeze his lithe young body through the hedge. Having squeezed it through the hedge, he found himself to his surprise in a field of sheep. He did not know that they were sheep. It was his first day in the country. He had only that morning left a London shop. But dim, wholly incomprehended, instincts began to stir in him. William, watching with mingled consternation and delight, saw him round up the sheep in the field, and begin to drive them pell-mell through the hedge into the road; then, hurrying, snapping, barking, drive them down the road towards William's house. On the way lay another field of sheep, separated by a hedge from the road. The collie plunged into this field, too, drove the occupants out into the road to join his first flock, and began to chivvy the whole jostling perturbed flock of them down the road towards William's house.

William stood and watched the proceeding. The delight it afforded him was tempered with apprehension. He had not forgotten the occasion when he had tried to train Jumble to be a sheep dog. He had learnt then that farmers objected to their sheep being rounded up and removed by strange dogs, however well it was done (and William had persisted at the time, and still persisted, that Jumble made a jolly fine sheep dog). William's mind worked quickly in a crisis. The white undulating company was already some way down the road. Impossible to bring them back. Still more impossible to separate them into their different flocks.

The collie had now made his way into a third field in search of recruits, while his main army waited for him meekly in the road. William hastily decided to dissociate himself from the proceedings entirely, to have been walking quietly to his dancing-class, and not to have noticed that one of his dogs had left him to collect sheep from all the neighbouring fields. Better to let one of his dogs go than risk losing both. . . .

He hurried on to the dancing-class, occasionally turning round to throw a glance of fascinated horror at the distant sea of sheep that was still surging down the road. At their rear was William's new pet, chivvying them with gusto, his tail arched proudly like a plume.

William reluctantly turned the corner that hid the wonderful sight from him, and walked up the drive of the girls' school where the dancing-class was held. Aware of a group of little girls in dancing-frocks clustered at the downstairs window, he assumed a manly swagger, and called out curt commands to his attendant hound. ("Here, sir. To heel! Down sir!") Near the front door he tied the collie to a tree with the lead, and entered a room where a lot of little boys—most of whom William disliked intensely—were brushing their hair and washing their hands and changing their shoes. William changed his shoes, studied his hair in the glass and decided that it really didn't need brushing, wiped his hands on his trousers to remove any removable dirt, and began to scuffle with his less sedate fellow pupils.

At last a tinkly little bell rang, and they made their way to the large room where the dancing-class was held. From an opposite door was issuing a bevy of little girls, dressed in fairy-like frills and furbelows with white socks and dancing-shoes. Followed them an attendant army of mothers and nurses, who had been divesting them of stockings or gaiters and outdoor garments. William greeted as many of these fairy-like beings as would condescend to look at him with his most hideous grimace. The one he disliked most of all (a haughty beauty with auburn curls) was given him as a partner.

"*Need* I have William?" she pleaded pitifully. "He's so *awful*."

"I'm not," said William indignantly. "I'm no more awful than her."

"Have him for a few minutes, dear," said Mrs. Beauchamp, who was tall and majestic and almost incredibly sinuous, "and then I'll let you have someone else."

The dancing-class proceeded on its normal course. William glanced at the clock and sighed. Only five minutes gone. A whole hour of it. The longest hour of the week. And on his birthday. His *birthday*. Even the

"NEED I HAVE WILLIAM?" SHE PLEADED PITIFULLY.
"HE'S SO *AWFUL."*

"I'M NOT," SAID WILLIAM INDIGNANTLY. "I'M NO
MORE AWFUL THAN HER."

thought of his two new dogs did not quite wipe out that grievance.

"Please may I stop having William now? He's doing the steps all wrong."

William defended himself with spirit.

"I'm doin' 'em right. It's her what's doin' 'em wrong."

The smallest and meekest of the little girls was given to William as a partner, because it was felt that she would be too shy to protest. For some minutes she tried conscientiously to dance with William, then she said reproachfully:

"You seem to have such a lot of feet. I can't put mine down anywhere where yours aren't."

"I've only got two," he said distantly, "same as other people. When I've got mine down, you should find somewhere else to put yours."

"If I do you tread on them," said the little girl.

"Well, you can't expect me not to have feet, can you?" said William. "Seems to me that what you all want to dance with is someone without any feet at all. Seems to me the best way to do is for me to put mine down first, and then you look where mine aren't and put yours there."

They proceeded to dance on this system till Mrs. Beauchamp stopped them, and gave William another partner—a little girl with untidy hair and a roguish smile. She was a partner more to William's liking, and the dance developed into a competition as to who could tread more often on the other's feet. The little girl was unexpectedly nimble at this, and performed a sort of *pas seul* upon William's dancing slippers. He strove to evade her, but she was too quick for him. It was, of course, a pastime unworthy of a famous Indian chief, but it was better than dancing. He unbent to her.

"It's my birthday to-day and I've had two dogs give me."

"*Oo!* Lucky!"

"An' I've got one already, so that makes three. Three dogs I've got."

"Oo, I say! Have you got 'em here?"

"I only brought one. It's in the garden tied to a tree near the door."

"Oo, I'm goin' to look at it when we get round to the window!"

"Yes, you have a look. It's a jolly fine dog. I'm goin' to train it to be a huntin' dog. You know, train it to fetch in the wild animals I shoot. One of the others is a performin' dog and the other's a sheep dog. They're all jolly clever. One of them's with the vet. now an' I don't know if he'll come out alive. They kill 'em as soon as look at 'em, vets. do. Chokin' 'em and stranglin' 'em. I bet what I'll do is to rescue him. Go with these other two dogs an' rescue him. I bet I can train 'em to hold the vet. down while I rescue Jumble from him. I'm not afraid of anyone and neither are my dogs."

Mrs. Beauchamp was watching his steps with a harassed frown, and it was evident that it was only a question of seconds before she interfered.

"Not of *her* or of anyone," said William, meaning Mrs. Beauchamp. "Got you."

"No, you didn't," said the little girl, neatly withdrawing her foot from William's descending slipper and placing it firmly upon the top, "Got *you*."

"Well, here's the window. Have a look at my dog," said William.

They edged to the window, and there the little girl halted, making a pretence of pulling up her socks. Then she glanced out with interest, and stood suddenly paralysed with horror, her mouth and eyes wide open.

But almost immediately her vocal powers returned to her and she uttered a scream.

"*Look!*" she said. "Oh, *look!*"

They crowded to the window—little girls, little boys, nurses and mothers.

The collie had escaped from his lead, and found his way into the little girls' dressing-room. There he had collected the stockings, gaiters and navy-blue knickers that lay about on tables and desks, and brought them all out on to the lawn, where he was happily engaged in worrying them. Remnants of stockings and gaiters lay everywhere about him. He was tossing up into the air one leg of a pair of navy-blue knickers. Around him the air was thick with wool and fluff. Bits of ravelled stockings, chewed-up gaiters, with here and there a dismembered hat, lay about on the lawn in glorious confusion. He was having the time of his life.

After a moment's frozen horror the whole dancing-class—little girls, little boys, nurses, mothers and dancing-mistress—surged out on to the lawn. The collie saw them coming and leapt up playfully, a gaiter hanging out of one corner of his mouth, and a stocking out of the other. It occurred to everyone simultaneously that the first thing to do was to catch the collie, and take the gaiter and stocking from him. They bore down upon him in a crowd. He wagged his tail in delight. All these people coming to play with him! He entered into the spirit of the game at once, and leapt off to the shrubbery, shaking his head excitedly so that the gaiter and stocking waved wildly in the air. In and out of the trees, followed by all these jolly people who were playing with him, back to the lawn, round the house, through the rose garden. A glorious game! The best fun he'd had for weeks. . . .

Meanwhile William was making his way quietly homeward. They'd say it was all his fault, of course, but he'd learnt by experience that it was best to get as far as possible and as quickly as possible away from the scene of a crime. Delayed retribution never had the inspired frenzy of retribution exacted on the spot.

As he walked along the road, his brows drawn into a frown, his hands plunged into his pockets, his lips were moving as he argued with an invisible accuser.

"Well, how could I help it? Well, you gave me them, didn't you? Well, how could I know it was a dog like that? It's not done any real harm either. Jus' a few stockings an' things. Well, they can buy some more, can't they? They're cheap enough, aren't they? Grudgin' the poor dog a bit of fun! They don't mind paying as much as a pair of stockings for a bit of fun for themselves, do they? Oh no! Then why should they grudge the poor dog a bit of fun? That's all I say. An' it wasn't *my* fault, was it? I never trained him to eat stockings an' suchlike, did I? Well, I couldn't have, could I?—seein' I'd only had him a few minutes. An' what I say is——"

He turned the bend in the road that brought his own house in sight, and there he stood as if turned suddenly to stone. He'd forgotten the other dog. The front garden was a sea of sheep. They covered drive, grass and flower beds. They even stood on the steps that led to the front door. The overflow filled the road outside. Behind them was the other collie pup, his tail still waving triumphantly, running to and fro, crowding them up still more closely, pursuing truants and bringing them back to the fold. Having collected the sheep, his instinct had told him to bring them to his master. His master was, of course, the man who had brought him from the shop, not the boy who had taken him for a walk. His master was in this house. He had brought the sheep to his master. . . .

His master was, in fact, with Ethel in the drawing-room. Mrs. Brown was out, and was not expected back

"WELL," SAID MR. DEWAR, "LOVELY PETS, AREN'T
THEY?"

ETHEL TURNED AND FACED HIM. "PETS!" SHE
SCREAMED. "I'VE NOWHERE TO KEEP THEM."

till tea-time. Mr. Dewar considered he was getting on very well with Ethel. He had not yet told her about the two collies he had brought for her. She'd said last week that she "adored" collies, and he'd decided to bring her a couple of them next week. He meant to introduce the subject quite carelessly when he'd reached the right stage of intimacy. He possessed the dramatic instinct and liked to produce his effects at the right moment. And so, when she told him that he seemed to understand her better than any other man she'd ever met (she said this to all her admirers in turn) he said to her quite casually:

"Oh! by the way, I forgot to mention it but I just bought a little present—or rather presents—for you this afternoon. They're in the drive."

Ethel's face lit up with pleasure and interest.

"Oh, how perfectly sweet of you," she said.

"Have a look at them and see if you like them," he said.

She walked over to the window. He remained in his arm-chair, watching the back of her Botticelli neck, lounging at his ease—the gracious, generous, all-providing male. She looked out. Sheep—hundreds and thousands of sheep—filled the drive, the lawn, the steps, the road outside.

"Well," said Mr. Dewar casually, "do you like them?"

She raised a hand to her head.

"What are they for?" she said faintly.

"Pets," said Mr. Dewar.

"*Pets?*" she screamed. "I've nowhere to keep them. I've nothing to feed them on."

"Oh, they only want a few dog biscuits," said Mr. Dewar.

"*Dog* biscuits?"

Ethel stared at them wildly for another second, then collapsed on to the nearest chair in hysterics.

Mrs. Brown had returned home before Ethel had emerged from her hysterics. Mrs. Brown had had literally to fight her way to her front door through a tightly packed mass of sheep. If Ethel hadn't forestalled her she'd have had hysterics herself. Mr. Dewar was wildly apologetic. He couldn't think what had happened. He couldn't think how the dogs had got loose. He couldn't think where the other dog was. He couldn't think where the sheep had come from. The other dog arrived at the same moment as a crowd of indignant farmers demanding their sheep. It still had a gaiter hanging out of one corner of its mouth and a stocking out of the other. It was curveting coquettishly. It wanted someone else to play with it. William was nowhere to be seen.

*   *   *

William came home about half an hour later. There were no signs of Mr. Dewar, or the dogs, or the sheep. Ethel and Mrs. Brown were in the drawing-room.

"I shall never speak to him again," Ethel was saying. "I don't care whether it was his fault or not. I shall always connect him with that horrible moment when I looked out and saw—it was like a nightmare—nothing but sheep as far as you can see. I've told him never to come to the house again."

"I don't think he'd dare to when your father's seen the state the grass is in. It looks like a ploughed field. You can hardly see where the beds begin, and everything in them's broken and trodden down. I shouldn't be a bit surprised if your father didn't talk of suing him."

"As if I'd want hundreds of *sheep* like that," said Ethel, who was still feeling distraught, and confused what Mr. Dewar had meant to do with what he had actually done. "*Pets* indeed!"

"And Mrs. Beauchamp's just rung up about the other dog," went on Mrs. Brown. "It evidently followed William to the dancing-class and tore up some stockings and things there. I don't see how she can blame us for that. She was really very rude about it. I don't think I shall let William go to any more of her dancing-classes."

William sat listening with an expressionless face, as if he didn't know what they were talking about, but his heart was singing within him. No more dancing-classes . . . that man never coming to the house any more. A glorious birthday—except for one thing, of course. But just then a housemaid came into the room.

"Please, 'm', it's the man from the vet. with Master William's dog. He says he's quite all right now."

William leapt from the room, and he and Jumble fell upon each other ecstatically in the hall. The minute he saw Jumble, William knew that he could never have endured to have any other dog beside him.

"I'll take him for a little walk," he said; "I bet he wants one."

The joy of walking along the road again with his beloved Jumble at his heels was almost too great to be endured. He sauntered along, Jumble leaping up at him in tempestuous affection. His heart was full of creamy content.

He'd got Jumble back. That man was never coming to the house any more.

He wasn't going to any more dancing-classes.

It was the nicest birthday he'd ever had in his life.

from *William's Happy Days*

The Christmas Truce

It was Hubert's mother's idea that the Outlaws versus Hubert Laneites feud should be abolished.

"Christmas, you know," she said vaguely to William's mother, "the season of peace and goodwill. If they don't bury the hatchet at this season they never will. It's so absurd for them to go on like this. Think how much *happier* they'd be if they were *friends*."

Mrs. Brown thought, murmured "Er—yes," uncertainly, and added, "I've *tried*, you know, but boys are so funny."

"Yes," said Mrs. Lane earnestly (Mrs. Lane was large and breathless and earnest and overdressed), "but they're *very* sweet, aren't they? Hubie's *awfully* sweet. I simply can't think how anyone could quarrel with Hubie. We'll make a *real* effort this Christmas to put an end to this foolish quarrel, won't we? I feel that if only your Willie got to know my Hubie properly, he'd simply love him, he would really. *Everyone* who really knows Hubie loves him."

Mrs. Brown said, "Er—yes," still more uncertainly, and Mrs. Lane continued: "I've thought out how to do it. If you'll invite Hubie to Willie's party, we'll *insist* on his coming, and we'll invite Willie to Hubie's, and you *insist* on his coming, and then it will be all right. They'll have got to know each other, and, I'm sure, learnt to love each other."

Mrs. Brown said "Er—yes," more uncertainly than ever. She felt that Mrs. Lane was being unduly optimistic, but still it *would* be nice to see the end of the feud that was always leading William into such wild and desperate adventures.

"Then we'll begin by——"

"Begin and end, my dear Mrs. Brown," said Mrs. Lane earnestly, "by making them attend each other's Christmas parties. I'm absolutely convinced that they'll *love* each other after that. I know anyway that Willie will love Hubie, because, when you really get to know Hubie, he's the most *lovable* boy you can possibly imagine."

Mrs. Brown said "Er—yes," again, because she couldn't think of anything else to say, and so the matter was settled.

When it was broached to William, he was speechless with horror.

"*Him?*" he exploded fiercely when at last the power of speech returned to him. "Ask *him* to my Christmas party? I'd sooner not have a Christmas party at all than ask *him* to it. *Him!* Why I wun't go to the *King's* Christmas party, if *he* was going to be there. Not if I had to be beheaded for it. *Him?* Well, then I jolly well won't have a party at all."

But Mrs. Brown was unexpectedly firm. The overtures, she said, had come from Hubert's mother, and they could not with decency be rejected. It was the season of peace and goodwill ("No one's ever peaceful or goodwillin' to me at it," put in William bitterly); and we must all bury the hatchet and start afresh.

"I don't want to bury no hatchet," said William

tempestuously, " 'cept in his head. *Him!* Wantin' to come to my party! *Cheek!*"

But William's tempestuous fury was as usual of no avail against his mother's gentle firmness.

"It's no use, William," she said. "I've *promised*. He's to come to your party, and you're to go to his, and Mrs. Lane is quite sure that you'll be real friends after it."

"*Me* friends with *him!*" exploded William. "I'll never be friends with him 'cept in a lunatic asylum an'——"

"But William," said his mother, stemming his flood of frenzied oratory, "I'm sure he's a very nice little boy when you get to know him."

William replied to this by a (partially) dumb and very realistic show of physical nausea.

But faced by the alternative of Hubert Lane and his friends as guests at his party or no party at all, William bowed to the inevitable.

"All right," he said, "I'll have him then an'—all right, I won't *do* anythin' to him or to any of them I'll wait till it's all over. I'll wait till he's been to my party an' I've been to his, an' then—well, you'll be jolly sorry you ever made us do it 'cause we'll have such a lot to make up."

Mrs. Brown, however, was content with her immediate victory. She sent an invitation to Hubert Lane and to Bertie Franks (Hubert's friend and lieutenant) and to Hubert's other friends, and they all accepted in their best copper-plate handwriting. William and his Outlaws went about sunk deep in gloom.

"If it wasn't for the trifle an' the crackers," said William darkly, "I wouldn't have had it at all—not with *him*. An' it'll have to be a jolly fine trifle, practic'ly *all* cream, to make it worth while." His mood grew darker and darker as the day approached. He even discussed with his Outlaws the possibility of making a raid on the larder before the party, and carrying off trifles and jellies and fruit salad into the woods, leaving the Hubert Laneites to arrive and find the cupboard bare and their hosts flown. It was a tempting plan, but after dallying with it fondly for a few days they reluctantly gave it up, as being not really worth its inevitable consequences. Instead, they steeled themselves to go through the affair in the dogged spirit of martyrdom, their sufferings allayed only by the thought of the trifle and crackers, and the riot of hostilities that could take place as soon as the enforced Christmas truce was over. For the prospect of the end of the feud brought no glow of joy to the Outlaws' hearts. Without the Hubert Lane feud life would be dull indeed.

As the day of the party drew nearer, curiosity lightened the gloom of their spirits. How would the Hubert Laneites behave? Would they come reluctantly, surlily, at the bidding of authority, or would they come in a Christmas spirit of peace and goodwill, genuinely anxious to bury the hatchet? The latter possibility was too horrible to contemplate. Rather let them come in the spirit in which the Outlaws were prepared to receive them—a spirit in which one receives a deadly foe in time of truce, all their thoughts and energies centred on the happy moment when hostilities might be resumed.

William, of course, could not watch the preparations for his party and maintain unbroken his pose of aloof displeasure. The trifle was, he was convinced, the finest trifle that had yet been seen in the neighbourhood; there were jellies of every shape and hue, there was a cream blancmange decorated with cherries and angelica, and there was an enormous iced Christmas cake. *And* there were crackers. In the eyes of William and his friends it was the crackers that lent the final touch of festivity to the tea.

The Outlaws and their supporters, as arranged, arrived first, and stood round William like a body-guard awaiting the arrival of the Hubert Laneites. They wore perfectly blank expressions, prepared to meet the Hubert Laneites in whatever guise they presented themselves. And the guise in which they ultimately presented themselves was worse than the Outlaws' worst fears. They were not surly foes, forced reluctantly to simulate neutrality, nor were they heralds of peace and goodwill. They advanced upon their host with an oily friendliness that was nauseating. They winked at each other openly. They said, "Thanks *so* much for asking us, William. It was ripping of you. Oh, I say . . . what *topping* decorations!"

And they nudged each other and sniggered. William clenched his fists in his coat pocket and did swift mental calculations. His party would be over in four hours. In four days' time Hubert's party would come, and that would last about four hours, and then, *then,* THEN they could jolly well look out for themselves. The right hand that was clenched tightly in his coat for safety's sake was itching to plant itself firmly in Hubert's smug and smiling face. Mrs. Brown, of course, was deceived by their show of friendliness.

"There, William," she whispered triumphantly, "I knew it would be all right. They're so nice really, and *so* grateful to you for asking them. I'm sure you'll be the *greatest* friends after this. His mother *said* that he was a nice little boy."

William did not reply to this because there wasn't anything that he could trust himself to say. He was still restraining himself with great difficulty from hurling himself upon his foes. They went in to tea.

"Oh, I saw how *ripping!* How *topping!*" said the Hubert Laneites gushingly to Mrs. Brown, nudging each other and sniggering whenever her eye was turned away from them. Once Hubert looked at William and made his most challenging grimace, turning immediately to Mrs. Brown to say with an ingratiating smile:

"It's a simply topping party, Mrs. Brown, and it's awfully nice of you to ask us."

Mrs. Brown beamed at him and said:

"It's so nice to *have* you, Hubert," and the other Hubert Laneites sniggered, and William kept his hands in his pockets with such violence that one of them went right through the lining. But the crowning catastrophe happened when they pulled the crackers.

Hubert went up to William, and said, "See what I've got out of a cracker, William," and held up a ring that sent a squirt of water into William's face. The Hubert Laneites went into paroxysms of silent laughter. Hubert was all smirking contrition.

"I say, I'm so sorry, William, I'd no idea that it would do that. I'm frightfully sorry, Mrs. Brown. I'd no idea that it would do that. I just got it out of one of the crackers. I say, I'm *so* sorry, William."

It was evident to everyone but Mrs. Brown that the ring had not come out of a cracker, but had been carefully brought by Hubert in order to play this trick on William. William was wiping water out of his eyes and ears.

"It's quite all right, dear," said Mrs. Brown. "It was *quite* an accident, we all saw. They shouldn't have such nasty things in crackers, but it wasn't your fault. Tell him that you don't mind a bit, William."

But William hastily left the room.

"Now let's go and have a few games, shall we?" said Mrs. Brown.

Ginger followed William upstairs, and found him on the hearthrug in his bedroom, kneeling over a bolster that he was violently pummelling. Ginger knew that to William the bolster was not the bolster, but Hubert Lane's plump, well-nourished body. William raised a shining purple face from his task, and then the glow faded from it as he realised that the prostrate form before him was merely the bolster, and that Hubert Lane was triumphantly sniggering among his friends downstairs, not yet overtaken by Nemesis.

"Why don't you go down and smash his face in?" said Ginger simply.

William, returning reluctantly to Reality, raised the limp form of the bolster, and threw it on to the bed.

"Can't," he said tersely, "can't do anything not while he's in our house. I——"

"William, darling," called his mother, "Come down, we're going to begin the games."

William and Ginger went downstairs, and the rest of the party passed off uneventfully. The Hubert Laneites said good-bye at the end with nauseous gratitude, and went sniggering down the drive.

"*There,* William!" said Mrs. Brown, as she shut the door, "I knew it would be all right. They were so grateful and they enjoyed it *so* much and you're *quite* friends now, aren't you?"

But William was already upstairs in his bedroom, pummelling his bolster with such energy that he burst his collar open. During the days that intervened between William's party and Hubert Lane's party, the Hubert Laneites kept carefully out of the way of the Outlaws. Yet the Outlaws felt uneasily that something was brewing. Not content with scoring over them at William's party, Hubert meant to score over them in some way at his own. The Hubert Laneites looked upon the truce, not as something that tied their hands for the time being, but as something that delivered their enemies into their power. William was uneasily aware that Hubert Lane would not feel the compunction that he had felt in the matter of his guests.

"We've gotter do somethin' to them at their party, same as they did to us at ours," said Ginger firmly.

"Yes, but what can we do?" said William. "We can't start fightin' 'em. We've promised not to. An'—an' there's nothin' else we *can* do. Jus' wait, jus' *wait* till their party's over."

And William's fists curled themselves zestfully as he danced his most fiendish war dance in the middle of the road (his bolster had been so badly used lately that nearly all the feathers were coming out. Mrs. Brown had asked him only that morning what on earth he was doing to it).

"But they'll never forget that water squirt," said Ginger mournfully.

"Unless we do somethin' back," said Douglas.

"What *can* we do in *their* house with them watchin' us all the time?" said Henry.

"We mus' jus' *think*," said William, "there's four days an' we'll think hard."

But the day of Hubert's party arrived, and they'd thought of nothing. William looked downcast and spiritless. Even pummelling his bolster had lost its charm for him.

They met in the old barn in the morning to arrange their plan of action, but none of them could think of any plan of action to arrange, and the meeting broke up gloomily at lunch time, without having come to any decision at all.

William walked slowly and draggingly through the village on his way home. His mother had told him to stop at the baker's with an order for her, and it was a sign of his intense depression that he remembered to do it. In ordinary circumstances William forgot his mother's messages in the village. He entered the baker's shop, and stared around him resentfully. It seemed to be full of people. He'd have to wait all night before anyone took any notice of him. Just his luck, he reflected bitterly. . . . Then he suddenly realised that the mountainous lady just in front of him was Mrs. Lane. She was talking in a loud voice to a friend.

"Yes, Hubie's party is this afternoon. We're having William Brown and his friends. To put a stop to that silly quarrel that's gone on so long, you know. Hubie's so lovable that I simply can't think how anyone could quarrel with him. But, of course, it will be all right after to-day. We've having a Father Christmas, you know. Bates, our gardener, is going to be the Father Christmas and give out presents. I've given Hubie three pounds to get some *really* nice presents for it to celebrate the ending of the feud."

William waited his turn, gave his message, and went home for lunch.

*   *   *

Immediately after lunch he made his way to Bates's cottage.

It stood on the road at the end of the Lanes' garden. One gate led from the garden to the road, and the other from the garden to the Lanes' shrubbery. Behind the cottage was Bates's treasured kitchen garden, and at the bottom was a little shed where he stored his apples. The window of the shed had to be open for airing purposes, but Bates kept a sharp look out for his perpetual and inveterate enemies, boys.

William approached the cottage with great circumspection, looking anxiously around to be sure that none of the Hubert Laneites was in sight. He had reckoned on the likelihood of their all being engaged in preparation for the party.

He opened the gate, walked up the path, and knocked at the door, standing poised on one foot ready to turn to flee should Bates, recognising him and remembering some of his former exploits in his kitchen garden, attack him on sight. He heaved a sigh of relief, however, when Bates opened the door. It was clear that Bates did not recognise him. He received him with an ungracious scowl, but that, William could see, was because he was *a* boy, not because he was *the* boy.

"Well?" said Bates sharply, holding the door open a few inches, "what d'you want?"

William assumed an ingratiating smile, the smile of a boy who has every right to demand admittance to the cottage.

"I say," he said with a fairly good imitation of the Hubert Laneites' most patronising manner, "you've got the Father Christmas things here, haven't you?"

The ungraciousness of Bates's scowl did not relax, but he opened the door a few inches wider in a resigned fashion. He had been pestered to death over the Father Christmas things. These boys had been in and out of his cottage all day with parcels and what not, trampling over his doorstep and "mussing up" everything. He'd decided some time ago that it wasn't going to be worth the five shillings that Mrs. Lane was giving him for it. He took for granted that William was one of the Hubert Laneites coming once more to "muss up" his bag of parcels, and take one out or put one in, or snigger over them as they'd been doing every day for the last week. But he *did* think that they'd have left him in peace on the very afternoon of the party.

"Yes," he said surlily, "I've got the things 'ere an' they're all right, so there's no call to start upsettin' of 'em again. I've had enough of you comin' in an' mussin' the place up."

"I only wanted to count them, and make sure that we've got the right number," said William with an oily friendliness that was worthy of Hubert himself.

The man opened the door with a shrug.

"All right," he said, "go in and count 'em. I tell you, I'm sick of the whole lot of you, I am. Mussin' the place up. Look at your boots!"

William looked at his boots, made an ineffectual attempt to wipe them on the mat, and entered the cottage. He had an exhilarating sense of danger and adventure as he entered. At any minute he might arouse the man's suspicions. His ignorance of where the presents were, for instance, when he was supposed to have been visiting them regularly, might give him away completely. Moreover, a Hubert Laneite might arrive any minute and trap him, in the cottage. It was, in short, a situation after William's own heart. The immediate danger of discovery was averted by Bates himself, who waved him irascibly into the back parlour, where the presents were evidently kept. William entered, and threw a quick glance out of the window. Yes, Ginger was there, as they had arranged he should be, hovering near the shed where the apples were sorted. Then he looked round the room. A red cloak and hood and white beard were spread out on the sofa, and on the hearthrug lay a sackful of small parcels.

"Well, count 'em for goodness' sake an' let's get a bit of peace," said Bates more irritably than ever. William fell on his knees and began to make a pretence of counting the parcels. Suddenly he looked up and gazed out of the window.

"I say!" he said, "there's a boy taking your apples."

Bates leapt to the window. There, upon the roof of the shed, was Ginger, with an arm through the open window, obviously in the act of purloining apples and carefully exposing himself to view.

With a yell of fury Bates sprang to the door and down the path towards the shed. He had forgotten everything but this outrage upon his property. Left alone, William turned his attention quickly to the sack. It contained parcels, each one labelled and named. He had to act quickly. Bates had set off after Ginger, but he might return at any minute. Ginger's instructions were to lure him on by keeping just out of reach, but Bates might tire of the chase before they'd gone a few yards, and, remembering his visitor, return to the cottage in order to prevent his "mussin' " things up any more than necessary. William had no time to investigate. He had to act solely upon his suspicions and his knowledge of the characters of Hubert and his friends. Quickly he began to change the labels of the little parcels, putting the one marked William on to the one marked Hubert, and exchanging the labels of the Outlaws and their supporters for those of the Hubert Laneites and their supporters. Just as he was fastening the last one, Bates returned, hot and breathless.

"Did you catch him?" said William, secure in the knowledge that Ginger had outstripped Bates more times than any of them could remember.

"Naw," said Mr. Bates, panting and furious. "I'd like to wring his neck. I'd larn him if I got hold of him. Who was he? Did you see?"

"He was about the same size as me," said William in the bright, eager tone of one who is trying to help, "or he may have been just a *tiny* bit smaller."

Bates turned upon him, as if glad of the chance to

vent his irascibility upon somebody.

"Well, you clear out," he said, "I've had enough of you mussin' the place up, an' you can tell the others that they can keep away too. An' I'll be glad when it's over, I tell you. I'm sick of the lot of you."

Smiling the patronising smile that he associated with the Hubert Laneites, William took a hurried departure, and ran home as quickly as he could. He found his mother searching for him despairingly.

"Oh, William, where *have* you been? You ought to have begun to get ready for the party *hours* ago."

"I've just been for a little walk," said William casually. "I'll be ready in time all right."

With the unwelcome aid of his mother, he was ready in time, spick and span and spruce and shining.

"I'm so *glad* that you're friends now and that that silly quarrel's over," said Mrs. Brown as she saw him off. "You feel much *happier* now that you're friends, don't you?"

William snorted sardonically, and set off down the road.

The Hubert Laneites received the Outlaws with even more nauseous friendliness than they had shown at William's house. It was evident, however, from the way they sniggered and nudged each other that they had some plan prepared. William felt anxious. Suppose that the plot they had so obviously prepared had nothing to do with the Father Christmas. . . . Suppose that he had wasted his time and trouble that morning. . . . They went into the hall after tea, and Mrs. Lane said roguishly:

"Now, boys, I've got a visitor for you." Immediately Bates, inadequately disguised as Father Christmas and looking fiercely resentful of the whole proceedings, entered with his sack. The Hubert Laneites sniggered delightedly. This was evidently the crowning moment of

BATES CALLED OUT THE NAMES ONE BY ONE. THE
FIRST WAS WILLIAM.

IT WAS THE MOST MAGNIFICENT MOUTH ORGAN THAT HE
HAD EVER SEEN. THE HUBERT LANEITES STARED IN
HORROR AND AMAZEMENT.

the afternoon. Bates took the parcels out one by one, announcing the name on each label.

The first was William.

The Hubert Laneites watched him go up to receive it in paroxysms of silent mirth. William took it and opening it, wearing a sphinx-like expression. It was the most magnificent mouth organ that he had ever seen. The mouths of the Hubert Laneites dropped open in horror and amazement. It was evidently the present that Hubert had destined for himself. Bates called out Hubert's name. Hubert, his mouth still hanging open with horror and amazement, went to receive his parcel. It contained a short pencil with shield and rubber of the sort that can be purchased for a penny or twopence. He went back to his seat blinking. He examined his label. It bore his name. He examined William's label. It bore his name. There was no mistake about it. William was thanking Mrs. Lane effusively for his present.

"Yes, dear," she was saying, "I'm so glad you like it. I haven't had time to look at them but I told Hubie to get nice things."

Hubert opened his mouth to protest, and then shut it again. He was beaten and he knew it. He couldn't very well tell his mother that he'd spent the bulk of the money on the presents for himself and his particular friends, and had spent only a few coppers on the Outlaws' presents. He couldn't think what had happened. He'd been so sure that it would be all right. The Outlaws would hardly have had the nerve publicly to object to their presents, and Mrs. Lane was well meaning but conveniently short sighted, and took for granted that everything that Hubie did was perfect. Hubert sat staring at his pencil and blinking his eyes in incredulous horror. Meanwhile the presentation was going on. Bertie Franks' present was a ruler that could not have cost more than a penny, and Ginger's was a magnificent electric torch. Bertie stared at the torch with an expression that would have done credit to a tragic mask, and Ginger hastened to establish his permanent right to his prize by going up to thank Mrs. Lane for it.

"Yes, it's lovely, dear," she said, "I told Hubie to get nice things."

Douglas's present was a splendid penknife, and Henry's a fountain-pen, while the corresponding presents for the Hubert Laneites were an indiarubber and a note-book. The Hubert Laneites watched their presents passing into the enemies' hands with expressions of helpless agony. But Douglas's parcel had more than a penknife in it. It had a little bunch of imitation flowers with an india-rubber bulb attached and a tiny label, "Show this to William and press the rubber thing." Douglas took it to Hubert. Hubert knew it, of course, for he had bought it, but he was paralysed with horror at the whole situation.

"Look, Hubert," said Douglas

A fountain of ink caught Hubert neatly in the eye. Douglas was all surprise and contrition.

"I'm so sorry, Hubert," he said, "I'd no idea that it was going to do that. I've just got it out of my parcel and I'd no idea that it was going to do that. I'm so sorry, Mrs. Lane. I'd no idea that it was going to do that."

"Of course you hadn't, dear," said Mrs. Lane. "It's Hubies's own fault for buying a thing like that. It's very foolish of him indeed."

Hubert wiped the ink out of his eyes and sputtered helplessly.

Then William discovered that it was time to go.

"Thank you so much for our lovely presents, Hubert," he said politely, "we've had a *lovely* time."

And Hubert, under his mother's eye, smiled a green and sickly smile.

The Outlaws marched triumphantly down the road, brandishing their spoils. William was playing on his mouth organ, Ginger was flashing his electric light, Henry waving his fountain-pen, and Douglas slashing at the hedge with his penknife.

Occasionally they turned round to see if their enemies were pursuing them, in order to retrieve their treasures.

But the Hubert Laneites were too broken in spirit to enter into open hostilities just then.

As they walked, the Outlaws raised a wild and inharmonious pæan of triumph.

And over the telephone Mrs. Lane was saying to Mrs. Brown:

"Yes, dear, it's been a *complete* success. They're the *greatest* friends now. I'm sure it's been a Christmas that they'll all remember all their lives."

from *William's Happy Days*

Not Much

William walked down the village street singing lustily. His strident, unmelodious young voice rang out harshly. His face was purple with vocal effort.

> *"Dare to be a Daniel,*
> *Dare to stand alo—o—o—one,*
> *Dare to have a purpose true—ue—ue,*
> *Dare to make it know—ow—ow—own."*

Becoming tired of that subject and not knowing the next verse, he abruptly changed his tune—

"I'm longing for the dear ole home agai—ai—ai—ain,
That cottage in the little winding la—a—a—ne,
I can see the roses climbing, I can hear the sweet bells
> *chiming,*
And I'm longing for the dear ole home agai—ai—ai—
> *ain."*

Inhabitants of the street along which William was passing hastily shut their front windows or fled from their front rooms or uttered loud objurgations of William according to their characters. William passed along, singing and unmoved. A parrot, who had refused all invitations to converse since its purchase, suddenly raised its voice with William's in piercing screams. The quiet street had become a nightmare uproar of inharmonious sound. A man threw a boot at William from an upstairs window. It hit a hen in a neighbour's garden. The hen added its voice to William's and the parrot's. William passed along, singing and unmoved—

"I've a girl in Navara,
I've a girl in Sahara,
I've got a few sweet girlies who—o—o—o I've promised
to—o—o be true—ue—ue—ue to—o—o—o."

He turned off the main street. The hideous sound died gradually away in the distance and quiet reigned once more in that vicinity. Windows were opened, people returned to their front rooms, the parrot relapsed into his customary silence.

William went on singing towards his home. At the gate of his garden he changed his song for a toneless penetrating whistle. He whistled his way blithely up the drive. His father flung up a window fiercely.

"Stop that noise!" he called.

William proceeded on his way.

"Stop—that—noise!"

William stopped.

"What noise?" he said.

"That—that foul noise you were making just now."

"Whistlin'? I din't know you meant whistlin' when you said noise," William went on, drawing near the window. "I din't know you was talking to me at all jus' at first. I thought——" William was obviously anxious to carry on a friendly conversation with a fellow-being. His father hastily slammed the window and returned to his armchair.

William opened his mouth as for a burst of song. Then he seemed suddenly to change his mind and pursed his lips as if for a whistle. Then, after a breathless moment of silence, he unpursed them and humming untunefully under his breath he entered by the side door.

The hall was empty. Through the open kitchen door he could see his mother and Ethel, his grown-up sister, cutting sandwiches at one table and the cook and housemaid at another. He went into the kitchen.

"Who're you makin' sandwiches for?" he demanded.

His mother surveyed him sadly.

"I do wish you could keep clean for more than two minutes together, William," she said.

William smoothed back an obstreperous mop of hair with a grimy hand.

"Yes," he agreed mechanically, 'but who're you makin' sandwiches for?"

Ethel paused with a butter-laden knife in mid-air.

"Don't for Heaven's sake tell him," she said, "and let's hope and pray that he'll keep out of the way till it's over. It'll be enough trouble without him hanging round."

William ejected the tip of his tongue in her direction behind his mother's back.

"Yes — but — who're — you — makin' — sandwiches —for?" he said slowly and emphatically, with an air of patience tried beyond endurance.

"I think he'd be rather a help than otherwise, you know," said his mother, carefully arranging pieces of tongue on a slice of bread and butter.

Ethel merely shrugged her shoulders.

"I s'pose," said William with heavy sarcasm, "you're makin' them jus' for fun?"

"Clever!" said Ethel, cutting off the crusts of a sandwich.

William, whose appetite was a never-failing quality, fell upon the crusts and began to eat them.

"Don't spoil your lunch, dear," murmured Mrs. Brown.

"No," promised William, "but—all—I—want—to—know—is—who're—you—makin'—sandwiches—for?"

"Oh, do say something and stop him saying that awful sentence," groaned Ethel.

"Well, dear," began his mother persuasively, "would you like a little party this afternoon?"

"People coming to tea?" asked William guardedly.

"Yes, dear, you'd be such a help—and——"

William interrupted.

"I'll eat up all they leave afterwards for you," he said obligingly; "but I think I won't come this time."

"Thank Heaven!" murmured Ethel.

"I'm not much good at parties," said William with perfect truth and with a perfunctory grimace at his sister.

"But wouldn't you like to help to hand things round, darling?" asked Mrs. Brown.

"No, thanks, but I'll eat up all they've left for you afterwards."

"How kind!" said Ethel.

William, goaded at last to verbal retaliation, turned on her.

"If you say much more to me," he said darkly, "I'll—I'll—I'll not help *you* at any of your parties."

He then echoed her derisive laughter in a piercing tenor.

"William, darling," sighed Mrs. Brown, "do go and wash your face."

William crammed a handful of crusts into his mouth, put the cushion from the armchair on to the top of the cat, and went out into the hall. Here he burst suddenly into a flood of raucous sound—

> *"Oh, who will o'er the downs with me?*
> *Oh, who will with me ri—i—i—i—ide?"*

Mr. Brown opened the library door.

"Will — you — stop — that — confounded — noise?" he demanded emphatically.

"I'm sorry," said William amicably. "I forgot you din't like musick."

* * *

After lunch William sallied forth once more into the world. He was feeling slightly bored. Ginger and Douglas and Henry, his three sworn allies, were all away on their holidays. William did not consider holidays unmixed blessings. Anyway, he considered that there ought to be a law that everyone should go on their holidays at the same time. He walked again down the village street. He did not sing this time. Instead he threw stones at the telegraph poles. He stood at one telegraph pole and tried to hit the one across the road. Every pole that was hit was to William a magnificent tiger, falling lifeless, shot by William through the heart. The parrot, catching sight of him again, gave an excited scream. This put William off his aim. He screamed back at the parrot, missed the telegraph pole and hit a King Charles spaniel in a garden. He then dropped the rest of his stones and fled from the indignant owner of the dog. She pursued him down the street. "You cruel boy—I'll tell your father—a poor dumb animal——" She gave up the chase at the end of the road, and William went on his way whistling, his hands in his pockets. At a bend in the road he stood suddenly silent. A group of children were walking along in front of him. They had evidently just come out of the station. At their head walked a tall, thin man. The children—boys and girls—were about William's age. They were clean and tidy, but badly dressed, and with pale cockney faces. William hurried along the road. A little girl turned round.

" 'Ullo," she said with a friendly grin, "did yer neerly git left be'ind? Wot's yer nime!"

William liked the almost incredible frizziness of her over-crimped hair. He liked the dirty feather in her hat and the violent blue of her dress. He liked her white stockings and yellow boots. He thought her altogether and entirely charming. He liked the way she talked. He found her whole personality intriguing. His grim freckled features relaxed into an ingratiating smile.

"William," he replied. "Wot's yours?"

"Heglantine," she said. "Noice nime, ain't it? Me sister's called 'Oratia. Loverly, comin' on the trine, weren't it?"

It was evident that she took him for one of her party. William grasped at the opportunity of continuing the acquaintance. "Um," he said non-committally.

"Din't see yer on the trine. Such a crawd, were't there? Some from St. Luke's an' some from St. Mary's. Oi dunno 'aft of 'em, an' don't think much o' some of 'em by their looks. Oi were jus' lookin' aht fer someone ter pal up wif."

William's heart swelled with delight at this implied superiority. A boy in front turned round. He was pale and undersized and wore a loud check cap that would have fitted a grown man.

" 'Ullo, Freckles!" he said to William.

William glared at him fiercely.

"You jus' mind wot you say to me," he began darkly.

Eglantine quickly interposed.,

"Nah then, Elbert 'Olmes," she said sharply, tossing her tight curls and feathered hat. "None of your fice 'ere! You mind wot yer syes ter me an' my frens."

The boy grinned and dropped behind with them.

"Wot we goin' ter do, anywyes," he said in a mollifying tone of friendship. "Not much ter do in the country, is there? No pishers, no nuffin'."

"There's gimes," said William, deliberately adopting the accent of his new friends. He decided to adopt it permanently. He considered it infinitely more interesting than that used by his own circle.

"Gimes!" said the boy in the check cap with infinite scorn. "Runnin' rices an' 'suchlike. An' lookin' at cows an' pickin' flowers. Thanks! *Not much!*"

William stored up this expression for future use.

"Well, yer needn't of come, Elbert 'Olmes," said Eglantine sharply, "if yer din't of wanted to."

"They said," said Elbert grimly, "as 'ow there'd be a tea, an' oi'm not one ter miss a tea—a proper tea wif cike an' all—*not much!*"

William was watching the large check cap with fascinating eyes.

"Where'd you get that cap?" he said at last.

"Dunno," said the boy. He took it off and looked at William's.

"Loike ter swop?"

William nodded. The boy whipped off the cap without a word and handed it to William, taking William's school cap in return. William, with a sigh of bliss, put it on. It enveloped his whole head and forehead, the large peak standing out over his nose. He pulled it firmly down. It was the cap of his dreams—the cap of a brigand chief.

"We hare smart, ain't we?" said Eglantine with a high-pitched laugh.

William felt blissfully happy walking along beside her.

"Wot does yer farver do?" demanded Elbert of William suddenly.

"Wot does yours?" replied William guardedly.

" 'E goes rahnd wiv a barrer sellin' things," said Elbert.

"Moine sweeps chimeneys," said Eglantine shrilly, " 'e gets that black."

They both turned on William.

"Wot does yours do?"

William bowed his head in shame. He could not bear to confess that his father neither sold things nor swept chimneys, but merely caught a train to London and his office every morning.

"Ain't got no father," he said doggedly.

"You're a horphin, then," said Eglantine, with an air of wide knowledge of the world.

"Umph," grunted William.

At this point the tall, thin man in front stopped and collected his flock around him. He wore a harassed and anxious expression.

"Now," he said, "are we all here? One—two—three—four," he counted to himself, wagging a thin forefinger round the group as he spoke.

"Plears, sir, William's a horphin," said Eglantine excitedly.

"Yes, yes," said the tall man. "Let me see—I seem to make you one too many, but no matter—William an

WILLIAM FELT BLISSFULLY HAPPY WALKING ALONG
BESIDE HER.

orphan? How sad! Poor little fellow! Come along. We're
going to play in the woods first, children, and then go to
a kind friend's to tea. The vicar rang her up this morning
and she very kindly offered to give you tea. Very kind!
Very kind! Yes, yes. This way, I think."

Again the little procession moved on its way.

"Softie!" commented Eglantine scornfully. " 'E's one
of the swanks, 'e is! 'E's a friend of the vicar's, 'cause the
vicar couldn't come. Ain't got no patience wiv 'em
myself. Whoi carn't they talk like other folks?"

William redoubled his efforts to acquire his friend's
intonation.

"Yes, whoi-oi'd loike ter know," he said aggressively,
pulling his large and loud tweed cap yet farther over his
eyes. The tall, thin man at the head of the procession
stopped again.

"I'll just go into this house, children," he said, "and
ask the way to the woods."

He went up the pathway and knocked at the door. The
group of children clustered round the gate and watched
him. The door was opened by a housemaid. The thin
man disappeared inside. The door was shut.

"Are we going to hang round *him* all the time?"
asked William discontentedly. "Won't be any fun—*not
much*," he added proudly, after a slight pause.

"Well, 'e knows the wye an' we don't," said Elbert.

"I do," said William. "You come with me—quick—
afore he comes out."

They followed William silently round the back of the
house and across a field. From the other end of the field
they had a glimpse of the tall man coming out of the
house, taking off his hat with a polite bow, then standing
at the gate and looking round in bewildered amazement.
Then they disappeared over a stile into another road.

Here a small person at the rear of the procession set up a plaintive cry.

"Oh—oo—oo," she sobbed, "I'm tahred of the country. Oo—oo—oo, I want to gow 'owm."

Eglantine came to the rescue.

"If you don't shut up makin' that noise, Christine 'Awkins," she said, "a cow or sumphin'll eat you up. Yer never knows in the country."

The sound ceased as by magic. William led his friends along the road. At a pair of iron gates leading past a lodge into a winding drive, Eglantine stopped.

"I'm tahred of walkin' along this 'ere road," she announced. "Let's go in here."

Even William was aghast.

"It's someone's garden," he explained.

"Fought yer could go anywhere yer loiked in the country," said Eglantine aggrievedly. "That's wot they said, anyway. They said yet could go anywheres yèr loiked in the country. Dunno whoi we cime," she ended wearily.

The shrill wail rose again from the back of the crowd.

"Oo—oo—oo—oo, I'm tahred of the country. I want to gow 'owm."

Eglantine entered the gate determinedly.

"Come orn!" she said.

"They'll turn us out," said William.

Eglantine squared her thin shoulders.

"Let 'em jes' troi turnin' *me* aht," she said.

"*Not much*," murmured William proudly.

They passed with no opposition up the first part of the drive. Then Eglantine saw a hedge with a gate in it and marshalled her party through that. Within they saw a lawn, some gardens, and a fountain.

"Looks orl roight," commented Eglantine loftily.

A young man rose languidly from a hammock in the trees.

"I beg your pardon?" he said politely.

"Grarnted," said Eglantine, not to be outdone in politeness.

"Can I do anything for you?" said the young man.

"We're St. Luke's and St. Mary's," explained Eglantine importantly.

"I see," said the young man. "You, I presume are a St. Mary, and he of the horsey headgear is a St. Luke."

" 'Im?" said Eglantine, pointing at William, " 'e's a horphin."

The young man adjusted a monocle.

"Really," he said, "how intensely interesting!"

"We've come into the country fer a 'oliday," went on Eglantine, "an' we jes' cime in 'ere ter see wot it was loike in 'ere."

"How extremely kind of you!" said the young man, "I hope you like it."

Eglantine surveyed the scene distantly.

"Wiv a band an' some swings an' a hice cream cart, it'd be orl roight," she admitted.

The young man sighed.

"I suppose so,' he said.

Most of the children were already making the best of their opportunities. Some were chasing butterflies, some picking flowers, some had taken off shoes and stockings and were paddling in the ornamental pond. The young man watched them rather despondently.

"If I'd known that you were coming," he said, "I'd have procured something in the way of a band and ice-cream cart."

Eglantine again was not to be outdone in politeness. She stood, a curious picture, in her blue dress, white stockings, yellow boots, with her over-frizzed hair standing out around her sharp little face beneath her feathered hat, and nodded slightly.

"Hits of no consequnce," she said graciously.

She had the situation entirely in hand. Even William, born leader as he was, was overshadowed by her, and was content that it should be so. Just as two small boys had climbed the pedestal in the middle of the ornamental pond and were endeavouring to stop up the fountain, a butler came down the path with an expression of horror on his face. The young man waved him away.

"It's all right, Thomson," he said.

"Yes, sir," said the man, "but her ladyship has arrived, sir. Her ladyship has had her boxes sent upstairs. I thought I'd better warn you, sir."

The young man groaned.

"Is there time for me to be summoned to town!" he asked.

"I'm afraid not," replied the butler. "She's coming to find you now, sir. Here she is, sir."

A large woman bore down upon them. She wore a large cloak and a large hat, and several Pomeranians trotted at her heels.

The young man rose to receive her.

"Here you are, Bertram," she said, "you didn't invite me, but I've come."

"How awfully good of you," said the young man dispiritedly.

The lady put up her lorgnettes and surveyed the children.

"Who—are—these—ragamuffins?" she said slowly and distinctly.

"Oh, just a nice little party of mine," said the young

man pleasantly. "St. Luke's and St. Mary's. You'll get awfully fond of them. They're very lovable."

The lady's face became stony.

"Are you aware," she said, "that they're trampling on the flowers and splashing in the pond and sitting on the sundial?"

"Oh, yes," he smiled. "Just jolly childish pranks, you know."

"And that one in the awful tweed cap——"

"He's an orphan," said the young man. "I'm going to give you the room next his. He's got quite a jolly voice. I heard him humming to himself a moment ago."

At this point four things happened.

One—William, who had wandered over the flower beds, was suddenly impelled by the general brightness of the day to give vent to his feelings by a burst of song—

*"One more river, an' that's the river of Jor—or—or—
    ordan,
One more river, there's one more river to cross. . . ."*

He yelled the words happily in his strident young voice.

Two—The small pessimist again lifted up her voice in a wail. "Oo—oo—oo—oo. I'm tahred of the country. I want to gow 'owm. Oo—oo—oo."

Three—Eglantine, who had surveyed the visitor in outraged silence for a few moments, at last burst forth. She set her thin hands on her thin hips and began.

"An' oo're you ter talk abaht ragamuffins? Queen of Hengland, are yet? An' wot abaht yer own 'at? A-hinsultin' of hother people in hother people's gardings."

Four—The five Poms, excited by the uproar, burst

WILLIAM YELLED THE WORDS IN HIS STRIDENT YOUNG
VOICE.

into simultaneous yapping.

Above the horrible sounds of William's song, the pessimist's wails, Eglantine's recriminations, the Poms' yapping, the lady screamed to her nephew.

"I'm going straight home, Bertram. When you have a Christian house to invite me to, perhaps you'll let me know."

"Yes, aunt," he screamed back. "Shall I see you to your car?"

He left them for a few minutes and returned, mopping his brow, in time to rescue three boys from an early death from drowning in the pond. William and a few other daring spirits were balancing themselves at a dizzy height on the top of the wall. The young man was beginning to look pale, when once more the butler appeared.

"There's a gentleman at the front door, sir," he said respectfully, "who seems in a great state, sir, and he says that he's lost some slum children——"

The young man's face brightened.

"Ah," he said, "tell him I've found some, and ask him to come and see whether they happen to be his. They've done me a very good turn, but I shouldn't mind being relieved of them now."

*   *   *

" 'E was one of the swanks an' no mistake," said Eglantine to William. "Oi'd no patience wiv 'im an' 'is wye of talkin'. Oi can plye the toff as well as anyone when oi loikes—oi did wiv 'im, din't oi? But oi despises 'em."

William was looking anxiously down the road where the tall man was taking them.

"Where we goin'?" he said distrustfully.

"To the kind lady's who invited us to tea," said the tall man, overhearing him.

William walked along in silence. Eglantine began to expatiate again.

"Look at all them 'ouses," she said, with a contemptuous glance at the houses between which they were passing. "Wot they want wiv such big 'ouses? Swank! That's all it is. Swank! Livin' in big 'ouses an' talkin' so soft. Oi've no patience wiv 'em. Oi wouldn't be one of 'em—not fer nuffin'."

But William was growing more and more uneasy.

"What we're goin' along here for?" he muttered truculently.

The tall man turned in at a gate. William moistened his lips.

"He's making a *mistake*," he murmured, pulling his check cap still farther over his eyes.

At the door stood Mrs. Brown and Ethel. Their glance fell first on Eglantine.

"What a dreadful child," whispered Mrs. Brown.

Next it fell on all that could be seen of Eglantine's companion.

"What an appalling cap!" whispered Ethel.

Then they advanced to welcome them.

"Here we are," said the tall man, with a note of relief in his voice. "Here we are . . . we've had a delightful time—er—quite a delightful time—er—on the whole—er—just a little misunderstanding at one point—a—temporary separation, but all's well that ends well. It's too kind of you. This is—er—Eglantine, and—er—this little boy is an orphan, poor little chap!"

Mrs. Brown laid her hand tenderly on the tweed cap. "Poor little boy," she began. "Poor little——" then she met the eyes beneath the tweed cap. "*William!*" she said sharply, "take off that horrible cap and go and wash your face."

*   *   *

William, clean and brushed and frowning, sat and glared across the table at his late friends. He felt himself disgraced for ever. He was a pariah, outside the pale, one of the "swanks" who lived in big houses and talked soft. His mother's and Ethel's intonation and accent seemed at that moment a public humiliation to him. He did not dare to meet Eglantine's eyes. Fiercely he munched a currant bun. Into his unoccupied hand stole a small grimy one.

"Never moind," whispered Eglantine, "yer carn't 'elp it."

And William whispered gratefully, "*Not much.*"

from *William Again*

The Sweet Little Girl in White

The Hall stood empty most of the year, but occasionally tenants re-awoke the passing interest of the village in it. This summer it was taken by a Mr. and Mrs. Bott with their daughter. Mr. Bott's name decorated most of the hoardings of his native country. On these hoardings citizens of England were urged to safeguard their digestion by taking Bott's Sauce with their meat. After reading Bott's advertisements one felt convinced that any food without Bott's Sauce was rank poison. One even felt that it would be safer to live on Bott's Sauce alone. On such feelings had Mr. Bott—as rubicund and rotund as one of his own bottles of sauce—reared a fortune sufficient to enable him to take the Hall for the summer without, as the saying is, turning a hair.

William happened to be sitting on the fence by the side of the road when the motor containing Mr. and Mrs. Bott—both stout and overdressed—and Miss Violet Elizabeth Bott and Miss Violet Elizabeth Bott's nurse flashed by. William was not interested. He was at the moment engaged in whittling a stick and watching the antics of his mongrel, Jumble, as he caught and worried each shaving. But he had a glimpse of a small child with an elaborately curled head and an elaborately flounced white dress sitting by an elaborately uniformed nurse. He gazed after the equipage scowling.

"Huh!" he said, and it is impossible to convey in print the scorn of that monosyllable as uttered by William, "*a girl!*"

Then he returned to his whittling.

*   *   *

William's mother met Mrs. Bott at the Vicar's. Mrs. Bott, who always found strangers more sympathetic than people who knew her well, confided her troubles to Mrs. Brown. Her troubles included her own rheumatism, Mr. Bott's liver, and the carelessness of Violet Elizabeth's nurse.

"Always reading these here novelettes, the girl is. I hope you'll come and see me, dear, and didn't some one say you had a little boy? Do bring him. I want Violet Elizabeth to get to know some nice little children."

Mrs. Brown hesitated. She was aware that none of her acquaintances would have described William as a nice little child. Mrs. Bott misunderstood her hesitation. She laid a fat ringed hand on her knee.

"I know, dear. You're careful who the little laddie knows, like me. Well now, you needn't worry. I've brought up our Violet Elizabeth most particular. She's a girlie who wouldn't do your little boysie any harm——"

"Oh," gasped Mrs. Brown, "it's not that."

"Then you'll come, dearie, and bring the little boysie with you, won't you?"

She took Mrs. Brown's speechlessness for consent.

*   *   *

"*Me?*" said William indignantly. "Me go to tea with that ole girl? *Me?*"

"She—she's a nice little girl," said Mrs. Brown weakly.

"I saw her," said William scathingly, "curls and things."

"Well, you must come. She's expecting you."

"I only hope," said William sternly, "that she won't 'spect me to *talk* to her."

"She'll expect you to *play* with her, I'm sure," said his mother.

"Play!" said William. "*Play?* With a girl? *Me?* Huh!"

William, pale and proud, and dressed in his best suit, his heart steeled to his humiliating fate, went with his mother to the Hall the next week. He was silent all the way there. His thoughts were too deep for words. Mrs. Brown watched him anxiously.

An over-dressed Mrs. Bott was sitting in an over-furnished drawing-room. She rose at once with an over-effusive smile and held out over-ringed hands.

"So you've brought dear little boysie," she began.

The over-effusive smile died away before the look that William turned on her.

"Er—I hadn't thought of him quite like that," she said weakly, "but I'm sure he's sweet," she added hastily.

William greeted her coldly and politely, then took his seat and sat like a small statue scowling in front of him. His hair had been brushed back with so much vigour and application of liquid that it looked as if it were painted on his head.

"Would you like to look at a picture book, boysie?" she said.

William did not answer. He merely looked at her and she hastily turned away to talk to Mrs. Brown. She talked about her rheumatism and Mr. Bott's liver and the incompetence of Violet Elizabeth's nurse.

Then Violet Elizabeth entered. Violet Elizabeth's fair hair was not naturally curly but as the result of great daily labour on the part of the much maligned nurse it stood up in a halo of curls round her small head. The curls looked almost, if not quite, natural. Violet Elizabeth's small pink and white face shone with cleanliness. Violet Elizabeth was so treasured and guarded and surrounded with every care that her small pink and white face had never been known to do anything else except shine with cleanliness. But the *pièce de résistance* about Violet Elizabeth's appearance was her skirts. Violet Elizabeth was dressed in a white lace-trimmed dress with a blue waistband and beneath the miniature blue waistband, her skirts stood out like a tiny ballet dancer's in a filmy froth of lace-trimmed petticoats. From this cascade emerged Violet Elizabeth's bare legs, to disappear ultimately into white silk socks and white buckskin shoes.

William gazed at this engaging apparition in horror.

"Good afternoon," said Violet Elizabeth primly.

"Good afternoon," said William in a hollow voice.

"Take the little boysie into the garden, Violet Elizabeth," said her mother, "and play with him nicely."

William and Violet Elizabeth eyed each other apprehensively.

"Come along, boy," said Violet Elizabeth at last, holding out a hand.

William ignored the hand and with the air of a hero bound to his execution, accompanied Violet Elizabeth into the garden.

Mrs. Brown's eyes followed them anxiously.

*   *   *

"Whath your name?" said Violet Elizabeth.

She lisped! She would, thought William bitterly, with those curls and those skirts. She would. He felt at any rate relieved that none of his friends could see him in the unmanly situation—talking to a kid like that—all eyes and curls and skirts.

"William Brown," he said, distantly, looking over her head as if he did not see her.

"How old are you?"

"Eleven."

"My nameth Violet Elizabeth."

He received the information in silence.

"I'm thix."

He made no comment. He examined the distant view with an abstracted frown.

"Now you muth play with me."

William allowed his cold glance to rest upon her.

"I don't play little girls' games," he said scathingly. But Violet Elizabeth did not appear to be scathed.

"Don' you know any little girlth?" she said pityingly. "I'll teach you little girlth gameth," she added pleasantly.

"I don't *want* to," said William. "I don't *like* them. I don't *like* little girls' games. I don't want to know 'em."

Violet Elizabeth gazed at him open-mouthed.

"Don't you *like* little girlth?" she said.

"*Me?*" said William with superior dignity. "Me? I don't know anything about 'em. Don't want to."

"D-don't you like me?" quavered Violet Elizabeth in incredulous amazement. William looked at her. Her blue eyes filled slowly with tears, her lips quivered.

"I like you," she said. "Don't you like me?"

William stared at her in horror.

"You—you *do* like me, don't you?"

William was silent.

A large shining tear welled over and trickled down the small pink cheek.

"You're making me cry," sobbed Violet Elizabeth. "You are. You're making me cry, 'cause you won't say you like me."

"I—I do like you," said William desperately. "Honest—I do. Don't cry. I do like you. Honest!"

A smile broke through the tear-stained face.

"I'm tho glad," she said simply. "You like all little girlth, don't you?" She smiled at him hopefully. "You, do don't you?"

William, pirate and Red Indian and desperado, William, woman-hater and girl-despiser, looked round wildly for escape and found none.

Violet Elizabeth's eyes filled with tears again.

"You *do* like all little girlth, don't you?" she persisted with quavering lip. "You do, don't you?"

It was a nightmare to William. They were standing in full view of the drawing-room window. At any moment a grown-up might appear. He would be accused of brutality, of making little Violet Elizabeth cry. And, strangely enough, the sight of Violet Elizabeth with tear-filled eyes and trembling lips made him feel that he must have been brutal indeed. Beneath his horror he felt bewildered.

"Yes, I do," he said hastily, "I do. Honest I do."

She smiled again radiantly through her tears. "You with you wath a little girl, don't you?"

"Er—yes. Honest I do," said the unhappy William.

"Kith me," she said raising her glowing face.

William was broken.

He brushed her cheek with his.

"Thath not a kith," said Violet Elizabeth.

"It's my kind of a kiss," said William.

"All right. Now leth play fairieth. I'll thow you how."

On the way home Mrs. Brown, who always hoped vaguely that little girls would have a civilising effect on William, asked William if he had enjoyed it. William had spent most of the afternoon in the character of a gnome attending upon Violet Elizabeth in the character of the fairy queen. Any attempt at rebellion had been met with tear-filled eyes and trembling lips. He was feeling embittered with life.

"If all girls are like that——" said William, "well, when you think of all the hundreds of girls there must be in the world—well, it makes you feel sick."

Never had liberty and the comradeship of his own sex seemed sweeter to William than it did the next day when he set off whistling carelessly, his hands in his pockets, Jumble at his heels, to meet Ginger and Douglas across the fields.

"You didn't come yesterday," they said when they met. They had missed William, the leader.

"No," he said shortly, "went out to tea."

"Where?" they said with interest.

"Nowhere in particular," said William inaccurately.

A feeling of horror overcame him at the memory. If they knew—if they'd seen. . . . He blushed with shame at the very thought. To regain his self-respect he punched Ginger and knocked off Douglas's cap. After the slight scuffle that ensued they set off down the road.

"What'll we do this morning?" said Ginger.

It was sunny. It was holiday time. They had each other and a dog. Boyhood could not wish for more. The whole world lay before them.

"Let's go trespassin'," said William the lawless.

"Where?" enquired Douglas.

"Hall woods—and take Jumble."

"That ole keeper said he'd tell our fathers if he caught us in again," said Ginger.

"Lettim!" said William, with a dare-devil air, slashing at the hedge with a stick. He was gradually recovering his self-respect. The nightmare memories of yesterday were growing faint. He flung a stone for the eager Jumble and uttered his shrill unharmonious war whoop. They entered the woods, William leading. He swaggered along the path. He was William, desperado, and scorner of girls. Yesterday was a dream. It must have been. No mere girl would dare even to speak to him. He had never played at fairies with a girl—he, William the pirate king, the robber chief.

"William!"

He turned, his proud smile frozen in horror.

A small figure was flying along the path behind them—a bare-headed figure with elaborate curls and very short lacy bunchy skirts and bare legs with white shoes and socks.

"William, *darling!* I thaw you from the nurthery window coming along the road and I ethcaped. Nurth wath reading a book and I ethcaped. Oh, William darling, play with me again, *do*. It *wath* so nith yethterday."

William glared at her speechless. He was glad of the presence of his manly friends, yet horrified as to what revelations this terrible young female might make, disgracing him for ever in their eyes.

"Go away," he said sternly at last, "we aren't playing girls' games."

"We don't like girls," said Ginger contemptuously.

"William doth," she said indignantly. "He thaid he did. He thaid he liked all little girlth. He thaid he withed

he wath a little girl. He kithed me an' played fairieth
with me."

A glorious blush of a rich and dark red overspread
William's countenance.

"*Oh!*" he ejaculated as if astounded at the depth of
her untruthfulness, but it was not convincing.

"Oh, you *did!*" said Violet Elizabeth. Somehow that
was convincing. Ginger and Douglas looked at William
rather coldly. Even Jumble seèmed to look slightly
ashamed of him.

"Well, come along," said Ginger, "we can't stop
here all day talking—to a *girl*."

"But I want to come with you," said Violet Elizabeth.
"I want to play with you."

"We're going to play boys' games. You wouldn't like
it," said Douglas who was somewhat of a diplomatist.

"I *like* boyth gameth," pleaded Violet Elizabeth, and
her blue eyes filled with tears, "*pleath* let me come."

"All right," said William. "We can't stop you
comin'. Don't take any notice of her," he said to the
others. "She'll soon get tired of it."

They set off. William, for the moment abashed and
deflated, followed humbly in their wake.

* * *

In a low-lying part of the wood was a bog. The bog was
always there but as it had rained in the night the bog to-
day was particularly boggy. It was quite possible to skirt
this bog by walking round it on the higher ground, but
William and his friends never did this. They preferred to
pretend that the bog surrounded them on all sides as far
as human eye could see and that at one false step they
might sink deep in the morass never to be seen again.

"Come along," called William who had recovered his

spirits and position of leadership. "Come along, my brave fellows . . . tread careful or instant death will be your fate, and don't take any notice of her, she'll soon have had enough."

For Violet Elizabeth was trotting gaily behind the gallant band.

They did not turn round or look at her, but they could not help seeing her out of the corners of their eyes. She plunged into the bog with a squeal of delight and stamped her elegant white-clad feet into the black mud.

"Ithn't it lovely?" she squealed. "Dothn't it feel nith—all thquithy between your toth—ithn't it *lovely?* I *like* boyth gameth."

They could not help looking at her when they emerged. As fairy-like as ever above, her feet were covered with black mud up to above her socks. Shoes and socks were sodden.

"Ith a *lovely* feeling!" she commented delightedly on the other side. "Leth do it again."

But William and his band remembered their manly dignity and strode on without answering. She followed with short dancing steps. Each of them carried a stick with which they smote the air or any shrub they passed. Violet Elizabeth secured a stick and faithfully imitated them. They came to a clear space in the wood, occupied chiefly by giant blackberry bushes laden with fat ripe berries.

"Now, my brave fellows," said William, "take your fill. 'Tis well we have found this bit of food or we would e'en have starved, an' don' help her or get any for her an' let her get all scratched an' she'll soon have had enough."

They fell upon the bushes. Violet Elizabeth also fell upon the bushes. She crammed handfuls of ripe blackberries into her mouth. Gradually her pink and white face became obscured beneath a thick covering of blackberry juice stain. Her hands were dark red. Her white dress had lost its whiteness. It was stained and torn. Her bunchy skirts had lost their bunchiness. The brambles tore at her curled hair and drew it into that state of straightness for which Nature had meant it. The brambles scratched her face and arms and legs. And still she ate.

"I'm getting more than any of you," she cried. "I geth I'm getting more than any of you. And I'm getting all of a *meth*. Ithn't it *fun?* I like boyth gameth."

They gazed at her with a certain horrified respect and apprehension. Would they be held responsible for the strange change in her appearance?

They left the blackberry bushes and set off again through the wood. At a sign from William they dropped on all fours and crept cautiously and (as they imagined) silently along the path. Violet Elizabeth dropped also upon her scratched and blackberry stained knees.

"Look at me," she shrilled proudly. "I'm doing it too. Juth like boyth."

"Sh!" William said fiercely.

Violet Elizabeth "Sh'd" obediently and for a time crawled along contentedly.

"Are we playin' bein' animalth?" she piped at last.

"Shut *up!*" hissed William.

Violet Elizabeth shut up—except to whisper to Ginger who was just in front, "I'm a thnail—what you?" Ginger did not deign to reply.

At a sign from their leader that all danger was over the Outlaws stood upright. William had stopped.

"We've thrown 'em off the scent," he said scowling, "but danger s'rounds us on every side. We'd better plunge into the jungle an' I bet she'll soon've had enough of plungin' into the jungle."

They left the path and "plunged" into the dense, shoulder-high undergrowth. At the end of the line "plunged" Violet Elizabeth. She fought her way determinedly through the bushes. She left remnants of her filmy skirts on nearly every bush. Long spidery arms of brambles caught at her hair again and pulled out her curls. But Violet Elizabeth liked it. "Ithn't it *fun?*" she piped as she followed.

Under a large tree William stopped.

"Now we'll be Red Indians," he said, "an' go huntin'. I'll be Brave Heart same as usual and Ginger be Hawk Face and Douglas be Lightning Eye."

"An' what shall I be?" said the torn and stained and wild-headed apparition that had been Violet Elizabeth.

Douglas took the matter in hand.

"What thall I be?" he mimicked shrilly, "what thall I be? What thall I be?"

Violet Elizabeth did not run home in tears as he had hoped she would. She laughed gleefully.

"It doth thound funny when you thay it like that!" she said delightedly. "Oh, it doth! Thay it again! Pleeth thay it again."

Douglas was nonplussed.

"Anyway," he said, "you jolly well aren't going to play, so there."

"*Pleath* let me play," said Violet Elizabeth. "Pleath."

"*No.* Go away!"

William and Ginger secretly admired the firm handling of this female by Douglas.

"*Pleath,* Douglath."

"*No!*"

Violet Elizabeth's blue eyes, fixed pleadingly upon him, filled with tears. Violet Elizabeth's underlip trembled.

"You're making me cry," she said. A tear traced its course down the blackberry stained cheek.

"*Pleath,* Douglath."

Douglas hesitated and was lost. "Oh, well——" he said.

"Oh, thank you, dear Douglath," said Violet Elizabeth. "What thall I be?"

"Well," said William to Douglas sternly. "Now you've *let* her play I s'pose she'd better be a squaw."

"A thquaw," said Violet Elizabeth joyfully, "what thort of noith doth it make?"

"It's a Indian lady and it doesn't make any sort of a noise," said Ginger crushingly. "Now we're going out hunting and you stay and cook the dinner."

"All right," said Violet Elizabeth obligingly. "Kith me good-bye."

Ginger stared at her in horror.

"But you mutht," she said, "if you're going out to work an' I'm going to cook the dinner, you mutht kith me good-bye. They do."

"I don't," said Ginger.

She held up her small face.

"*Pleath,* Ginger."

Blushing to his ears Ginger just brushed her cheek with his. William gave a derisive snort. His self-respect had returned. Douglas's manly severity had been overborne. Ginger had been prevailed upon to kiss her. Well, they couldn't laugh at him now. They jolly *well* couldn't. Both were avoiding his eye.

"Well, go off to work, dear William and Douglas and Ginger," said Violet Elizabeth happily, "an' I'll cook."

Gladly the hunters set off.

                    *   *   *

The Red Indian game had palled. It had been a success while it lasted. Ginger had brought some matches and over her purple layer of blackberry juice the faithful squaw now wore a layer of black from the very smoky fire they had at last managed to make.

"Come on," said William, "let's set out looking for adventures."

They set off single file as before, Violet Elizabeth bringing up the rear, Jumble darting about in ecstatic searches for imaginary rabbits. Another small bog glimmered ahead. Violet Elizabeth, drunk with her success as a squaw, gave a scream.

"Another thquithy plath," she cried. "I want to be firtht."

She flitted ahead of them, ran to the bog, slipped and fell into it face forward.

She arose at once. She was covered in black mud from head to foot. Her face was a black mud mask. Through it her teeth flashed in a smile. "I juth thlipped," she explained.

A man's voice came suddenly from the main path through the wood at their right.

"Look at 'em—the young rascals! Look at 'em! An' a dawg! Blarst 'em! Er-r-r-r-r!"

The last was a sound expressive of rage and threatening.

"Keepers!" said William. "Run for your lives, braves. Come on, Jumble."

They fled through the thicket.

"Pleath," gasped Violet Elizabeth in the rear, "I can't run as fatht ath that."

It was Ginger and Douglas who came back to hold her hands. For all that they ran fleetly, dashing through the undergrowth where the keepers found it difficult to follow, and dodging round trees. At last, breathlessly, they reached a clearing and in the middle of it a cottage as small and attractive as a fairy tale cottage. The door was open. It had an empty look. They could hear the keepers coming through the undergrowth shouting.

"Come in here," gasped William. "It's empty. Come in and hide till they've gone."

The four ran into a spotlessly clean little kitchen, and Ginger closed the door. The cottage was certainly empty. There was not a sound.

"Ithn't it a thweet little houth?" panted Violet Elizabeth.

"Come upstairs," said Douglas. "They might look in here."

The four, Jumble scrambling after them, clattered up the steep narrow wooden stairs and into a small and very clean bedroom.

"Look out of the window and see when they go past," commanded William, "then we'll slip out and go back."

Douglas peeped cautiously out of the window. He gave a gasp.

"They—they're not goin' past," he said. "They—they're comin' in at the door."

The men's voices could be heard below.

"Comin' in here—the young rascals! Look at their footmarks, see? What'll my old woman say when she gets home?"

"They've gone upstairs, too. Look at the marks. Blarst 'em!"

William went to the window, holding Jumble beneath his arm.

"We can easily climb down by this pipe," he said quickly. "Then we'll run back."

He swung a leg over the window sill, prepared to descend with Jumble clinging round his neck, as Jumble was trained to do. Jumble's life consisted chiefly of an endless succession of shocks to the nerves.

Ginger and Douglas prepared to follow.

The men's footsteps were heard coming upstairs when a small voice said plaintively, "Pleath—pleath, I can't do that. Pleath, you're not going to leave me, are you?"

William put back his foot.

"We—we can't leave her," he said. Ginger and Douglas did not question their leader's decision. They stood in a row facing the door while the footsteps drew nearer.

The door burst open and the two keepers appeared.

"Now, yer young rascals—we've got yer!"

*   *   *

Into Mr. Bott's library were ushered two keepers, each leading two children by the neck. One held two rough-looking boys. The other held a rough-looking boy and a rough-looking little girl. A dejected-looking mongrel followed the procession.

"Trespassin', sir," said the first keeper, "trespassin' an' a-damagin' of the woods. Old 'ands, too. Seen 'em at it before but never caught 'em till now. An' a *dawg* too. It's an example making of they want, sir. They want prosecutin' if I may make so bold. A-damagin' of the woods and a-bringing of a dawg——"

Mr. Bott who was new to squiredom and had little knowledge of what was expected of him and moreover was afflicted at the moment with severe private domestic worries, cast a harassed glance at the four children. His glance rested upon Violet Elizabeth without the faintest flicker of recognition. He did not recognise her. He knew Violet Elizabeth. He saw her at least once or almost once a day. He knew her quite well. He knew her by her ordered flaxen curls, pink and white face and immaculate bunchy skirts. He did not know this little creature with the torn, stained, bedraggled dress (there was nothing bunchy about it now) whose extreme dirty face could just be seen beneath the tangle of untidy hair that fell over her eyes. She watched him silently and cautiously. Just as he was going to speak Violet Elizabeth's nurse entered. It says much for Violet Elizabeth's disguise that her nurse only threw her a passing glance. Violet Elizabeth's nurse's eyes were red-rimmed.

"Please, sir, Mrs. Bott says is there any news?"

"No," said Mr. Bott desperately. "Tell her I've rung up the police every minute since she sent last. How is she?"

"Please, sir, she's in hysterics again."

Mr. Bott groaned.

Ever since Violet Elizabeth's disappearance Mrs. Bott had been indulging in hysterics in her bedroom and taking it out of Violet Elizabeth's nurse. In return Violet Elizabeth's nurse had hysterics in the nursery and took it out of the nursery maid. In return the nursery maid had hysterics in the kitchen and took it out of the kitchen maid. The kitchen maid had no time for hysterics but she took it out of the cat.

"Please, sir, she says she's too ill to speak now. She told me to tell you so, sir."

Mr. Bott groaned again. Suddenly he turned to the four children and their keepers.

"You've got their names and addresses, haven't you?

Well, see here, children. Go out and see if you can find my little gal for me. She's lost. Look in the woods and round the village and—everywhere. And if you find her I'll let you off. See?"

They murmured perfunctory thanks and retired, followed by Violet Elizabeth who had not uttered one word within her paternal mansion.

In the woods they turned on her sternly.

"It's you he wants. You're her."

"Yeth," agreed the tousled ragamuffin who was Violet Elizabeth, sweetly, "ith me."

"Well, we're going to find you an' take you back."

"Oh, *pleath*, I don't want to be found and tooken back. I like being with you."

"Well, we can't keep you about with us all day, can we?" argued William sternly. "You've gotter go home sometime same as we've gotter go home sometime. Well, we jolly well want our dinner now and we're jolly well going home an' we're jolly well goin' to take you home. He might give us something and——"

"All right," agreed Violet Elizabeth holding up her face, "if you'll all kith me I'll be found an' tooken back."

*   *   *

The four of them stood again before Mr. Bott's desk. William and Ginger and Douglas took a step back and Violet Elizabeth took a step forward.

"We've found her," said William.

"Where?" said Mr. Bott looking round.

"Ith me," piped Violet Elizabeth.

Mr. Bott started.

"You?" he repeated in amazement.

"Yeth, father, ith me."

"But, but—God bless my soul——" he ejaculated peering at the unfamiliar apparition. "It's impossible."

Then he rang for Violet Elizabeth's nurse.

"Is this Violet Elizabeth?" he said.

"Yeth, ith me," said Violet Elizabeth again.

Violet Elizabeth's nurse pushed back the tangle of hair.

"Oh, the poor poor child!" she cried. "The poor child!"

"WE'VE FOUND HER," ANNOUNCED WILLIAM, AND VIOLET ELIZABETH TOOK A STEP FORWARD. "ITH ME," SHE PIPED.

"God bless my soul," said Mr. Bott again. "Take her away. I don't know what you do to her, but do it and don't let her mother see her till it's done, and you boys stay here."

"Oh, my lamb!" sobbed Violet Elizabeth's nurse as

"GOD BLESS MY SOUL!" EXCLAIMED MR. BOTT, PEERING AT THE APPARITION. "IT'S IMPOSSIBLE."

she led her away. "My poor lamb!"

In an incredibly short time they returned. The mysterious something had been done. Violet Elizabeth's head was a mass of curls. Her face shone with cleanliness. Dainty lace-trimmed skirts stuck out ballet-dancer-wise beneath the pale blue waistband. Mr. Bott took a deep breath.

"Now fetch her mother," he said.

Like a tornado entered Mrs. Bott. She still heaved with hysterics. She enfolded Violet Elizabeth to her visibly palpitating bosom.

"My child," she sobbed. "Oh my darling child."

"I wath a thquaw," said Violet Elizabeth. "It dothn't make any thort of a noith. Ith a lady."

"How did you——" began Mrs. Bott still straining Violet Elizabeth to her.

"These boys found her——" said Mr. Bott.

"Oh, how kind—how noble," said Mrs. Bott. "And one's that nice little boy who played with her so sweetly yesterday. Give them ten shillings each, Botty."

"Well, but——" hesitated Mr. Bott remembering the circumstances in which they had been brought to him.

"Botty!" screamed Mrs. Bott tearfully, "don't you value your darling child's life at even thirty shillings?"

Hastily Mr. Bott handed them each a ten-shilling note.

*   *   *

They tramped homewards by the road.

"Well, it's turned out all right," said Ginger lugubriously, but fingering the ten-shilling note in his pocket, "but it might not have. 'Cept for the money it jolly well spoilt the morning."

"Girls always do," said William. "I'm not going to have anything to do with any ole girl ever again."

"'S all very well sayin' that," said Douglas who had been deeply impressed that morning by the inevitableness and deadly persistence of the sex, "'s all very well sayin' that. It's them what has to do with you."

"An' I'm never goin' to marry any ole girl," said William.

"'S all very well sayin' *that*," said Douglas again gloomily, "but some ole girl'll probably marry you."

from *Still—William*